CITADEL OF SERVITUDE

'You see, Simbulan, there is always one who refuses to obey. What makes me Servitrix is that I know what will happen to them. Come – drink, my little deviant. And don't look to your friends. From now on you have none. You shall not be moved from here without my say-so. And I shall not let you go until you come to heel.'

Toinile burst into tears.

The Servitrix, sighing, unbuckled her heavy belt. 'Get against that wall!' Toinile scampered – for her deliverance from the cold claws of terror and into the comforting hands of burning pain. 'Face it! Arms folded behind your back! Tighter!'

CITADEL OF SERVITUDE

Aran Ashe

This book is a work of fiction.
In real life, make sure you practise safe sex.

First published in 1997 by
Nexus
332 Ladbroke Grove
London W10 5AH

Typeset by TW Typesetting, Plymouth, Devon

Printed and bound by CPI Group (UK) Ltd, Croydon, CR0 4YY

ISBN 978-0-753-54016-9

Printed and bound in Great Britain by Clays Ltd, St Ives PLC

Contents

1

Riders

In twos and threes the naked beauties – the pride of Servulan – gradually emerged from the shallows of the lake but made no move to disperse. The stillness of the cove was eerie. No one spoke a word. Several-dozen nubile initiates were eventually clustered on the grassy shelf, standing or kneeling, staring in awed silence at the cross of Tormunil over the open gateway of the vast citadel lodged impregnably against the side of the mountain. The Abbey from which they had only yesterday been taken now seemed very far away. Its orderly domain of discipline and infixation was displaced by the unknown.

Sianon drifted into the shallows and stood up unsteadily. Her breasts pulled heavily as they emerged from the water. They were overfull with milk. They had been trained that way, to provide sexual pleasure. In the Abbey, at least one specific trait of each young woman's body had been groomed to some fleshly rite. And here, in Tormunil, their training would be brought to full fruition by the lords and masters who dwelt beyond those giant walls. That was all Sianon knew of her fate. Her breasts and sex felt frightened at the thought of what their new masters might want to do to them.

Roslin took Sianon by the hand, helping her over the shingle. Sianon was shivering. Fine water droplets clung

1

to the downy erect hairs upon her skin. Roslin rubbed her and held her against her own smooth body, which was already warm. The sun's heat gradually seeped into Sianon's skin. There was gentleness in Roslin's fingers and tenderness in Sianon's breasts.

Sianon stared again at the place above the gateway: set into the keystone, as if poured there as molten metal, was the Tormunite symbol – a giant gold icon shaped like a curved-armed cross. It captured and distilled the sunlight. Within the archway was cavernous shadow.

Behind her, the broad grassy shelf swept along the lakeshore towards brush-covered rocks. Towering above the shelf was the long, unscalable fortress wall faced with huge glass-smooth blocks of blue-black stone. It followed the perimeter of the cove then struck inland behind a harbour protected by a tower on a rock. Far beyond the harbour buildings she could see the great wall stepping up the mountainside and into the hazy distance. What sort of world did it enclose?

Sianon looked back: the ferry was moving away. She jumped up in a panic, scanning the water. Then she saw one last tiny figure swimming for the shore.

'Josef!' Heart surging, Sianon ran stumbling along the grassy shelf, waving her arms, crying out to him: 'Josef!' But the distance was great. She wasn't sure that he could even hear her. The current was taking him out towards the promontory, where the water would be deep and cold. And he was already weak from the sexual punishments the boat-women had meted out because he had tried to save her.

Breathless, she reached the rocks and began scrambling towards the point. Then suddenly she stopped in her tracks. Sounds were coming from behind her, chilling sounds, echoing from the walls – animal cries, hollow, blood-curdling whoops, then women's screams. The screams got louder. She couldn't make out the cause of the commotion until she had clambered back on to the

2

ridge. Then she crouched there, terror-riven: in those few seconds, the scene had been transformed.

Everyone was running, scattering, stumbling and falling in their panic-stricken efforts to escape. Frantic ponies wheeled in twisting curves amongst them. Bareback riders clad in studded leather mesh clung precariously to the ponies' manes. The men's arms, legs, sex and haunches were exposed. And their whips – short, quick and multi-stranded – whirred then swooped like stinging bees upon the naked breasts and buttocks stampeding by. There was no escape for their victims, no cover. They were given no chance to co-operate; some were whipped back towards the shore, others to the walls, and others towards the rocks where Sianon cowered.

She felt a terror then as never before. She turned and ran blindly away from the tumult. Only when she reached the point did she remember Josef. But she couldn't see him in the water, couldn't see him on the land.

A group of riders had dismounted. They were swarming hungrily towards her, surrounding her. She was poised on the brink, about to jump.

Then she saw him – below her, a little way along the shore, sprawled upon the shingle. Swallowing her fear and turning back, dodging the approaching wild men, ignoring their rabid cries, Sianon scrambled down the rocky slope. There was only one thing on her mind now – to reach Josef.

He wasn't moving. She fell to her knees beside him. His body was stone cold. His legs were still in the water. His eyes were closed; they never opened when she turned him over. He was barely breathing! She tried to drag him on to land.

Her pursuers had hesitated at the top of the bank. They stood grunting to each other and pointing. Sianon finally cried in desperation to them: 'Help! Please help him!'

One of them, his naked sex bouncing, loped down the face, brandishing his whip at her and growling: 'Move back!' She didn't budge. This time he showed no hesitation: even as she knelt there he used the whip. And Sianon still did not budge, nor ever would she.

'Please help him . . .' she pleaded, sinking back, tears in her eyes, her arms stretched outwards, her breasts exposed for punishment. In offering up her breasts, she sacrificed herself. And therein lay for her the deep and peculiar eroticism to which she had been trained. Images flashed within her mind, of her former mistress and master on the farm and their usage of her breasts for sexual comfort in such very different ways; and of the intimate punishments in the Abbey – novices being shaved smooth then kissed and smacked between the legs while Sianon's breasts were being being pinched and gently whipped and played with until they yielded up their milk.

As her breasts now shook beneath the stinging strokes, her eyes tried to fix upon the Tormunite cross upon the rider's chest. And suddenly her viewpoint seemed to shift to a point above his head: she was seeing herself – nude, pale-skinned, kneeling for him, her belly thrust out, her arms splayed back across the shingle. Her breasts were soft and full, shaking, sliding gently back and forth, the nipples brown, excited. Sweet feelings were coming in her belly.

His penis was filling out, thickening. She felt his thick, gloved fingers taking hold of her by the nipple to steady her, for she could not keep still, not fully still. It seemed he wanted to make both breasts, both underbellies, share each stroke, to bring them on together, but her breasts were too full for him to be able to take both nipples in the fingers of one hand. They swayed, they swelled, trembling; they were tight now, sexually stimulated by the whipping. Deep hollows opened under Sianon's arms. Her rider whipped until her gasping body rolled from side to side and her nipples kept slipping from the clutches of his fingers.

Then he stood over her, his nostrils flared, his penis irretrievably erect. Sianon, open-mouthed, lay on her side, breasts heaving, hot, heaped upon the moist cold shingle.

'Get someone to see to him,' he shouted to his men. 'Quickly! My lady brooks no delay!' He stared high up towards a turret at the outermost corner of the fortress wall. A point of light upon it glinted like the reflection from a window. When he saw Sianon's perturbed gaze, he shook his head, declaring: 'Ladyseer – beyond there – where a man might die of pleasure, it is said.'

He watched Josef's limp form being carried away. Then he turned again to the frightened Sianon, grasped her wrists behind her head and hauled her to her knees. 'But they are welcome to my lady's wiles. I would as soon die here of giving it you.' So saying, he drew her wrists backwards. Her belly arched up, her breasts bulged out, her nipples stood in tight erection. His lecherous gaze feasted upon Sianon's body. Leaning over her, he edged her thighs more open with the toe of his boot. Her labia touched the shingle: its wet smooth pebbles, piled coolly up between her legs, slid against each other, rasping. 'Oh – beautiful, beautiful . . .' And she could see his pulse inside his rigid penis as the pile of shiny pebbles coaxed her belly open, as her knees sank ever wider, as her sex pressed down.

'Ohhh!' she gasped, 'Uunh!' For he whipped her breasts – again holding them by the nipples – while her sex was suckered like a fleshy slippy sea-thing to the smooth round pebble. 'Nnn! Ahh! Ooohh!' she cried. His swollen penis bounced from the exertion. And the fiery tongues of pleasure-pain licked round Sianon's shuddering breasts and underneath her arms.

Taking her by the elbows he lifted her from the pebbles and set her down on the grass. He meant to take his time with her. She felt his hard shiny muscles against the softness of her arms. She smelt the scent of his chest through the leather mesh of his tabard. And when he turned she saw the firmness of his haunches, deeply split by the studded thong. It reminded her of what the monks used to do to her, using a leather cord.

Two of the other riders had returned. They had the same short-jointed physique as their leader, with muscles as smooth as polished bronze.

The leader, wanting to display her, thrust his burly arm under her two arms to draw her shoulders sharply up and back. He pointed out her breasts – their generous size, their tautness, saying how attractive he considered them to be with the marks of the whipping. He twisted her body this way then that, showing off her breasts individually, jolting her to make them move. He slipped the strands of the whip beneath them and lifted them, squeezing them together. And Sianon knew that such treatment, should it continue, would make her breast milk come.

She sank back, her breasts rising and falling quickly, thin raised lines of chastisement sculpted over their skin. All three men were rigidly erect, their penises thick, veined and sunbrowned.

As the leader made her kneel up again, legs splayed open, thighs held wide, and now whipped her bottom for his comrades, all these emotions were welling inside her: the fear, the anxiety for Josef, the stinging pleasure-pain that bathed her bloated breasts, the sexual feelings now stimulated by the steady whipping of her bottom, the sight of the stiff cocks up above her – men's pleasure because she was being punished, firm brown penises, fleshy bronzed balls that they might make her kiss. And suddenly she was moaning as the man beside her had taken hold of her face and turned it and drawn her long brown hair aside and pressed his hot stiff penis hard against her cheek. She could smell this special maleness and the scent of pony on his naked thighs. 'Come on, girl . . .' Her lips were open. She was moaning; the smell of sex was good; she had learnt well what the monks had taught her. They had kept her in a state of permanent arousal; now the wanting was there again between her legs, the need for release. The leader's whip kept smacking the open cheeks of her bottom all the time that this strong heady scent of ripe penis was being rubbed against her nose and cheek. And it had leaked very recently; she could smell it. Sianon put her tongue out, licked the salty bulb of the penis. Its skin was smooth and waxy. She sucked the bulb on its underside, just as the monks had shown her. Then her lips burst away from it. She moaned in pleasure and sank sideways. The whipping stopped. The third rider pulled off his gloves and crouched between her legs, touching, exploring. Her belly writhed. 'Lift up, girl. Up . . .' Sianon gasped as he touched it again. 'Look at it . . .'

'Oh, lord . . .' The leader cast the whip aside and bent over her. 'By Lady Belangaria's precious need . . . Just keep it open. Let me hold it for her. Lie her down, with it open.' She was on her back on the grass, her knees pushed back. The leader held her naked sex lips spread. Sianon's mouth reached up around the shiny proffered penis, not sucking it, just allowing it to slide. Her nose touched the curly black musky hairs. The rider groaned.

'Keep still, girl. Still,' murmured the leader. 'There – look, it's weeping. And her knob – her knob up, just like ours. By fuck, is she not beautiful?' He pursed his lips and kissed it, then put his bare fingers up inside.

Sianon wriggled and moaned, spat on the penis and the prurient fingers. She felt a second penis kiss between her legs. Her slippy wet sex lips clung to its bulb. Her clitoris poked stickily into the mouth of this teasing penis. Fingers wet from up inside her sex now toyed with her nipples, pulling them, testing them. Then suddenly she was lying gasping on the grass, the three

7

men standing over her again, tightening their thongs, their penises bulging almost to bursting. 'Turn her over, flat.' They whipped her bottom again. She lay spread-eagled, thighs stiff for it, legs open, her buttocks spread by her own trembling fingers, her belly and breast-tips pushed into the grass.

The sweet stinging tracks of the whip crisscrossed her naked skin. Her anus throbbed; the sexual pulse was there though the whip had not delved deep enough to kiss it properly. 'She punishes well,' said one man.

'That she does. Tag her.'

They rolled her over, again gently tugging her erect nipples. A loose, coloured braid bearing the Tormunite icon was fastened round her neck and she was hauled upright by her wrists. Then they showed her how they wanted her to stand – with back hollowed, arms folded behind it, so her breasts and belly stood out; and always with legs open, so her sex lips could be seen and felt and punished from behind. One rider then stood to each side and started slapping between her legs with little alternating slaps that made her labia stand open.

As they walked Sianon back across the ridge, she saw what was happening to the other novices: Roslin, cut off from the rest, was kneeling in the water, the knob of a penis in her mouth; Samarkin was being pinned and spread against the polished convex foot-stone of the wall. She was held under the arms and under the thighs. Her feet were off the ground, her toes pointing outwards. The riders had already discovered what happened to Samarkin during masturbation. Their eager hands were between her legs. Her sex was responding by swelling. Its thick shiny wet pink swollen folds were gently spilling out. One rider's hungry lips were poised to drink.

Then Sianon saw Leah. Her small nude form was standing stiff-legged, open, belly down, round split buttocks jutting behind her. The two men with her sported powerful erections: it could not be otherwise for they were examining Leah's bottom. For in the Abbey, with her pubic lips sealed by a little chain, Leah had been trained to anal coitus – masturbated continuously while her anus was being gently stretched to accommodate the most ardent of suitors. So now, any touching of that place made Leah hunger for this masturbation. Sianon glimpsed the first knob probe tentatively between Leah's bottom-cheeks. Leah moaned and buckled. The second rider caught her by the shoulders and rubbed her little breasts as they hung down. She spread her legs wider yet for her rider, but his knob never went deeper; it was as if it was being put inside not to satisfy her craving but just far enough to tease.

Women were now being herded together and driven towards the gateway. Anyone who broke ranks or unfolded her arms from behind her back was punished with the whip. The open-legged, pushed-out posture during whipping gave unbridled access to the intimate places.

Sianon's breasts throbbed. But the men made her run, down from the rocks and across the grass. They chased her. With her arms now tightly folded behind her back, she could not hold her breasts to stop them bouncing. The squealing riders ahead descended upon her; those on foot tried to block her way. The whip-strands teased afresh her breasts and bottom. Her tears began to blind her. Frequently she stumbled; her tormentors caught her but kept whipping her from behind, whipping her aroused sex as it protruded, driving her onwards, through the swelling double line of riders that surrounded the entrance and into the pens of the vast stable yard.

2

Danime

High on the ramparts, guy-ropes unwound, pulleys
squealed and the giant bellows yawned, inflating, wavering, then creaking as the power of three strong men
was brought to bear to try to close it. The bellows
groaned in protest; the pullers gasped and heaved,
sweated and crouched. And suddenly the bellows yielded; with a trembling rush the air accelerated down the
shuddering pipe and blared from the mouth of the
mighty horn. The wooden trestles shook beneath it. The
ropes fell slack; the bellows gulped again; then the
sweating workers heaved. And again the horn blared,
out beyond the fortress walls, over stables and rooftops,
past the harbour, through the barracks.

Far below, tiny figures spilled from the doorways and
swarmed down the narrow streets towards the slaves'
gate and the stables. The outer stairways seethed; runners darted out atop the crisscrossing maze of precipitous sandstone walls of the labyrinth to reach the prime
viewpoints before the start of the chase. And the area
around the pens thronged with the eager peering faces
of these artisans, off-duty soldiers, merchants and fields-
men who dwelt around the periphery of the citadel. To
them, who could never have first call upon such lovely
creatures, each landing of slaves was special; each nubile
form that might be lost to the inner sanctum, never to
caress their eyes again, was uniquely perfect; homage

must be paid while the opportunity availed. And sometimes there might fall upon the watcher a gaze, a single pleading glance that would strike right through the heart to leave a pang of wanting that would never go away.

Such a fate befell Danime. She stood at the front of the crowd. She stood amongst men and watched women. Her pulse raced; her cheeks burned. No other girl had come to watch. Many had wished to. None would; no matter.

The captives were her own age. They tried in vain to hide their nakedness. Danime's pale-blue eyes, innocent yet desirous, flitted excitedly from one to the next. She pushed along the front row, elbowing aside the men, who did not really notice she was different. Some in the crowd were calling to the captives, wanting to make them turn and so display to better advantage. There were girls of every beautiful shape – lovely faces, lithe girls, some with breasts to make you shiver. Behind them lay the labyrinth. Soon they would be made to run. Some were being tagged: these would be brought back here tonight, to the stables, for the citadel guards. Tonight was such a long time away. Danime could not wait. Her lover had promised to take her to watch.

Danime clambered up the bars until she could see the dome of the Meganopticon glistening beyond the parapet of the inner walls. One day, very soon, she would stand inside there. And she stared down at the finger which, upon that near day, would proudly bear the ring, not a ring that she was given but a ring she had earned: Ring-elant – not mason's, nor limner's, but bright-smith's – artisan in gem and gold.

On tiptoes, she gazed up at the forbidden palace: she had been inside there only once. But every tiny jewel her fingertips had fashioned now lived there, adorning and provoking the most intimate of sexual parts.

She peered through the cage at the sweet nude

11

recipients, in her mind's eye matching skin tone with gem and mounting. She was hoping – with all her heart – there might be a girl with shiny blonde beaded hair. She knew just how she would dress such a slave with body jewellery. Then in the midst of her musings the pang struck without warning: glancing up at her was a quite different girl – brown-haired, full-breasted. Then the girl turned away.

Danime watched, she knew not why; the glance came again, fleetingly, then the girl was dragged away. Danime jumped down and fought her way through the crowd. At the end of the pens, she climbed up again. Her eyes darted round the group of guards moving among the captives, then they found their quarry. Heart pounding, Danime waited for the special glance to come again. It did not. The girl, with others, was being readied for the run. The crowd waited with bated breath. Danime strained to hear the first stilted gasps of forepleasure. One by one the girls began to succumb, trying to sink to their knees, moaning gently, sometimes pleading. The ones awaiting their turn were trembling. In the vast bowl at the foot of the stables, there was not a sound save from the women at centre stage. And no one could see exactly what was being done, exactly what in those fingers was bringing on such effects.

One day Danime's lover had made her run bare-bottomed through the Lindrene meadows, with the plump grass-heads tickling her naked thighs. Danime made nectar that day and knew not what it was; her lover painted it on the grass-heads. It was as if the captives were having these feelings now because of what the guards were doing. Danime, clinging to the bars, knew that she too could be a lover with the brown-haired one in the Lindrene grass. She waited for that look again. Still it did not come. And so it came about that Danime found herself hanging on every murmur of pleasure that this girl made, and when she was driven into the labyrinth, Danime was sprinting up the flights of steps, leaping them, until she caught sight of her far below. Then, above the labyrinth, she followed the girl, watching her progress, becoming her lover in all but deed.

Long after the girl had disappeared into the tunnels, Danime was still sitting on her heels, dreaming in the airy space at the top of the labyrinth.

'I thought I might find you here.'

The words were icy fingers at the back of Danime's neck, making her afraid to turn. She did not need to: with a sudden exhalation of breath, the speaker landed directly in front of her on the crumbling narrow wall.

'Janna . . .' Danime whispered, almost afraid to say out loud her lover's name. For when the lover is from within the citadel . . .

Danime could feel the ring her lover had given her coming to life in her lover's presence. That was the sensation – as though her lover was communicating to Danime's body through the piercing. Her legs were shaking. She had been crouching, staring down the labyrinth wall. And now she was still on her knees, but kneeling upright, head bowed, all the confidence drained from her body. She glanced up at her lover's sunbronzed face.

Janna, clad in a grey suede riding jacket and thigh boots, was balanced as precariously as a tightrope walker. Her beaded hair dangled round her proud beautiful face in straight blonde waxy strands. She extended her hand, wanting Danime to take hold. Danime shook her head and crouched down. Only Janna could make her feel so unsteady. Janna laughed but in her gaze was the look, the dark look that sometimes came, and she was tight-lipped. 'Take my hand.' A small group of men had gathered on the lower parapet. Janna always drew onlookers. They did not come any nearer. 'Come on, take it.'

Danime had to stand up. Suddenly she was afraid of heights. Suddenly the wall was very narrow. She had to take two steps with feet of lead along the crumbling masonry. Janna made no move to help her. Danime, half crouched again, reached out a trembling arm; her clammy hand clasped Janna's cool dry fingers. A wave of relief swept up her arm. For a second she closed her eyes.

'With me . . . Jump!' Without warning, Janna sprang across the chasm. Her tugging hand slipped through Danime's off-guard fingers. Danime overbalanced. She had neither stride nor impetus to span the gap. She fell forward twisting. For a split second nothing happened; she floated through the air. She heard the onlookers gasp. Then the vertical walls slid up past her as if propelled; she felt the abrasions on her knuckles; she saw the ground racing to meet her. Then a hand snapped round her wrist; her body smacked against the wall.

Janna, crouching, dragged her up. The men were cheering. The beaded blonde locks tickled Danime's breathless ashen face.

'Your eyes – so wide. Your heart – so fit for bursting.' Danime could not close her lips around her lover's, so deeply was she breathing. But her lover took her upper lip between hers and sucked it slowly and long. When the kiss was finished there remained a fat contusion upon Danime's upper lip as if she had been smacked there. 'Let me see the ring; let me touch it – now, here,' Janna whispered lewdly.

In her own world, her small corner of the brightsmiths' workshops, in the glow of her miniature furnace, fashioning her jewellery, Danime felt secure. With Janna there was nothing of which Danime could be sure. For Janna was of noble blood – a princess of the citadel. But that first time, in the flickering light, under the steadfast gaze of Janna's groom, with men still working in the nearby bays, and Danime shuddering, crying out, Janna had taken first love of Danime with her mouth. Then she had pressed her flesh against Danime's, driving her upwards to a second pleasure. 'Today you find me running with the tribe,' she had said disparagingly to the groom. Yet all her fondling of Danime had been loving and gentle. Then she had asked Danime to fashion a special ring. A few days later, following the tryst in Lindrene, Janna took her to a room at the inn. There were two boat-women in the room. While Janna watched, they shared Danime. They kept her naked through the night, naked and aroused while the ring was being fitted. The piercing and insertion were slow and progressive. Danime had never experienced pleasure like it. Before morning the boat-women were gone. So was her lover, having left her mark – the ring, an intimate token of possession. As Danime crept down the stairs, the smell of smoky beer hung in the air. Her bare feet chilled against the scrubbed oak planking. Every step brought sinking pleasure. A group of waggoners were playing cards by the window. The inn-keeper was huddled across the bar, talking to a soldier. He glanced up and she felt her cheeks flush red. At work she had to stand: she could not sit.

Every night since the fitting of the love-ring, Danime had lain face down on her bed, legs spread, offering herself in her mind to Janna and living dreams so sexually vivid that by morning her thighs were wet with this new nectar and her bitten lip was smeared with blood. Without Janna, release only happened while she was sleeping. Awake she kept herself for her lover's return. Now that she had tasted fleshly love, each day of waiting ached like a year.

In the outer stable yard, now empty of spectators, Janna set Danime down. Danime knew that her lover's touching of her was only the beginning; Danime had waited

15

many days; her body was attuned to the things her lover did. Janna again put her fingers down the front of Danime's soft leather trousers, past the deep well of Danime's navel, past the silky orange hairs and past the burning soft moist place. Two fingers slipped through the thick gold ring and pulled. Danime moaned. Her tongue protruded between her lips. Janna gently kissed it. Her free hand, at the back, wrenched the buttons of the braces and tugged Danime's trousers down, exposing Danime's tight round buttocks to the kiss of daylight.

The groom arrived leading Janna's stallion. 'She's my slave,' said Janna.

He nodded approvingly. Danime turned bright red but did not counter Janna's words. They had made her pulse run, her breathing shaky. Janna stared into her face. 'I knew it,' she said with quiet satisfaction, 'from the start. That was why I chose you – why I had your hair shorn, why I put you with the boat-women and had you ringed. There is a doting innocence in these eyes, more heady than full wine.' She looked to the groom. 'Hold her – under the arms.' He supported her from behind. Janna drew the braces over Danime's shoulders and dragged the trousers completely down. They snagged on the heels of Danime's boots and turned inside out. Janna tugged them. Danime's body stretched between the two contenders. She could feel the groom's sex boning through his trousers, pressing between her shoulders. Her pale naked thighs were kicking; her buttocks touched the ground; the trousers, now inverted, came free. Janna tossed them to the groom. 'Keep them till we get back.' She grasped the reins of the black stallion. 'Now lift her up – astride.' Janna jumped up behind her.

They cantered uphill through the narrow streets towards the outer wall and the deep flower-strewn meadows of Lindrene. But at the last moment, Janna

turned the stallion to the right, towards the headland.
Before Danime knew what was happening they had
swept under the archway of the barracks and the gates
were closed behind them. Janna dismounted and handed
the reins to a soldier. He stared in disbelief at Danime,
naked from the midriff to the boots. Janna hauled her
from the horse and carried her into the building. At the
end of the corridor she climbed the stairs before setting
Danime down.

Danime, hunched to try to hide her nudity, stared
anxiously around.

'Hold your head high. Let me look at you. Your
mouth – so beautiful; these lips . . .' Gently she prised
them open. A group of soldiers had gathered round the
foot of the stairs. There were low whistles. Danime was
trembling. The intimacy of Janna's gaze invaded her so
deeply that she almost wanted to cry. Janna's hand slid
round her neck, caressing her. 'I could never tire of you,
never.' Danime's lips reached for her lover's wrist. And
her tears flooded. Janna stared defiantly down at the
men. Then she kissed Danime very slowly. But it was
Danime's lips which clung – for succour and with the
hunger of innocent youth. Janna drew back but put her
fingers quickly there to prevent Danime's lips from
closing. Danime's thighs ached from the short naked
ride, as if she had been slapped there. Bowing down,
Janna again took between her lips the contusion she had
put on Danime's upper lip and she sucked it hard. A
tingling feeling moved down Danime's spine; Janna
again pulled away. Then she stroked the love-bite.
Deliberately she turned Danime to face the men.

'Oh,' Danime turned her head away. Janna carefully
turned it back and opened her lips. 'We have come so
far – we two,' she whispered. She held out her hand.

She led the nervous Danime to the rail of the stairs.
Her naked legs were visible between the bars. The men
were staring up from below. 'Let them look. Let them

see it. They cannot touch it. They are not privileged. I am proud of you.' A surge of new emotion swamped Danime. She twisted her head and kissed Janna open-mouthed as Janna spread open Danime's legs. 'I wanted it like this – the gauge a little thick for the piercing. It makes it stand out like an erection; you can feel its path under the skin.' The ring was a large split circlet of gold. If Danime stood up straight it faced down and back between her legs; now she leant back against Janna so the men could see it. It threaded through the bridge of skin between her sex and her anus; it held this place nipped while Danime walked. It prevented her from sitting properly; it taunted her. On the stallion, her knees had kept sliding as she had tried to grip his back. Her thigh muscles ached, but between her legs the feeling was quite different.

Janna took hold of her by the jacket and led her deeper into the barracks. Still inside the building they emerged above a kind of quadrangle subdivided into many cells. 'The military prison,' said Janna, 'where the scapegraces amongst the ranks are brought to heel by assiduous retraining.'

As Janna marched her round its periphery, Danime could see through the grille ceilings into the cells. There were men, semi-naked, wearing short wool vests. Some of these prisoners were bound to the walls. In one larger cell were two sturdy female soldiers with a naked man who was crouching for them. Danime glimpsed his wet erection. Tubes and instruments lined the walls. She saw these things fleetingly. Then Janna took her downstairs to watch. There was a gagged inmate secured in the shape of a cross in the middle of the cell. Being put into him was a nozzle connected by a tube to a tap. Janna found for Danime a very small prison vest which she put on her in place of her jacket. It barely covered her breasts. She was still putting it on Danime when the tap was turned on. Janna stood her against the wall, holding her by her chin, touching her open lips, while opposite, the low sexual gasps of the male escaped through the gag. With the tap still running, Janna let Danime watch the erection until it did not come any bigger. Every so often, the sex would jerk and try to gulp the air. Then she led Danime back upstairs. At the far side of the quadrangle, Janna opened a door without knocking: she was expected. Danime meekly followed her in.

Again there were two soldiers. And again both were female. One wore the uniform of a captain. She had a razor poised in one hand. Her tunic was half unbuttoned. The other woman soldier was naked from the waist up. She was on the bed where a nude male lay tied and prostrate. But she was watching her captain and seemed ill at ease. A second male, semi-nude, handsome, well-endowed, was being shaved between the legs. He had been placed like a work of art in the bay window. Behind him lay the sunlit panorama of the cove with the round tower and the citadel beyond. He was fastened by the wrists to the ceiling. Every sweep of the blade provoked a small involuntary jump of his stiffly erect lathered sex.

'Remember – you told me you had never really seen one at close quarters?' Janna loosened her silk scarf and closed the door. 'Well today you shall learn in detail about men. Our captain will help me teach you.'

The captain pursed her lips. She eyed Danime, clad like the miscreant males. She placed the razor carefully down. Then standing in front of Danime she straightened the short wool vest. 'Hmmm,' she nodded. 'With her cropped hair and no breasts to speak of, she even looks the part.' She turned Danime round then saw the ring. 'And we even have a tether.' She had addressed the woman on the bed, who nodded nervously. 'Lara is our commandant's kickshaw. She knows all too much about men. The commandant is away. So today she learns how to please herself.'

Danime, unnerved but curious, was edged closer to the proceedings.

'They say that men are harder to discipline than girls. It is not true. They are uncommonly responsive to the clyster.'

'As we saw in the cells,' said Janna.

The captain smiled. 'The dark one on the bed – I trained him myself. The blond one in the window is my princess's.' She returned to him and took up the razor.

'He was given by some fawning despot to my cousin,' Janna said, relaxing on the bed. 'She tires quickly. I like to keep myself amused.'

'My princess must reveal her secrets.' The captain continued to shave the victim. Each delicate upstroke, deep between the spread cheeks, sent little shivers up Danime's spine.

He was clothed in one of Janna's short lawn shirts, too small by far. His wrists were fastened to a ring in the ceiling so his heels were off the floor. His sex stood very erect, and seemed to be stimulated by the strokes against his lathered anus. 'The more you do to this one, the more juice you get,' said the captain.

Danime shivered again; she wondered exactly how it would be made to come out; she knew that it was white. His legs were trembling just as hers would have.

Janna had picked up a heavy brass nozzle. On the walls were short whips and leather strings threaded with lead balls. On a table were jars of lubricant and tubes like those she had glimpsed in the cells.

Danime glanced at the male on the bed. Lara was turning him on to his side. His sex was only half erect, still thick, but soft and malleable. Danime wondered how Lara had been used by the commandant – whether she had been held for his exclusive use, or held in common. Dark and attractive, she was very graceful – but intent about what she was doing. She put her hand around his sex and spread his buttock-cheeks. The lumps of flesh – the balls – were loose inside the bag. Danime almost had the urge to touch.

The shaving of the one beside her in the window was almost finished. All the shaved skin was soft, pink, naked. The captain wiped it with a towel. There were no hairs inside the legs or in the buttock crease. From behind, the shaft of his sex looked longer than Danime had expected; but she had never seen one close by. Underneath, there was no real join to the belly; the true connection seemed much further back, as if the stem was rooted in the anus.

'Touch it,' Janna said, and to the captain, 'Let her feel it properly, she needs to know what it is like.'

Janna crept up behind Danime, propelling her closer, whispering over her shoulder: 'How would my bright-smith bedeck it? What stones would she choose? Where would she put them?' When Danime touched it, the feelings inside her were prodigal, pleasurable; she could see her fingers holding it; and she could see the response – even where the stem curved up and underneath. Janna showed her where to feel it. She directed Danime's fingers to where the stem seemed rooted, explaining that up inside him was a pleasure centre where the juice was formed. She said she liked to keep her slaves with this gland full swollen; there were many ways to stimulate it – things to be put inside, selective ways of whipping, unctions, instruments of penetration on which he could be made to sit.

Danime had often seen sexual excitement in the male guards driving girl-slaves, but she had never thought in terms of men being heeled to pleasure by women, let alone that she might experience satisfaction from bringing it about. But suddenly her mind flashed back to what she had seen in the labyrinth – the brown-haired girl and what she was doing to stimulate the guards enjoying her. And it was as if Danime's fingers did not

21

now belong to her, though she could feel the smooth-ness of the male slave's skin, the smoothness of the shaved inner cheeks, the direct hotness of the anus, and all the tight congestion that seemed focused where the lower stem converged with it. When her fingers bunched and tentatively pushed, the balls, no longer loose, be-came lumps against the shaft, which wavered as she moved her wrist.

Before now, she had only ever received pleasure – exquisite pleasure – at her lover's behest. A new world was opening up before her.

A surge of dominant desire swelled inside her as she watched the prisoner on the bed being entered. The captain had a fat dildo strapped below her belly. Danime had seen them used on girls. She had even had it done to her once. With the male, it made his erection come on; with each push, his sex responded. Lara watched enthralled.

The tips of Danime's dissolute fingers felt hot; she could hear the shaved slave's catch of breath; she tried to cup his tight balls in her hand; when she squeezed them, they retreated up inside him, almost disappearing. She closed her eyes, trying to find the rhythm she would use, were he a girl. Her heart was thumping in her throat. Janna's lips closed round hers; Janna's fingers searched between her thighs and nipped the seating of the ring. And up inside her sex it felt as if a swelling lump was there. Janna drew Danime away from the gasping slave; her fingertips pulled against the inside skin. She saw the mouth of his anus contract. She wanted to push her fingers back in – to make his sex, already stiff, come stiffer, as had happened through penetration to the male on the bed.

'You do well – my protégée,' said Janna, running her fingers through Danime's short hair. Danime in her vest stood breathless and proud. Janna led her to the win-dow. She said nothing at first. She was staring at the citadel. 'What happened?'

'When?'

'Down there, with the new consignment – I saw you following someone. You ran across the yard. And on the walls, you were watching – someone in particular.'

Danime's eyes widened. Janna stared into them. They slid away. Guiltily she shook her head.

'I'm not blaming you. I simply want to know.' Janna's fingers toyed gently at the hem of Danime's vest. Below it she was belly-naked. The thick moist gold ring felt cold against the top of her leg. Janna took hold of it again from behind.

'I don't know who she was,' murmured Danime, edging one leg open in acquiescence.

'I want to know what happened.' Janna's finger rubbed the skin through which the ring was threaded. The ring rocked, sending funny feelings up Danime.

'It wasn't like that, I only . . .' She tried to reach up for her lover.

Janna took her wrists in one hand. 'Look at me – look.' Again she stared down into Danime's eyes – not brave, nor adventurous now, but obedient pools of desire.

Danime heard a sigh, distant, softened. The room slewed gently sideways; she could not resist, nor did she want to. She slumped against Janna. She could feel the press of Janna's lovely breast against her cheek. When the Gaze comes everything in the real world turns dreamy; all pleasures are subdued – until the vision strikes. Danime watched with eyes half-closed, half-drugged, the sling being fastened to the ceiling. She was half carried to it. The loop hung down at the level of her belly. She felt her wrists being fastened up above her head. She felt the leg that she had earlier edged open now being lifted and slid through the loop, which supported it round the inner thigh. She was stretched but half sitting in the sling, with one foot on the floor. And during a timeless while, Janna was crouched on a stool in front of her, milking her between the legs, milking then kissing, with Danime's sex gradually opening, softening and spreading, and with Janna sucking, feeding, and the ring standing out stiffly, taunting Danime's body sweetly, as Lara watched her, fascinated, and the captain played with Lara's nipples. Danime closed her eyes and suddenly nothing was dreamy; everything was real. And she was in the labyrinth. The sexual feeling swelled between her legs. But she was inside another's body, not her own. The breasts were full, so full it seemed they would burst. And the swollen nipples of shiny brown were now the toys of male flesh not servile, but demanding, unshaven, pungent and strong.

Far above was a narrow slot of blue-grey sky; underfoot was dry soft sand: the walls were too high and closely spaced for rainwater ever to reach the floor. No one seemed to have noticed her abduction. She was afraid of being left behind, afraid that these guards would use her then leave her in the labyrinth and she would never find her way out. This was what the brown-haired one was thinking as her trembling legs were coaxed open, as she was lifted, as her toes unsteadily left the sand, as her frightened thighs slipped round the guard's waist, as her naked aroused sex was slotted to his hot stiff penis. Its broad base spread her, made the stretching feeling come inside, made her hood draw back, her clitoris protrude, just as it had done in the stable yard while she was bent over and masturbated. His mate's fingers found her erect clitoris from behind. Gasping, she tried to lift away: for as he was holding her clitoris, lightly tickling, softly squeezing, he was attempting to insert the knob of his whip into her bottom, gently and slowly turning it, pushing it deeper. Her sex was already fully distended by the penis.

'Ahh!' she cried softly. 'Hhhu! Hhhhuuu!' she panted.

The whip had a shiny handle, ornamented with faces and little knobs and bumps. It would not go fully home. He took it away, moistened it, relocated it against the half-admissive fleshy cup and pressed again, but continued to milk her clitoris with ever slower strokes, until she gave a long sighing moan and the slippy stem with its shiny little knobs and bumps at last cajoled the anal muscle fully open and the length of the handle slid slowly up inside her.

'Ohh!!' Reaching back, she put her hand against his shoulder, trying to ease the pressure-pleasure of this feeling. Her anus tightened; and every bump and pimple of polished sliding whip-shaft licked and petted up inside her.

'Oh, fuck . . .' the first guard moaned, 'sweet fuck . . .' for her bottom, involuntarily clasping, pressed the knobbly whip-shaft up against his captive penis. His legs began trembling. His eyes glazed. The strands of the whip dangled from her bottom, shaking, drawing curving patterns of wanton pleasure in the sand. Suddenly the guard groaned and pulled out of her. The other guard supported her as the head of the withdrawn penis, wet with her juices, gulped and bulged under the action of the restraining muscle which was vainly trying to keep the floodgates closed.

Reaching with her feet, she closed her toes around the head of the penis, making a little soft cage for the glans, probing it, squeezing. His breathing suddenly snagged; her toes just held the hot glans very gently and the thick slippy fluid came in burning spasms, jetting to her belly, squirting hotly between her toes, running in tickling warm streams of whiteness and clearness, dripping from her feet to make dust-coated balls of sexual fluid nested in little craters in the sand.

Looking up, she saw a solitary figure of a girl high above, watching her with a curious gaze.

* * *

25

Danime opened her eyes. Her lover was staring at her. Danime tried to conceal the deep feeling of warmth in her heart for that lovely girl. Her sex felt hot and open. The ring stood out and down between her legs. Janna had been playing with her throughout the vision.

'Are they ready?' Janna asked.

Danime remembered the male slaves.

'Very ready,' said the female captain. 'This one cannot wait.' The one in the window was writhing as if something had been put inside him to cause a pleasure so intense that his body arched away from it. The bone of his shaved sex poked thickly upward. The balls were almost buried at the base of the stem. The captain was simply leaning against the window, watching in satisfaction.

'You'd better bring her very soon.' The captain knelt back on the bed. The slave there crouched obediently forward, offering his anus to the dildo she was wearing.

Janna unfastened Danime and carried her to the window. She placed her kneeling on the floor. Danime looking up could now see a leather loop dangling from whatever source of pleasure had been put inside him. There were fine beads of sweat on the shaven belly; there was the smoothness of nudity running from the tip of the sex, underneath, in an unbroken sweeping curve seemingly bedded in the anus. So erect was it that the thickness of its root seemed to push the anus back and constrict the leather loop.

'Open your mouth,' Janna instructed. 'Open wide and proud. Lift your chin. Head back. Under it. Keep watching. Don't touch it.'

Her lover masturbated Danime, while she gradually and slowly rolled Danime's vest up under her arms. When Danime herself was close to coming, her mouth now desirously wide, her lover gripped the dangling leather loop with one hand. With the other, she held Danime's sex, which was wet and could now be clearly seen because the vest was rolled up all the way. She slipped her finger in and with her thumb she pressed the knob – applying only pressure, not moving, so it came slowly. The tight rolls of vest trembled, threatening to fall. Danime's hot gasps welled up under the naked penis. Then the drawing of the leather made the white fluid come. The slave was well trained. His semen did not shoot over Danime's eyebrows to soak into her short-cropped hair; it rapidly dripped then poured in hot aromatic gobbets into her hungry mouth. 'Let it slide,' Janna directed, crouching, kissing Danime's throat and continuing slowly to draw the leather to keep up the sexual flow.

It was like strong essence, burning the back of Danime's throat, its vapour stinging up inside her nostrils. And when her lips were finally allowed to close, there was not a drop of liquid there. There was no need for Janna to lick them. She had swallowed every weighted drop. And she could see the pleasure in Janna's eyes.

'Again,' Janna whispered, looking to the one undergoing dildoing on the bed. His sex was already smeared with leaked fluid. 'Take it deep.'

She put Danime on her back with her head between his knees. He arched upright as his sex slipped ever deeper through her lips. Danime had never sucked a cock, yet her head pushed back to take it. Janna kissed her throat, sucked it, slipped two fingers through the ring. The dildo in the slave kept thrusting very slowly in and out, each instroke scooping deeper, with Danime swallowing ever more of the stem. Janna's lips lifted from her throat. She took the razor and nicked the vest, then ripped it open, completely freeing Danime's small shaking breasts. Janna's tongue licked, pointed and wet, down the centre line of Danime's body, between the breasts, into the navel, on and down. And when it reached the pointy knob it enveloped it and pressed.

This cool wet traced line of sexuality opened Danime from her sex to her throat. Her body jerked. Her lips clamped wetly round the base of the penis. Janna held the ring. And the fluid, driven by the thrusts of the dildo, pumped thickly, bypassing Danime's mouth, alternately squirting and sliding down the tube of her throat.

When the penis came out, again there was not a drop of male fluid on her lips. She was the same perfect girl whom Janna had first chosen in the flickering light of the brightsmiths' shop. Except she now wore a man's ripped, rolled-up vest, and she was on her back near-naked. And the thick gold ring was bedded through the skin between her sex and anus. Janna held the swollen reddened skin through which it passed, squeezing it tightly to the metal while Danime moaned. Up the centre line of her body from throat to sex was the lingering line of wet.

'Tonight, I take you to the stables,' whispered Janna. 'Do you think she will be there?' Into Danime's mind came the image of the breasts of the girl swaying gently full as she languished in the guards' arms while the fluid jetting from between her toes shot out towards the lovely shiny brown nipples that Danime so dearly wanted to suck and squeeze. Still holding the ring, Janna began to finger-slap Danime's sex until her body stiffened, and the skin around the embedded circlet turned slippery with Danime's spillages of pleasure on Janna's nipping fingers.

3

Under the Servitrix

The slit of daylight above the captives disappeared and
the labyrinth gave way to a new and more sinister place
like the dark heart of a huge sprawling living thing.
They were being driven downwards, ever downwards,
through tangled branching tunnels lit by dusty shafts of
yellowing light. Their soft cries wavered through the
galleries as the guards positioned at every junction
whipped them on their way.

Each portal was carved to the shape of a sexual
opening – a pouted, thick-lipped female sex; a stretched,
cylindrical swollen anus; a giant open glans. Every so
often the space expanded into cavernous excavations
spanned by walkways connecting passages at various
levels. Mosaics displaying styles of perverse punishment
adorned the walls. Whipping posts fashioned to the
shape of phalluses projected from the sand. A strong
musky scent pervaded the air.

Their destination proved to be a long vaulted chamber which narrowed at its far end. The captors herded
them in, secured the iron gate then retreated.

The only sound was spent breathing. Large-eyed and
fearful, the women stared around. The floor was soft
deep sand. The walls were made of ancient crumbling
stone, covered in worn carvings; and there were tether-
ing points whose iron rings had recently been replaced.
Soft anxious whispers gave way to wary explorations.

No one was aware of the deft opening of a shutter near the apex of the far wall. Through the circular black grille, a pair of grey discerning eyes, well-practised in the art, stared obliquely down, studying hawkishly the naked creatures, searching out the most sexually breasted, and the most vulnerable and unsure. The eyes narrowed with silent certainty and satisfaction; the lank fingers sealed the shutter, retreated, straightened, pressing mirror-like, prayer-like, to the other palm. The tips of the paired fingers touched pensively the underthrust lower lip. The figure now turned; his eyes stared straight ahead. The brown sleeves of his cassock, turned deeply back, exposed arms of unusual narrowness. In appearance, somewhere between gaunt grey sage and rakish monk, the Chamberlain hovered, poised in thought.

Beneath his booted feet the imbricate stone floor of the viewing gallery swept a circle overlooking the domed chamber, a circle of exactly ninety-seven paces which the Chamberlain would repeatedly encompass in the hours to come, as the power-elite paid homage to their new supplicants for zealous and untiring love.

Stepping forward, he gazed down upon the means whereby promiscuity would be engendered as these sweet nymphs lay displayed. Arranged radially were the examination couches; suspended from the ceiling were the hooks and rings; the walls were densely clothed with instruments of close investigation; and there were racks of bottles, capsules, chrisms and philtres.

Stationed around the chamber were the Entires, full-male semi-naked keepers bearing short cane whips. And moving heavily yet methodically round the tiled floor, arranging, checking, testing – engrossed – was the Servitrix, garbed in clinical grey. Large and awkward, pale-skinned, tiny-eyed, she looked like a scrub nurse from some macabre place. But here she was queen. Something caught her attention; she straightened up. Her grey, stained, double-breasted tunic tightened across her hulking shoulders. And her tiny eyes fixed upon the Gothic doors beyond which her subjects lay.

Sianon examined the walls inlaid with soft erotic carvings. There were images of prolonged arousal, of deep intimacy, and of practices she found strange. Looking at them caused peculiar feelings in her belly. For the riders had brought her to the brink and left her unfinished. She was not the only one: watching the women, she saw time after time their gaze avert only to return, drawn to the unusual images; she saw cheeks flushed hot by sexual thoughts.

There were iron rings half-buried in the sand along the foot of each wall. Some of the women began to touch these tentatively. Their bending and crouching drew attention to the marks of punishment on their skin. Soon they began to examine each other. Their whispers echoed lightly from the vaulted ceiling. It reminded Sianon of the Abbey – of the vigils and Sister Sutrice. As she watched the soft fingertips caressing the weals, she felt goose-pimples all over her skin. It was the caressing after punishment that made her feel this way. It brought to mind the things her former mistress used to do to her. Then her eyes met Roslin's and a sweet shiver moved through Sianon.

When Roslin came to Sianon, the scent of maleness was on her lips. She caressed the tingling whipmarks on Sianon's breasts. 'They did you well,' she said. 'More on the breasts than any of the others had. Do you think they knew?' And she clasped Sianon's swollen nipples like beads in her fingertips and slowly squeezed them.

'Please – don't make it come. Not here,' Sianon pleaded gently but equivocally, stroking Roslin's flushed cheek, toying with the braid tagged round her neck. For in Sianon's belly was the feeling, very sexual, very strong, that she would have liked to kneel, breasts out, for Roslin, and let Roslin pump her nipples cruelly slowly until her milk dripped to the sand.

31

Roslin found the dried semen on Sianon's belly. 'Oh, how I wish that I had been there with you,' she whispered. 'How I wish that I were he.' Now Sianon's cheeks flushed.

Roslin slipped her hands under Sianon's arms, gently pressed her thumbs into Sianon's armpits and lifted. Roslin's nipples poked the undersides of Sianon's breasts. She made of her lips an 'o' for Sianon's stiff tongue to slip inside like the rider's stiff penis had done when Roslin was kneeling in the water. There was the taste of semen in Roslin's mouth, and the scent of it in her hair. Sianon was very aroused; Roslin surely knew it; if she were to put her fingers up between Sianon's legs, she would surely feel it in the lippy softness of her sex and the firm hot kernel of her knob. Sianon's legs opened, offering herself. She wanted to climb Roslin and let her sex lips spread upon Roslin's belly and her hard erection slip and slide within that smooth umbilicus that she had never had the chance to lick. Roslin pulled away and went over to a large wooden door at the far end. She tried the heavy handle.

'No!' cried Sianon. Roslin smiled.

Sianon's anxiety spread to some of the others. A red-headed girl nearby whispered fearfully:

'W – What will they do to us?'

Sianon put her arms around her to comfort her. She asked her name.

'Toinile,' the girl answered shyly.

'In the Abbey, Toinile,' Sianon then coaxed her, 'did the sisters not teach you about men and pleasure?'

Toinile nodded. 'But when they pierced me, I was frightened.'

Roslin had returned. 'And her training was hardly started,' she said, 'before the soldiers came.'

Glancing down over Toinile's softly freckled body, Sianon saw between the girl's legs the prominent ruby stud which had been set through one labium. It meant that Toinile had been a watcher, kept restrained and sexually awake whilst others all around her were being brought to pleasure. Some said it was the sweetest, cruellest training. The insides of Toinile's thighs bore marks of the whip but her sex was unblemished; the riders must have known the meaning of the ruby stud.

Sianon kissed Toinile; the kiss was gentle, yet Sianon felt a sweet electrifying tremble move through Toinile's lips, as if Toinile's sexuality was distilled by the constant deprivation. It made Sianon want gently to touch her. But the girl's fear of direct contact was very deeply rooted in her training. Sianon glanced at Roslin. Roslin understood. Toinile, trembling, bit her lip. 'It is nothing to be frightened of – such feelings can be good,' murmured Roslin. 'As just now – when Sianon kissed you.' Toinile glanced furtively at Sianon.

Roslin now kissed Toinile, and tentatively touched her pointed nipples. Sianon brushed her lips up Toinile's freckled downy back. She edged her thighs apart. Toinile was near the centre of the long tapering chamber. She was apprehensive at the prospect of the women around her while this was being done. 'They are the watchers now,' Roslin whispered. Toinile shyly hid her face against Roslin's breast. Her braided green tag brushed loosely over Roslin's nipple. She was trembling all over. When Sianon's fingers slipped a little way into the crease of Toinile's buttocks, Toinile shuddered. Roslin lifted up her chin. She stroked her tag, then held it. 'Look at me,' she told her. 'Let her tease your bottom.' Toinile shuddered again, more deeply. 'There ... Let these feelings take you. Kiss – gently. Tongue kiss ... Mmmm.' Toinile, with tongue extended for Roslin to suck upon and nip, moaned. Her knees went weak. Sianon's fingers toyed inside the crease. Roslin eased Toinile's breast to the side and stroked her pointy nipple. Willing fingers now came from several directions, caressing Toinile's beautiful red hair and slender

33

freckled back and soft round buttocks, wanting to bestow upon her all the pleasure that had for so long been denied. Sianon's fingers found the ruby labial stud. Her thumb coaxed Toinile's firm little velvety bottom hole. It was firm from sexual fright. Toinile's legs went rigid as Roslin lifted her on to her toes. Other fingers held her buttocks open and Sianon milked her sex and bottom gently in her hand, coaxing the frightened muscle. 'Gently, slowly,' Roslin whispered. The muscle opened. Toinile, panting, twisted her head and put her gasping lips to Roslin's inner wrist. Sianon milked between Toinile's legs. Toinile's bottom opened wider than her sex. It sucked the base of Sianon's thumb. 'So hungry . . .' Roslin sighed. Toinile bent forward, moaning, her legs trembling, her bottom thrust out behind her, her studded moist sex seeking Sianon's fingers.

But the climax was never taken: the heavy door swung open.

Toinile, still panting, swathed in new-found pleasurable feelings, stood there, guilty-eyed, terrified. Sianon's heart was thumping too. She held Toinile protectively. 'Don't be afraid,' Roslin whispered to Toinile. 'Stay close by us. We will keep you safe – I promise.' But it was already too late for poor Toinile; the guilt of sexual complicity was written in her eyes.

Two people marched into the chamber. One was dark-skinned and nearly nude. He wore an orange and brown skullcap and jewelled armbands. Arms folded, he held across his breast a cane. Like the riders, he made no attempt to hide his sex, which hung heavily, smooth and black. He stood by the door and stared straight ahead. But everyone's eyes were instilled with fear by the person standing beside him.

She carried no instrument of punishment. But her gaze was terrifying, hollow, dark, cold. She stood head and shoulders above the women. And she wore a scuffed grey double-breasted tunic, which was stained and much too small for her gawky frame. It stretched tautly round the shoulders, making her back appear humped and her arm movements awkward and restricted. Her hands – large, pale and doughy – were covered in small itchy-looking lesions. She kept rubbing them on the coarse cloth of her tunic as if to salve the irritation. The line of her meagre mouth was straight. Her hair was silver-blonde, but fine, drawn tightly back from her solid square face and fastened with a coarse ebony comb. Her eyes were tiny, buried in their sunken pits, cruel wiles their shady bedmates: so it seemed to Sianon.

Suddenly the woman drew herself up to a towering height. 'I am the Servitrix!' she bellowed. 'Here to prepare you.' Then she raised a single grisly finger. 'Defy me at your peril!' Her wicked eyes searched the frightened faces round the chamber. 'But there is always one. There must always be one who tries it. So who is it to be?'

With false patience she waited, hands on hips, her tunic-breast creaking with each powerful inflation of breath.

'Line up!' she ordered abruptly. 'Quickly! Legs open; heads back; arms folded behind you!' And hawkishly she watched for anyone slow to comply. But she could single out no one. So she lumbered down the line of nude forms, each body curving back, displayed and vulnerable, with belly arched and breasts projecting, lifting and swaying, trembling and pointing with fright and stilted breathing.

'These tags . . .' She touched the braid collar round one girl's neck. 'I see many of you bear them. It means your riders hope to lay temporary claim upon you – once we are done here.' She stopped at Sianon. Her cruel eyes narrowed. 'Though some of you, we cannot spare.' Suddenly she grasped Sianon's collar, clenched her teeth and dragged it roughly over Sianon's head. Sianon, thrown off balance, stumbled. Her ears felt on fire. 'Head back, I said!' the woman snapped. 'And stand still! Did they teach you nought but laxity in that self-indulgent place?' Her raised fist clenched tighter than her teeth. The skin was marble-white, veined by the small red lesions.

Toinile, next in line, began helplessly to whimper.

'Stop crying,' the Servitrix growled liplessly without even looking at Toinile. Suddenly the fist splayed and shot out diagonally; Toinile sprang back; the fist clutched only air.

The Servitrix slowly clasped the cringing girl in her large hands and stared hard at her averted tear-filled eyes. Perhaps she saw there some residual flicker of the previous warm unsanctioned pleasure Toinile had enjoyed. Perhaps she would now extinguish that completely. She sighed insidiously. 'There *is* always one. Simbulan!' Her guard stepped forward. 'See to it.' And she moved along the line, removing some collars, exchanging others, until she reached Leah. An evil glint came into the woman's eye when she saw the jewelled chain between Leah's legs. Smiling cruelly, she took hold of Leah's collar. Leah stiffened; the woman towered awesomely above her, tugging the collar as Leah shrank away. 'How then shall she please her riders when her chain denies access?' Leah's lips trembled. 'Turn round! Bend over. Bend! Let me see. I knew it! Wicked girl!' The Servitrix straightened up. 'Well, if that is where she likes to take it, who are we to lay restraint? Simbulan!' Her guard had returned with Toinile's collar. The Servitrix took it and fastened it anew round Leah's neck. Then she fastened Sianon's collar there too. 'There. Tonight, three teams shall plumb her wickedness. Keepers!' Two other half-naked guards appeared. 'Tie her with her split exposed.' Poor Leah was lowered backwards until just her shoulders rested on the sand. Her legs were drawn above her head then almost straight out to each side before her ankles were fastened to rings in the floor.

'And now the disobedient one.' She marched back to the shaking Toinile, then nodded to her guard. 'Bring the elixir.' He disappeared into the next chamber and returned with a conical glass bottle. The Servitrix turned to Toinile. 'Because you are young and inexperienced, your Servitrix allows you one more chance.' She held up the bottle embossed with the Tormunite motif. Toinile stared askance. The Servitrix drew the stopper. 'Open your mouth,' she instructed.

The administering of this unknown liquid in so unfeeling a manner, instilled into Toinile a fear so intense that, under those harsh sunken eyes, her mouth would not open; she could not drink.

'You see, Simbulan, there is always one. What makes me Servitrix is that I know. Come – drink, my little deviant. And don't look to your friends. From now on you have none. You shall not be moved from here without my say-so. And I shall not let you go until you come to heel.'

Toinile burst into tears.

The Servitrix, sighing, unbuckled her heavy belt. 'Get against that wall!' Toinile scampered – for her deliverance from the cold claws of terror and into the comforting hands of burning pain. 'Face it! Arms folded behind your back! Tighter!'

Upon the innocent, words may rain harsher than deeds, but that day the Servitrix did with Toinile all in her power to redress the cruel balance.

Every smack seared through the watching women. Toinile had done nothing to deserve so severe a punishment. But what the Servitrix had said was true: Toinile had no friends. Not one finger was lifted to attempt to save her. Roslin stood ashen-faced. The nostrils of the Servitrix dilated. Her powerful arm drew back. The body of the belt lay sprawled behind her in the sand. Her fist gripped the buckle; every muscle in her body was brought into play, every pound of strength. Then the belt whipped, snake-like from the floor. And there was a final forceful grunt as the leather lashed its broad red stripe across Toinile's pale tender innocent buttocks. The riders' whip-strokes that had smarted inside her thighs were now as nothing. They had melted under the burning evil strength of the Servitrix's lashing. Toinile's breasts and belly squashed themselves against the wall; choking sobs rose up inside her until she could not breathe. It was the harshness, not the punishment itself – so harsh, this woman was, so evil, loveless. After four such strokes, Toinile collapsed whining to her knees.

'Get up. Get up! Arms folded behind you.'

'Oh – please . . . *Please!*' she blubbered.

'Turn round. Back to the wall. Eyes open. Open, damn you! Devious little slut!'

The words were vehement, the belting was worse. It needed but three more strokes. And all their cruelty was reflected in that wicked gaze. They were laid across the front of Toinile's legs and belly – bright-red stripes that she would not forget, delivered for no other reason than malice.

'Now bring the elixir. And let her drink.' Toinile took it without refusal. And after the elixir came the reward. 'Open your legs – push it out!' She leant, panting against wall, spread-legged, her smooth bare sex exposed. 'Now – just so that it remembers . . .' In one quick lash, the belt-tip stung her ruby-studded innocence. Her legs gave way. Knees splayed, she sank down the wall. Her sex pouted open, one lip still swelling. Her hair was tousled; her gaze was pleading. The tears were streaming down her freckled cheeks, dripping from her chin, splashing on her lovely breasts.

'On your knees, now – come to heel. Keep your arms tight behind you. Mouth open. Knees spread. Look up at the ceiling.'

She had to progress by small shuffling movements of her knees. Her back was strongly hollowed; her breasts

38

projected; her buttocks rippled; the stripes stood out as weals. The guard Simbulan watched and was affected. His cock was semi-erect.

She arrived trembling, sobbing, at the Servitrix's knees. 'Kiss it.' The Servitrix held up the tongue of the belt. Toinile shivered when she saw at such close quarters the lesions on the woman's hand, but she obediently offered her frightened lips. 'No – kiss it with this.' The woman pushed her backwards. Toinile shuddered at the touch of that blemished hand. 'Open it and kiss. Open it wide. For we'll have this pussy well and truly stretched before we're done here.' And she pressed the leather up against the shivering Toinile. One lip of her sex protruded thicker than the other. 'And every time you disobey, we'll smack it when it's open. It will take me time, but I'll get you right.' Toinile started to cry again. The Servitrix drew away the tongue of leather, threaded it loosely through the buckle of the belt, then fitted it like a collar round Toinile's neck. She led her on her knees to a low chair which Simbulan had fetched and placed facing into the chamber. The Servitrix sat on the chair.

'Simbulan – the things.'

One was a white felt cloth splashed with stains; this she spread upon her ample lap. Sianon now understood the nature, though not the distribution, of the marks upon her tunic. The other 'thing' was a pair of muslin gloves. She put them on. But they were so thin they merely veiled the lesions on her hands. 'Come up now. On here.' And she lifted Toinile's frail slender form as if she were weightless. She made her sit open.

Whether through suasion by the elixir or by the spanking, Toinile was very visibly aroused.

It was a prolonged treatment, during which time Simbulan's penis stood up very hard, and the cloth acquired subtle new shading – billowing overlapping clouds of expressed liquid pleasure. The wetness came in waves. Toinile's pussy had never made so much before this day. And it had never stretched so wide. The muslin gloves had turned transparent. And below her pale freckled belly, her little knob stood proud and shiny as if another wet ruby stud now adorned its naked lips. Though her mind did not want these damaged fingers up inside her, her pussy clearly did. Her knees were up against her armpits; no one held them there. The wet was oozing out of her and running down. The cup of Toinile's anus, no longer velvet, stood thick-lipped, pink and wetted by her liquid.

The Servitrix, losing patience with any barrier to her tactile pleasure, peeled one glove from her hand; its fingers of muslin stayed inside Toinile. The fleshy lesioned fingers, bunching, slowly stretched open the little cup of Toinile's anus. Toinile moaned as they went inside. The stabbing, gripping movements of the fingers showed that they were nipping inside Toinile. The gloved hand drew back the hood from Toinile's shiny clitoris. 'You want to polish my buttons?' The Servitrix temporarily took her nipping fingers out of Toinile. 'More elixir! It gives her strength.' Toinile was drugged with pleasure. The Servitrix had her kneel up on her lap. 'Polish hard now.' She pressed Toinile's belly to her ample breast. One of the hard brass buttons slipped between Toinile's legs. 'Open it – spread.' Between the lips of Toinile's pussy, soft yielding moist sweet sexual flesh rubbed the hard metallic button. Toinile groaned sensually; she had never experienced such acute feelings. 'Rub harder. Good!' Then Toinile gasped, frightened, unsure of what was happening to her. The Servitrix, knowing well, eased her undulating belly away. The tunic button was quite wet. A stain of wetness had spread around it. The knot of Toinile's sexual flesh stood out, tender to the touch yet very stiffly willing. 'Again.' She put her to a different button, until it too was wet, then to another. Toinile's sex was inflamed.

40

The Servitrix applied to the buttons an unguent which drove Toinile wild. The Servitrix had to steady her. 'Slowly. Rub it gently now. Is it nearing again? Then slower.' Toinile's legs had spread wide and trembling. She wanted to ride the button. 'Slow. Steadily.' The Servitrix's naked, galled fingers slowly spread that tight small anus yet again and wormed themselves inside it.

'Ooo . . .' groaned Toinile.

'Still . . .' crooned the Servitrix. 'Fight it. Fend off those deviant feelings. It must not come.'

'Oooooo!'

'There now. Rest your chin upon my shoulder.' The fingers delved deeper up Toinile's bottom. 'I can feel my brass button through you. Let me rub it. Let me pinch it through this soft warm skin.' Toinile hunched. She was panting. Fine sweat glistened down the runnel of her spine. 'Simbulan!'

The brown glans of the stiff black penis slid into Toinile's gaping hungry mouth. The shaft rubbed the threadbare shoulder of the tunic. The Servitrix cradled Toinile's head, pushing gently, pumping Toinile's lips around the broad girth of the stem. When the ejaculate came, Toinile tried to pull back. Gripping the leather collar firmly, the Servitrix held her head in place. Her lips stretched wide to try to break contact with the wet glans of the pumping penis. Toinile gurgled as the jets of glutinous whiteness spurted inside her mouth and overflowed. Pushing aside the penis, the Servitrix's thick pink tongue licked the goo from Toinile's lips. Dribbles of escaping semen ran down her tunic. Toinile moaned. Her sex tried to mate with the buttons on the tunic breast. Her bottom tightened round the fingers that were still nipping up inside her. 'Steady. We have a long, long time together, we two. Gratification must come slowly.' The Servitrix eased Toinile's excited flesh away. She examined the enlarged clitoris then rubbed the ruby stud. Toinile groaned with sexual deprivation. The Servitrix lowered her to the floor. 'Hold her legs open,' she said, retrieving her belt. 'Cane the insides of her thighs.' Her teeth clenched. 'Harder!'

While it was being done, she walked down the now ragged line of women, studying their response. And she stood close to Sianon, towering over her, while the caning continued. Sianon was trembling; she had not witnessed such calculated and intimate cruelty since being with her mistress; but her mistress had been frail; this creature before her was strong. But Toinile was not strong, she was innocent. Sianon watched her legs shake; her feet had now been fastened apart; she saw her open sex. The shiver came again between Sianon's legs. The Servitrix was staring at Sianon's breasts. Would she want to do cruel things to them too? All these feelings, all these images, coming to Sianon . . .

'Enough caning!'

Pointedly, the Servitrix still stared at Sianon's breasts. And she knew. None of the men had realised, but this woman knew. 'Let down,' she instructed her, taking hold of Sianon's nipple. Both nipples came erect. Both breasts were bathed in luscious fear. 'Let down – you understand me?' Sianon closed her eyes and the feeling came, of floating, slowly spinning, her breasts full, sweeping upwards, outwards, her nipples fat, the pressure building. 'Let down!' Jarred back to earth like that, her breasts could not do it.

The Servitrix sighed. She took from her tunic a roll of muslin bandage and Sianon started breathing shallowly, quickly: her mistress used to bind her breasts. 'Arms up,' the Servitrix ordered, moving behind Sianon. Her fingers were warm against Sianon's breasts, not cold as she had expected, Her skin was soft and clammy. Even the fingertips were blemished with scabs and soft cracks. But they knew how to work her breasts, how to knead her nipples. She kept kneading them then supporting Sianon's swollen breasts on her thick splayed fingers.

42

'Ohh . . .' Sianon murmured. 'Mmmh.' All the feeling bulged inside her breasts. Her nipples fattened, softened, waxed. The soft, scabbed fingers smoothed them, smacked them. 'Ohhhh!'

'Hands up, behind your head.'

Her breasts stood out, bursting. The wide muslin bandage was unrolled, measured against her. Two slits were cut in it. They captured her nipples. When the band was drawn tight and held, it stretched like a second skin over Sianon's bulging breasts and her nipples poked through the slits. 'Kneel down.' Her breasts stood rigidly; her nipples made fatted caps. Then the band was oh so slowly tightened round her breasts. Tighter and tighter it bridled her, taking her breath. The substance of her breasts had nowhere else to go but to push, polished and naked, through the slits. 'Ohhhhh,' she murmured. The blemished fingers pulled them, slapped them gently, slapped the waxy polished skin. The feeling was unstoppable, exquisite. Her milk wanted to come.

The Servitrix stopped slapping. 'Lean forward.'

Suddenly the inner doors to the circular chamber opened again. A gaunt man clad in a dark-brown cassock strode over to where Sianon knelt.

'Servitrix!' he announced.

'Chamberlain?' Standing up, looking doubly ungainly beside this gaunt new arrival, the Servitrix began to retreat.

'I see you are begun with them. No, no – pray continue. That is good. The masters will soon be here to make their inspection.' His gaze moved quickly over to Toinile and then to Leah, where it lingered. In the background, in the circular chamber, there was light and activity. Preparations were under way. The Chamberlain tilted his head towards Leah. She was unfastened for him and drawn by her ankles across the sand. Her hair stretched out behind her. Her feet looked small in the woman's hands. Her breasts formed little pale jellied mounds, capped by rosy nipples. Stiff-bodied, apprehensive, breathing rapidly, Leah lay there. Between her thighs, the gold chain that linked her labia glinted. It captured the Chamberlain's interest.

'Let us see what little treasures Servulan has produced.' Leah, biting her lip, looked in vain to Sianon. The Chamberlain's gaunt grey gaze was fixed upon her unblemished belly. 'Has no one taken the trouble to chastise you properly? No? But there is yet time – before the matings.' Crouching, the Chamberlain held her chin. Leah swallowed softly and looked away from his searching gaze. She trembled as his gathered thin fingers were drawn across her naked belly. 'Cheer up, my little beauty.' Sweeping her up in his arms he declared: 'This is why you are here, why all of you are here – a circus for the pleasure and gratification of the few. Your Servitrix is mistress of the first ring of this circus. For what has come to pass thus far is but a prelude. She will now prepare you – help the juices flow,' he whispered wistfully, touching Leah's jewelled sexual chain. 'Keeper!'

The Chamberlain indicated to Simbulan the three collars around Leah's neck. 'I trust these betoken your strongest teams? In due course she shall need them – but that is after she has tasted the larrup.' Leah began to struggle a little, which goaded the Chamberlain to spread her bottom-cheeks wider yet, exposing her anus. 'Oh yes, we shall surely need the larrup on this one. Hold her so she cannot close.'

The larrup was a broad leaf of leather on a rigid handle. In the few minutes that it was used directly upon her anus, Leah came to know it well. It turned moist with the musk she expelled during spanking. Her chain was glistening and the mouth of her bottom was soaked. The Chamberlain kept Leah in his arms; he held her like a doll; he turned her this way then that. Simbulan kept her legs spread wide. The other keepers took turns to do the spanking. Sianon ached softly between the legs as she watched Leah brought ever nearer to the brink of pleasure by such means. She watched her being turned over, belly supported, bottom overhanging the Chamberlain's arm; legs wide, knees bent, angled, her feet in Simbulan's hands; her studded chain glowing on her glistening nude mount, the wet smacks splashing down.

'Take her in.' The Chamberlain finally passed her over to Simbulan. Leah looked small and frail against Simbulan's powerful body. She clung to his breast. Her legs dangled over his arms. There were fine droplets of perspiration on Leah's back; her skin was flushed with colour – not simply in the place where she had been spanked; her cheeks and breasts were pink, her earlobes red; her lips were full; her eyes were heavy lidded. Her thighs opened. And the place between them still glistened with her musk. Simbulan's penis was erect again. It kept brushing her buttocks as he carried her.

Beyond the Gothic doors was a circular domed chamber. Arranged radially around its centre were some twenty carved, shaped couches, each sloping in a convex curve from waist-height almost to the floor.

The Chamberlain retreated up some diagonal steps to a gallery above the chamber. Sianon was conscious of his watching over the proceedings; there were other figures up there who seemed to retain a more discreet presence but he remained to the fore, his gaunt face staring down at her, his arms arched out on each side, the thin fingertips resting insect-like on the capstone of the balcony.

The women were initially placed on the couches but not kept there all the while. The keepers would move them constantly from place to place around the room, perhaps to please the hidden watchers. When arousal was strongest a move would come: the woman might be lifted, murmuring gently, hair ruffled, breasts and belly

45

shiny with half-dried liquid. Sometimes a woman might be made to watch what was being done to the others; sometimes made to stand against the wall, or to crouch. Crouching would modulate the feelings of pleasure and there were instruments of exploration for use during crouching.

Loops of leather dangled from rings in the ceiling. They were for the wrists or for the feet. The couches sloped away from them. On a sloping couch, every position in which the naked captive might be placed was sexual. And once secured with one or both feet fastened in the air, she might be played with till her sex stayed open, with no instrument of dilation to assist it.

This was how these examinations proceeded – interludes of toying, exploration, sexual spanking, spillages of pleasure. 'If it comes, embrace it,' the Servitrix would say. For some recipients it came more than once. The keepers, their erections bone-hard, would take them aside and continue. There were small rooms leading off the main chamber. Sianon saw Leah being carried up to the gallery. A short time later, the keeper returned and selected from one of the shelves a very stout short spiral candle. As he hurried back up the stairs, this broad slug of wax hanging heavily from his hand appeared thicker than his engorged penis.

The Chamberlain no longer stood at the balcony, passively overseeing. He had left that to the others. His mission was more direct. Leah, the beautiful young sexual creature with the collars round her neck, now lay curled up in his lap, her promiscuous nude bottom against his functional brown cassock. The larrup was cast aside, no longer needed. His thumb was in her sweet umbilicus and his middle finger was slipped under her pubic chain, just pressing, bestowing light attention. The nodule of her clitoris was against the ball of the second joint of his finger. The tip of this finger gently dipped into the lubricant she was yielding. The Entire stood next to him, saluting her with his penis. Her scent was delicious, a rich musk her sex had expelled during anal spanking. The new liquid, coming warmer and thicker, clung in shiny strands to his dipping fingertip. The finger-joint gently rocked and twisted; young Leah moaned; her lips opened as if to take suck. He asked her again about the ferry – the male slave tethered on deck; and exactly what had happened with the one called Sianon.

'She suckled you?' He had to be sure.

The Entire's penis swelled almost to bursting as Leah recounted in detail the means of Sianon's milking.

When she had finished, the Chamberlain slid his hand under her bottom and lifted her legs until her knees sank down beside her ears and her pubic chain dangled above her in the air. 'The larrup again!' For so nicely balanced and exposed upon his lap was she, that he had changed his mind. Leah groaned a soft half protest. The Chamberlain's hand closed very gently over her mouth. And after each smack, he could feel, tickling the hairs on the backs of his fingers, the sharp explosive gasps of breath expelled through Leah's nose. After each sting of the larrup, her anus tightened, then expanded in harsh quick rebounding pulses, and little drops of musky fluid dripped on to the back of his hand from Leah's jewelled chain. He smacked until her small slippy tongue thrust out between his fingers.

He did not wipe her spittle from his fingers. He sniffed her musk like snuff from the back of his hand.

'Who had you opened here?' he whispered, touching the swollen pink anal ring with his moist fingertips.

'The Lady Abbess,' Leah replied.

'Ah, yes. She did you well. With what?' His eyes glinted.

'Dildos. And sometimes the monks would . . .'

'Use their . . . cocks?' he whispered.

Nodding, Leah closed her sweet submissive eyes. 'And the soldiers . . .' she murmured.

'Soldiers too. Oh, my! This Abbey I must one day visit. But how did they resist this little treasure?' He put both his hands flat against her naked pubes linked by the virgin's chain. His thumbs slipped tightly a little way inside her sex and prised the hard smooth lips apart until her chain stood tautly – five tiny rubies set in gold. She was like a little chained oyster, that would grace any master's table. His thumbs smoothed the walls of this delectable shell, coaxing its wet pink oyster flesh, touching its minute pee-hole, then dipping back into the narrow sealed entrance funnel filled with her exuded saline liquid.

But such was Leah's sexuality that only when he examined her anus again, and this time very much more intimately and deeply, did her erection truly begin. She made small stifled sexual moans and her belly tried to move to meet him. The more fingers that he eased inside, the more excited she became. Her eyes, innocent yet wanton, watched him. Female sexuality is a beautiful and diverse thing. 'Your soldiers must have been big,' he encouraged. 'In Tormunil we have creatures so endowed that even this exquisite place could never stretch wide enough to oblige.' Her toes curled up. 'The riders will help you; as will this . . .'

The Chamberlain nodded to the Entire. 'The candle . . .' When she saw its girth, she gasped, shaking her head pleadingly. Then her mouth fell slack. Her eyes closed.

Throughout the sweet stretching and insertion that he performed, he watched her lovely face. Her eyebrows, dark and dense, were quite superb. Her lips never closed. Her eyes never opened. Her head sank back, further and further, softly back, with little grunts and murmurs accompanying each deep slow screw of the candle.

'Ohhh,' she cried, and her fingertips reached down to try to stay its progress. The Chamberlain gazed in pleasure at these lovely fingers so delicately poised around the thick yellow shaft, as if it were a penis on the brink of spillage. Her labia were so soft beside her slender wrist. He hooked a finger under her chain and stretched them, drew the hood fully back and now, with his other hand, having left her bottom to clutch the candle, he took the wet knob of her clitoris and twisted it back and forth between his fingertips, screwing it very slowly, letting it come stiffer yet, a hard little nutmeg, but trembling like the glans of a penis. Leah let out a long, deep moan. His fingertips kept screwing her clitoris. Her love-juice began exuding from between her labia in luscious virginal clinging droplets. He unclamped his fingertips from her flesh and opened the breast of his cassock, drew the brown serge aside, and Leah's soft hot mouth searched moistly inside across the whiskers on his cool salt skin, over rib and hollow of his breast, and found the brown fleshy beak-like nipple like the nubble on a turkey's nose.

'Turn the candle,' he told the Entire. When the man touched it, the simple pressure of his hand, transferred so deeply inside her through the candle, made her climax come. Leah's bottom could not close. The Chamberlain kept her labia stretched up, sealed tightly together, and felt them tugging at the chain. He felt her teeth like needles round his nipple. And he felt the fine satin locks of her hair slip inside his cassock, under his arm, sliding coolly down, exquisitely tickling.

Laying her gently down he said: 'Leave her thus, with her candle inside until she goes down to the stables for the real thing.' When Leah groaned he shook his head and told her: 'It will be better prepared, my dear, more soft, more swollen, more sweetly presented.' And he took one of her hands and placed it modestly cupping her sex; the other he placed in the attitude of simulated love, delicately caressing the projecting candle. Then he kissed her mouth, her lips still hot, still moist with wanting, unrepentant. 'What tales of fulsome pleasure could these sweet lips spill?' he murmured. 'How was Servulan ever prevailed upon to part with you?'

By force of will the Chamberlain dragged himself away to resume his mission. At the top of the stone stairway he paused. His nostrils dilated, drinking the rising air, his languid gaze perused the scene – of love-flowers, petals spread open, pistils dripping nectar over stiffly teasing penises and over damaged probing fingers sealed in wet transparent gloves. Stifled moans of pleasure burgeoned and broke.

Sianon listened as she lay on her back. Her legs were open, her feet in the air. The tethers round her ankles felt softened by long usage. Her sex and bottom overhung the high end of the couch. Her back was arched by the curve of the couch. Her belly stood out. Her breasts throbbed gently. The muslin restraint had been drawn up from one nipple, trapping the breast and pushing it down. Her sex was soft and moist from the slow and intermittent masturbation the keepers were performing. She could hear the subdued moans of the others alongside her. The Servitrix moved among them, seemingly at random across the centre of the chamber, examining the expressions on their faces, examining the sexual place between their legs. 'Eyes open!' she instructed the girl beside Sianon. 'Look at me.' She tucked the whip into her belt and peeled off one glove. Sianon saw her bare hand rise, then pause, suspended. The girl groaned gently. The hand descended swiftly between her legs. *Smack!* The girl gasped. Her legs shook in their tethers. 'No – look at me,' the Servitrix said firmly. 'And hold it open.' The girl's moans came pleadingly. *Smack!* The sound was moist. There was a pause filled by the girl's strained breathing. Then *Smack!* Her belly curved upwards more strongly than the couch.

She did not use the whip on the girl. She finished her with her naked fingers. Then one of the keepers said:

'This one beside her is in milk.'

Sianon's breasts had begun to leak. The Servitrix stood between her open legs. The soft deep ache was in Sianon's belly. Her hands lay obediently by her sides. The Servitrix asked her to masturbate. When she was near to coming, the Servitrix put her hand over Sianon's. 'Still,' she whispered. Then after a short respite she made her masturbate again. Again Sianon wanted so desperately to be allowed to come. 'Lift her up.' Two men did it. The act of being lifted while she was so near, concentrated all the sexual feelings. Her feet were still fastened to the ceiling; her knees were up beside her ears. Her sex opened. Her buttocks were on the edge of the seat. And she could now see all the other women, being opened, played with, sexually smacked. Near the wall were two keepers with a girl, her belly arched back over one man's knees. The other was simply examining her with his bare fingers.

The Servitrix coaxed the rose-mouth of Sianon's anus open. Her thumbs slipped back to back inside it. She prised it wide. Sianon moaned and tightened. The Servitrix said she wanted Sianon's anus to be fully dilated when the pleasure came. Sianon could feel, brushing against her arms, the hot erect penises of the men who were supporting her. She could see the Servitrix's cruel expression. She could hear the lovely girl moaning near the wall.

When they lowered Sianon gently, the Servitrix's thumbs were still inside her and the sinking action again triggered feelings so strong that her anus could not help but tighten round the thumbs. When they were taken out, the soft skin of her rose was pulled. Her sex had stayed open. 'Simbulan – three lashes, just there, just inside it.'

Sianon's hips lifted in their moorings. 'Tongue out!' Needles of burning ice pushed up inside her. The whip-strands wetly drew away. Again the Servitrix's enquiring thumbs prised Sianon's anus open. Her knob remained untouched save by the warm musk trickling out of her.

'Now her breasts – use a crop.' The muslin band was drawn completely aside. The crop licked her breasts, over them, under, in urgent crisscross lines. 'Keep still, girl!'

It happened quickly for Sianon. But it was good. It left her breathless, wanting, with the ache still there between her legs, the sweet stinging feeling in her breasts, and in her mouth the taste.

She groaned. Her bottom tightened round the thumbs. Her nipples began spurting milk. It flooded over the plump brown areolae. It wetted the muslin. It wetted the crop. It made the men's erections come harder. The crop-strokes made it spray over the penises and run down under her arms. The spraying induced ejaculation. She felt the splash of hot semen over breast and nipple and neck and chin. The wet sticky tip of a penis wiped her shuddering open lips, probed gently up against her dilated nostril, touched her burning earlobe.

'It seems we have a milch-maid.'

Sianon looked up to see the gaunt figure with calm grey eyes watching her. Simbulan moved away. Her milk continued pulsing.

'Leave us, Servitrix. Take your men.' The Chamberlain's fingers drew back the dark-brown sleeves of his cassock and closed coolly and testingly around the leaking teats, so richly christened with the keepers' sprinklings.

Sianon stared up at the eyes searching hers. She murmured open-mouthed as the fingers helped her breasts keep up the flow. His face moved very close. 'On the shore,' he whispered, 'you were with a male slave?'

'Josef!'

'Shhhh,' he hissed. His thin fingers, warmed with her milk, closed over her mouth. 'Do not speak of it – to anyone. Do not even speak his name.' He moved back, took his hand away.

'But . . .'

The calm eyes glinted. A single finger returned to reseal her lips. 'Obedience . . . Yes?' The gaunt face tilted. The finger, lifting away, remained poised above her. Her lips stayed sealed. Inside she was in turmoil. Her breasts were rising and falling quickly. Little dribbles of her milk zig-zagged down her ribs. A teardrop seeped into the corner of her eye.

He straightened up, smoothing his bistre-brown cassock with the backs of his hands. His fingers slid through the slit of his gown to extract a small empty glass phial. Opening it, then reaching down, the tips of the fingers gently squeezed her plump brown nipple. 'Beautiful . . .' he whispered, and the zig-zags swelled, running continuously, creamy white, shiny, filling the small glass phial to overflowing. The Chamberlain carefully screwed down its gold filigreed cap and held the glass up to the light. He called the Servitrix over. 'You are certain there are no others here like this one?' he asked.

She shook her head.

'Then mark her for the Magus.'

He pocketed the phial, then bowing low, mouthed the words softly to Sianon: 'Your companion lies under the wing of the Lady Seer, Belangaria. When she is done with him, if she gets her way –' he hesitated – 'he may never be the same.'

4

Succubus

Josef remembered the icy water, remembered seeing Sianon on the shore. Then reality slid away.

He was floating in a warm blue sea far from land, his body rising and falling softly on the swell. The taste of salt was on his lips. But he was pinned by his wrists and ankles. He closed his eyes; the soft pulp of an open shellfish seemed to touch him and his lips ran wet. His tongue slipped into it but the flesh inside was hot. There were silken hairs about the mouth and a stiff tiny tongue half-buried in its warm wet folds. It pulsed as he licked it, and the mouth of this shellfish squeezed his tongue. A trickle of its salty wetness ran into his open mouth.

Inside him, deep behind his ball sac, was an ache, a good warm ache because the gland was full. The feeling at the tip of his penis was strange – as if something was being inserted and twisted round inside it, only at the tip. He pictured the head of a fine paintbrush, swollen, charged with oil, being fed inside him and slowly turned. The sensations were coming, peculiar ones – a gentle twisting inside the tube; the presence of a fetter; fluid rising against it; a dull ache of pleasure below the head; a soft wetness on the outside of the glans, as of warm lips kissing; and the pressure of a tongue against it. Inside the tube, an exquisite pleasure was focusing just below the tip as the desire to ejaculate continued building. And from under the sea waves came a soft coldness probing between his buttocks, then a delicious sinking feeling as it went inside. He felt his will to resist it yielding. The cold smooth creature began wriggling in slow motion, stretching him, sliding up, adding to the heavy pleasure-pressure deep inside until it lay coiled coldly and snugly up behind the warmly swollen gland. And the centre of pleasure was slowly shifting from his penis to within, spreading contentment like morphine out into his body, through his belly, chest and arms.

Then Josef felt the coldness slipping away: he was awake with his eyes still closed. He was afraid but knew not why. His penis was heavy but soft and hot against his naked leg. There was a feeling on his belly of a stickiness that had dried. He could smell the scent of a woman's sex. It was on his face; the skin of his cheek and neck was tight where her juices had dried to a glaze. The ache was still inside him, the ache of wanting to come. He was on his back, on a heap of soft quilting, his arms and legs stretched but not fastened. The place between the cheeks of his buttocks throbbed. He felt as if he had been forced open; there were dull throbbing pains at the mouth and itchy tickles deep inside.

He thought he heard gentle laughter like the tricklings of a stream. Then he opened his eyes.

He was on the edge of an enormous circular bed at the perimeter of a palatial circular room. Above him draped a velvet canopy, fawn on the underside, emerald-green on the outside and richly embroidered with gold thread. The princely room was captured in a giant oval gilt mirror on the opposite wall. Tall windows reached from floor to ceiling. Spars of dusty light balanced across spindle-legged malachite furniture floating on the polished beige marble floor. And strange phosphorescent liquids languished in sparkling decanters.

When Josef sat up, he felt the weight pulling through the end of his penis. Then he saw the thick gold torc there. It entered though a piercing on the underside an inch below the tip and it emerged through the mouth. Shivering, he recalled its recent insertion – Sister Sutrice's busy fingers working the metal through his skin, then her cool lips moistly sucking semen bubbling from the piercing. Even as these memories of sexual torment played upon his mind, his penis stirred. The feeling was like no other – polished smooth metal sliding inside the tube of skin. It kept coming as he watched his penis fill, the mouth spreading to take the thickness of the ring, swallowing it, reaching along the curving band of gold, stiffening until the glans was downbent from having to fit so unnaturally to the convexity of the ring. As his sex continued pumping up, the feeling became exquisite. It centred on the pierced flesh under the tip, where the bunch of nerves was stretched so tightly round the rigid metal intrusion through the skin.

Josef gasped and fell back into the softness of the emerald quilting. It took every ounce of self-control to stop himself from coming as the tip of his penis pulsed and sucked the partly swallowed ring. Many things passed through his mind – the thought of urination this way, with the tube obstructed; the thought of being tethered by it; the thought of what might happen to his ejaculate when he came. With the boat-women, when they had whipped his penis with the ring in place, it had felt as though the pleasure was being drawn out of him on a length of knotted string. Thoughts such as these came, but he was too squeamish to examine the piercing now, even to look at it for more than a second. Then he saw the girl.

It was as if she had appeared from nowhere, but she must have been there the whole time; she was not three yards distant on the bed. She slept motionless, half-submerged, moulded into the ruffled sheets, her breathing hardly perceptible. She had the posture as of floating in a sluggish stream, her silken yellow hair drawn out in lazy curves behind her. Her skin was china white. Her lips were crimson. When Josef moved, he saw glints of gold – on her lip, her nose, her cheek, her nipples. He crawled towards her across the yielding quilted surface. Still she slept.

The glints of gold were rings and rods and fine chains – one of these entered the corner of her mouth and was attached to a stud through her cheek; she had other body piercings – on her belly, on her foot; and she was secured by a heavy gold chain round one ankle. But her lips – so red and warm against skin so cool and pale; her limbs so long and lithe; her flesh so smooth – the punctures in it made him shiver.

Her eyes flicked open and Josef froze. But there was no sign that she was seeing him. She was staring vacantly up at the fawn canopy, her azure-blue eyes glazed over, her breathing coming slowly but more deeply, inflating her lovely breasts, which seemed to pause and shudder before subsiding into the mould of crumpled sheets. He looked again at the multiple piercings: her nipple-rings were linked together by a chain so thin it could have been broken by the pull of a finger. Her umbilicus was pierced by a rod; the tube of flesh had somehow been drawn out and then pierced, so it could not be retracted; the concavity had been reversed. Her leg moved, exposing her sex. The labia were standing as if they had been stimulated; they were pierced by a pair of thin interlinked rings. There were rings through the skin between several of her toes, and others between her fingers. A ring nestled at the top of her leg, in the crease of her thigh. There was a heavy clasp locked around her ankle and the gold chain passed down through the very bed.

Tentatively, Josef reached across to test it. Her eyelids flickered and she seemed to come awake, though her eyes had been open for some time. Suddenly she stared at him as if she were in shock; she seemed terrified.

'You must lie down,' she lisped, then coughed, because of the chain in her mouth.

'I only wished to free you.'

Her eyes widened as she turned to face him. 'Without the key you cannot. And they will be back.' Again her speech was stilted by the chain in her mouth.

'Show me – in your mouth,' he said. 'Let me look.' It opened slightly. Then slowly, nervously, her tongue peeped out. It trembled; there was a large gold barbell set through it and attached to the chain. Josef nodded softly but his heart was thumping. His hand, reaching out to reassure her, had come to rest against her belly; her skin was warm; she had been sweating. He saw that her nipples were engorged; they bulged like bright-red berries in a china-white surround.

The fear in her voice had turned to concern. 'Lie down. Pretend you are asleep. They must not find you with me.'

'Who?' But her hand was now on his.

'The Seerguard,' she lisped. 'They brought you here. They did things to you. You were moaning. Do you not remember?' Her wide, azure eyes sparkled at him.

'No. Seerguard?'

'They only want to punish me,' she frowned. 'Chained, I can never escape their torments. You are in grave danger if they find you with me.'

'But who are they?'

'All they do is punish me. Please – you must save yourself. You cannot help me.' Her lower lip trembled.

He tried the clasp around her ankle. He tested the chain; he tried pulling it up through the bed, but it was firmly anchored to the marble floor.

Leaving the bed, he crossed to one of the windows. The room was in the uppermost storey of a building set on a grassy slope in extensive grounds which called to mind the gardens of a palace. They were enclosed in the distance on three sides by giant walls. The view overlooked a cluster of curiously shaped buildings distributed around a large pool. To the right was woodland, still within the walls. A stream cascaded down the higher hill slope and through terraces of flowering plants. Josef followed the view round at the windows on the left. In this direction were fewer trees and many more buildings, including a huge vaulted glass-topped structure dominating the skyline.

The bedroom and the gardens spoke of opulence and space, yet Josef felt confined. None of the windows had any visible means of opening. The glass was extremely thick. There was one door, oval in shape, panelled with malachite, and it was locked. The only other possible exit was a skylight in the high ceiling.

Josef returned to the bed. 'Tell me your name,' he said gently to the lovely girl.

She stared at him, nonplussed. Then she whispered: 'They come through there.' And she pointed to the single door. It seemed a peculiarly unnecessary thing to have to state, almost as if she thought they might as easily have drifted through the skylight. 'I must lie with them. I am their reward.' She looked at him. He felt the nearness of her gaze. 'They can do whatever they wish with me. I cannot stop them. I am chained.'

He took her chained foot gently in his hands; it seemed so warm and slender and vulnerable. Her toes splayed out voluptuously; between them he could see the pierced skin and the rings. A delicious shiver ran through him. 'Why are you kept this way? Have you done wrong?'

'Yes,' she whispered.

'What wrong?'

'I dare not tell.' She was sitting up. Her gaze slid down his body and came to rest upon the place between his legs. Her breathing had altered; she no longer seemed frightened, but sensual and spellbindingly beautiful. The red lips and nipples pouted. She was toying with him. Her captive tongue was moving in her mouth. His hands had turned weak. She smiled; her foot pushed out, its splayed toes softly brushing his thigh.

59

'I cannot escape,' she lisped. 'Will you show me any mercy?' Josef looked at her and knew not what to make of her. 'I am their slave,' she whispered beguilingly. 'Each night they add another ring.' Then sinking down, she turned over to show him. His penis responded so quickly that it hurt.

There were two rings. Her fingers stretched herself gently open so he could see them both. One went through the skin between her anus and her sex. The other ring . . . Oh.

'It tickles. It makes me want to come,' she murmured. A thin chain connected the first ring to a large gold ball protruding like a bubble from the mouth of her bottom. A second, larger ring was threaded at four points through the velvet skin surround. It encircled the bubble. And it trapped the sensitive anal skin, which was squeezed between the ring and the bubble.

'I am not allowed with men. If I come too soon, they punish me.' It was unnerving; she was picking off his disjointed thoughts.

'But you are with a man now.'

'But I am chained and you are free to do your will upon me; I cannot stop you.'

He had edged nearer. She now turned. Her fingers reached out to him hesitantly – so sweetly and gently; he was powerless to stop her. She touched the torc where it fed inside him; she gently squeezed the punctured skin. He wondered – the ankle clasp, the chain, they were solid, but was it truly she who was the victim? And the diffuse memory returned as her gentle fingers squeezed him – her sitting on him, the hotness there, the taste, the clitoris like a tiny tongue, the feeling as the torc was rotated inside his tube – it had been her fingers, he was sure.

She slid back; her belly arched and the narrow rod of gold stood out from her speared umbilicus; one leg moved open and the linked rings between her labia glinted. Her eyelids were heavy, her lips apart. 'If I come too soon, they punish me,' she repeated. 'Kiss it.' He was looking at her protruding umbilicus, pierced by the gold. She reached tentatively again and took his penis, just the tip. It was aching with the deep sweet pleasure as she now masturbated it against his gold torc. Because she was reaching, chin down, all the pressure in her breasts seemed pushed out to the bulbous tips. Her nipple-rings stood out; the fine chain between them slid like liquid as her fingers provoked his aroused penis. He could smell her sex. 'You like it?' she whispered. For a second he thought she had read his mind. 'I will make it better for you.' She closed her eyes. He was looking at her face until he heard the tiny squirt. Her hand had momentarily left him. The fingers came back to wet his glans; the scent was in his nostrils; the droplets hung on the sheets between her legs; the ache of desire was in his belly. Who was this uninhibited creature?

Facing him she curled up on her side, her cheek beside his lap, her breasts and belly touching the sheets. She put her tongue out; its wet barbell stroked the sheet suggestively; his penis swelled until it ached; her fingers squeezed the torc inside his tip. Then she raised her free leg, exposing the protruding gold bubble. The velvet skin squeezed round it as if attempting to shed it. 'Take it out,' she moaned. He did not move. Her lips reached up. She kissed him – he felt her lip chain tremble then the barbell slipped inside his mouth as if inviting him to bite it and to hold her tongue-tip captive in his teeth. He felt for the chain attached to the bubble and he pulled it. Her tongue turned rigid. Through the chain, he felt her anus tremble, then yield the bubble. Then he felt the tip of his middle finger pressing through the large gold ring into the soft warm widened mouth that the bubble had just vacated. She gasped and pulled away from the kiss but pressed her open lips against the inside of his thigh. He could feel the wet gold barbell through her tongue, tickling his skin then tapping against the torc at the tip of his penis. Her lips began advancing and retreating moistly up and down the glans.

Gently he spread her sex to make a thick-lipped partial opening constricted by the rings. He sucked her speared umbilicus and licked her thickened clitoris. Then he began to work the gold plumb weight slowly back into the mouth of her bottom; he felt her shudder as it slipped inside. Suddenly her tongue swept down under his penis. Her lips sucked moistly behind his balls. The sucking moved ever further back until her tongue, aroused now, pointed, gold-tipped, touched him. It licked him, there. He froze. Her lips descended sucker-like and her tongue thrust through the rim. His stifled moans of pleasure served only to drive it onwards, upwards, opening him, stretching, slipping, moving deeper. How could a tongue go up so deeply? He could feel the barbell rubbing his swollen gland inside. She was licking this gland, insistently licking it, searching, her tongue-tip rough now, cat-like in its licking. His penis pulsed and throbbed, stimulated ever closer to ejaculation by this inner licking.

Quicker and quicker the raspings came. Then it was as if her tongue-tip had exposed the trigger she had known was there, for it suddenly stopped probing; and now he squirmed in pleasure – for the pressure inside him just kept building. Then very, very slowly the rigid point of her tongue pressed into this over-gorged sexual gland; and the feeling that followed was so exquisite – exquisitely defenceless pleasure rooted there, inside. His cock convulsed and his climax spurted, round the constriction of the gold ring, full and hot upon the quilt, with her tongue still in him, stretching him open, skewering his gland.

She rolled back, belly-rod pulsing, nipple-rings shaking, her plumb-line chain drawn tight. Her tongue, curved, pointed, thick and moist, was still thrust out impossibly far, and like no human tongue. Josef shuddered when he saw she had no leaf of skin beneath it to restrict its movements.

She disturbed him: she had kindled within him such contradictory feelings. But when she curled up against him, how he caressed her.

Immediately she wanted to do it to him again. She kept licking his penis insistently, sucking the spilt semen from his gold ring. And when he felt her tongue begin sliding down and back between his legs, he knew his desire was unassuaged. Over the next hour, he sucked her sex and gave her pleasure. And he let her tongue go up inside him three more times. Three more times it brought his climax, each time more pleasurable than the last. And each time, the rasping by the cat-like tongue-tip was the trigger. He never wondered why his potency seemed suddenly so enhanced; any fear of the untoward was swamped in the drowning floods of sexual pleasure she kept inducing. She seemed to want to persist in doing it to him this way, so he spread himself yet again. Her lips sealed limpet-like against him and her tongue went up inside and he burst and spilled – repeatedly, until he gave up all pretence of resistance, until finally he stopped touching her in return and lay there passively and just let her do it. He thought the soft raw ache inside him was the price of an excess worth having. Her hands and breasts were sticky from the continual floods of semen which they intercepted; how he was making it, he did not know and did not consider. She was draining him, but he was never being emptied. She put her tongue in from the side, then from the front, lifting his balls aside so she could get closer and deeper. Her hair was dripping.

Then the door opened. She pulled away terrified. Josef turned – not quickly enough. Four women clad in black leather tunic tops grasped him by the wrists and ankles.

'Seerguards – do not hurt him. Not yet.' The speaker could not have appeared in greater contrast to her semi-nude young guards. She was a mature woman in a narrow green velvet dress which matched the malachite surfaces in the room. Her hair, arranged in large lacquered tubular rolls, was set on her head like an inverted bluish-grey triangular hat. She sat slowly and gracefully on the bed. 'Josef?' She smiled at his surprise. 'I know all about you – everything. I am Belangaria, your mentor. You yourself are not to speak my name. To you, I am your lady. And I expect great things of you. Do not disappoint me.' She stared at him searchingly, then glanced aside. 'There are those who wish to see me fail in my endeavours.' Her astute gaze returned. 'I cannot afford that you let me down. I shall therefore be a zealous lady for you.' She turned to her guard. 'Has the Succubus been inside him?'

The word sent chilling feelings through to his marrow. 'I need to see it being done. Sometimes they pull away when her seed is being planted. Remove his torc first. Turn him over.'

And what had happened consensually before, now required the full strength and weight of the four guards.

Lady Belangaria stood up and went to the malachite table. There she poured some phosphorescent liquid from a decanter to a glass. Sipping it, she watched the beautiful creature at work between the buttock-cheeks the Seerguards held apart. It gave her a controlled inner pleasure to see the young man opened out, spread sexually in the way more usually reserved for women, with the surreal tongue curving like a wet smooth penis as it thrust inside him to the hilt. He started to moan – the tongue-tip must have found the place.

Lady Belangaria floated to the bed. 'Get his cheeks more open.' Reposefully she sat down. She could see his balls, which were good balls, already comparatively full ones, heavy against the bed. She touched them, squeezed them. Soon they would come fatter. She pressed them down so she could see the tongue of the Succubus entering from above. She touched it where it went inside the anus, then she let the lips descend again, so the deep penetration could occur. He gasped in sweet priapic pleasure. For if sexual desire was an essence – a magical venom – then the Succubus was surely the snake. Belangaria stroked the beads of sweat upon his forehead. 'Sweet youth, what are you feeling? Let her get to you. Let her swell your flow of delicious juices. Oh ... Your knob-end, Josef, let your lady see it.' And as his leg was drawn aside and the knob emerged from under his lifted belly, he shuddered and his semen began pouring thickly over his lady's hand. 'He has not learnt to stem it. We shall teach him. I shall teach you many things, Josef. And oh, you have such good young balls.' She clasped them in her wet fists. 'Dense, firm and thick. How I shall put them through their paces.'

Then she clamped a heavy metal split ring around his genitals. 'Take him somewhere quiet. It is important that the needs of the body become so attuned, so focused, that sexual desire and forced pleasure control his every waking thought and move. Let the seed which she has planted take nurture before we begin with the whipping of the sexual parts.'

There are four organs of depravity in the male slave – the penis, the anus, the deep gland and the balls. Belangaria understood that climax may be triggered by stimulation or irrigation or punishment of any of the four. She felt that the balls were all too frequently neglected. There was something about balls in harness – the shape, the smoothness, their detached roundness, aching sensitivity, and their weight – that cried out loud for retribution to be exacted.

There were two preferred restraints for this organ of debased male pleasure: one a rigid double clasp of gold, the other a supple oiled cord. The latter could be used during whipping. It forced the balls to protrude separately and polished. There were also instruments and halters for the penis – teats with a soft thick leather spike that slipped through the mouth of the glans and down inside the stem. By constricting the flow they prolonged the climax: the perpetratrix, at her leisure, might pour herself a drink and watch the soft teat slowly filling with the chaser.

There was a captive metal ball in a collar which fitted around the base of the penis. Light thumb-pressure held the ball against the tube and controlled the rate of emission. The naked penis could be kept inside a person's mouth throughout the stilted climax without the danger of a rapid choking spillage. And these practices always deepened the climax yet made it sweetly unfulfilling for the male. Once emission was complete, the stimulation would be recommenced to keep the seminal vesicles exercised to overflowing. The pleasure could be made unbearable. But Belangaria made her victims bear it.

No ejaculation was ever permitted to occur by conventional means. She – the Lady Seer – must direct its progress, all the pumping serving only to salute her. A sweetly sinking pleasure came to her when she saw such penises arching up, for a third or fourth time, polished, gasping, pulsing – the fluid so hot and the egress so constricted that it sprayed. She liked semen in all its forms, liked to see it, smell it, store it, taste.

The floor of her whipping room was smooth tiles. Sometimes she would go barefoot. Semen, cold and slippy between your toes was a feeling quite different from hot inside your mouth.

Belangaria, her hands now wet with warm ejaculate, drifted along the line of male slaves squatting on the long table. Each penis curved up, untouched yet stiffly erect – black ones, bronze ones, pale or sun-warmed yellow. Each pair of balls in varying degrees clung to its master-staff for absurd protection. Here and there, a belt buckle emerged from a distended anus. A Seerguard flexed her crop. Belangaria selected an appropriate pair of balls – ones that seemed to dangle perhaps a little more vulnerably than the rest. And a few seconds later, amid the exquisite groans, and the quick lashes of the crop, the hot spice of servile love gushed helpless pleasure over Belangaria's cool prepotent fingers.

And each time she asked for a lashing to be delivered harder, or a belt to be pulled more quickly through the tight love-ring, she was thinking of her new acquisition, as yet untouched, upon which so much depended and which in time she must display.

5

The Farbesian Girl

The Chamberlain left the domed chamber by a door which led directly from the viewing balcony to a covered straight gallery. About a quarter of the way along this, some steps on the right descended swiftly through several short flights to emerge at street level. He followed the cobbled slope down twisting alleys to the cluttered buildings of the artisans' quarter in the shadow of the inner wall. From the host of narrow and diverse entrances he selected a dim coffin-shaped archway, crowned by a sculpture of the sun being plucked from the heavens by a celestial hand. A worn spiral stone staircase led him down and down, through billowing warm air laced with wisps of acrid smoke, into a low, extensive catacomb-like suite of chambers – the brightsmiths' workshops. Far below the level of the pavement, these were dark, poorly ventilated places, lit by candlelight. The stalls had been excavated from the living stone. The workforce was large; space was very precious; no cranny was left unfilled.

Tiny charcoal furnaces spurred by miniature bellows glowed with orange light; minute ladles spat pure white sparks of burning spelter into sizzling oil baths. Ever present in the background were the whirrings of the polishing laps and the urgent tappings of the copper hammers. And the unkempt craftsmen, a proud caste of freemen, thick-fingered yet keen-eyed and meticulously precise, huddled intently over spangled microcosms of perfection in jewel and precious metal. No one here showed deference to the Chamberlain, for no one seemed aware of his presence. The master-smith, a few stalls distant, was bent in conversation with a leather-clad apprentice. The Chamberlain allowed his gaze to roam across the workbenches.

Sparkling in peculiarly mean containers of singed wood and chipped earthenware were the priceless raw materials of this micrurgy: spun gold, gold leaf, gold dust, thread silver, raw opal, amber, and a multiplicity of uncut precious stones.

Placed haphazardly on a nearby bench were some of the partly finished products: gold spatulas; fine, necked lengths of silver tubing; shaped cups in which to capture spillages of potable sexual fluids; netmeshed pouches for the vulva; jewelled personalised sheaths; gold balls and bells; tiny weights on gold twine to keep the girl-slaves open during masturbation or whipping; ornamented nipple clamps; nipple sheaths; gold baubles to adorn and stimulate the various body piercings.

At length the master-smith noticed him and hurried over.

'Apologies, my lord. I was . . .'

The Chamberlain cut him short with a wave of his hand. Then he saw that the apprentice was a girl.

The master-smith smiled apologetically.

'Her name is Danime, my lord.' When the Chamberlain continued to stare quizzically at her without saying anything, the smith shook his head and added: 'I was doubtful too, but . . .'

'But what?'

'Well, she has proved herself, and more,' he nodded. 'So nimble. And quick. And there's a spark there – like skittish spelter.'

'I see she has her master's good opinion.'

'That she does – but not the way you're thinking.

She's her own woman here – a worker, and a good one too.'

The Chamberlain moved closer to the stall where she was bent over her work.

'Shall I?' asked the smith.

'No. Don't disturb her.' Because of the noise and her intentness she was quite unaware of being watched. Her small attractive face was lit by the warm light of the workbench candles. The space was confined. She wiped her brow. Her hair was short and orange-yellow. Her hands were slender. She wore a soft leather jacket and trousers.

When the Chamberlain finally turned, the master-smith was holding out a small velvet-covered box.

'They are finished,' the smith simply said.

The Chamberlain quickly took the box and opened it. His sucked his breath, nodding weightily. 'So fine – and so precisely executed. Masterly. We must reward you – over and above the put price.'

'Not me, sir . . .' He tilted his head towards the girl.

When the Chamberlain looked again, the perpetrator of this masterpiece was once more bowed intently. But she had removed her jacket against the warmth. And she wore no shirt underneath it.

The straps supporting her trousers crossed unevenly on her slender naked back. One of the buttons was missing. Her elbows rested on the workbench. 'I shall speak with her,' the Chamberlain announced loudly. She looked up, surprised but unselfconscious. Then she saw the open box in his hand. 'They are perfect,' he said. 'You are very skilled.'

'My lord is generous.' She swung round to face him. On her upper lip was a contusion, like a little bruise, perhaps a lovebite. He glanced around, looking for likely swains amongst the other young apprentices. Her nipples pointed slightly up. Her naked breasts were small but nicely swollen. The straps of her trousers deformed around them to the sides. Her navel crowned a belly that was small and round enough to cup within the palm. The waistband of her trousers did not grip and mark this perfect belly; there was a gap which that selfsame palm might easily slip down in order to hold her, just to hold it, as she sat thus, forwards on her stool.

'Then you yourself measured her for the Princess Janna?' he asked, staring at her lithe fingers.

She nodded unassumingly. Would that he had been there. In the sweet blackness of her pupils he saw the spark. Again he looked upon the contents of the box. 'What reward will you take?'

Her reply shocked him: 'To be at the muster. And to take full part, along with the masters.'

'You cannot have her.'

'No,' she said cryptically.

The Chamberlain glanced at the bemused smith then stared again into the box. His fingers, unable to resist the touch, roved lambently across the castings, so recognisably Farbesian and so perfectly finished in every beautiful minute detail. Looking up, he saw the glow of the furnace reflected in the girl's eye. 'We shall see,' he told her.

There was one special vantage point atop a turret of the inner wall which at sunset remained brightly lit to the very last, after every other part of the citadel was cloaked in the young soft tide of summer night. The Chamberlain, arms folded, sleeves rolled back, stood sunlit and motionless under the waxing moon. Welling up from below was the sweet warm scent of disturbed hay. Lights flickered in the tiered stables; coarse laughter drifted skywards. The displaced ponies, stripped of their harness, murmured in the yard. Two hours hence was the appointed time: in two hours the Chamberlain was to bring the Farbesian to his master who would effect the fitting. By day she slept in the Milanderan dormitory, that she might recoup. But now it was night. And he had two hours. Under his cassock, against his naked breast, was the phial of Sianon's milk, kept warm by the heat of his body. The Chamberlain extended his arm over the parapet: the wispy grey hairs spangled metallic in the horizontal light; his spindly fingers crossed the crest of shadow and dipped into the night.

A few minutes later he was standing at the head of the broad sweeping green marble stairway overlooking the concourse of the vast Milanderan dormitory. The Farbesian had been kept separate from the others, so separate that only the matron knew precisely where.

In the interim the Chamberlain walked a short distance around the first level of this magnificent building wherein pulchritude could be savoured in palatial splendour by the emissaries dispatched here from every corner of the empire. Here contracts would be sealed – for precious metals, gems, silk, spicewood, and resin of Carne – in exchange for quotas of Tormunil's matchlessly beautiful slaves.

The true dormitories were restricted to the uppermost floor; in the body of the building were the reception halls, drawing-rooms, libraries and galleries; above these were the suites of intimacy, bathing, selection, and training.

The matron arrived and beckoned him to follow, taking him upstairs again, unlocking a large side door and leading him through, then along a wide candle-lit corridor decorated with a frieze of beautiful languorous women set against a backdrop of the orchards of Elysium. In the subsidiary corridors, no less ornate, the imagery was much more specific. Few free men had ever seen these works. They were intimately detailed studies of self-stimulation and mutual masturbation, of bondage and deep penetration. The only people depicted in them were women. The artists were men, personal slaves

72

to the Lady Seer Belangaria, and each picture was said to be based upon a living scene which she herself had orchestrated. While the artist worked upon the picture, the Lady Seer's own fair hand worked priapic inspiration deeper and deeper into the artist, keeping him erect indeed, both at the time of sketching and subsequently, by continuous stimulation, during transfer of the image to the frieze. Such was the rumour, and the Chamberlain did not doubt it.

At the end of a side corridor the matron halted at the red lacquered door of a private room. 'The seal?' she asked cagily. He placed into her hand his master's small engraved serpentine cylinder, which she fastened by its loop alongside the other seals already on her belt. Then she unlocked the door and glanced within. Seemingly satisfied, she touched her finger to her lips before finally admitting him and closing the door quietly behind him.

There was no feeling quite like it – to be a man admitted deep into the heart of this cloistered place. The room was comfortably appointed, upholstered in orange satin. But the first thing he had noticed was the light, delicious scent. The Farbesian was asleep in the bed. The housegirl beside her scarcely stirred when he eased the coverlet aside. Then her eyes opened up like saucers when she saw his gaunt brown figure towering above them. 'My lord,' she whispered agitatedly, crossing her arms over her naked breasts and staring guiltily at the Farbesian.

The Chamberlain raised a single narrow finger. 'Lie down again,' he whispered. 'Turn away.' And as she lay there, he could see in the mirror on the wall her anxious eyes, and her lovely breasts heaped one above the other with her pert young nipples poking from beneath her crossed forearms. Beautiful she was, but not Farbesian. Farbesian was perfection.

And so the Chamberlain turned to this perfect creature. She wore her own short yellow seersucker waistcoat. It was embroidered and buttonless. It sheltered her nipples. Her sex was sheathed in a narrow cotton band fastened to a cord round her waist. Her limber arms and legs were naked. The Chamberlain bared his arms and lifted her. Such was the nature of a Farbesian, that a man would always have this urge to lift her bodily and to strip her belly-naked and to hold her in his arms. The skin of her thighs was very warm against his bare arm. Farbesian skin was smooth and oily; it had its own aroma too, like warm beeswax. After sleep this scent was stronger. It was in her hair – black hair, long, fine and shiny – her dense black eyebrows, her skin of palest brown. Her waistcoat had fallen open. Her breasts were conical, firm, pumped up, upwards and outwards pointing, capped by smooth dark areolae. They swelled to his fingertips before she had fully woken. Her mouth opened, then a little afterwards, her eyes. They focused. Automatically she gasped. The Chamberlain shook his head and put his finger over her lips. Then, remembering her training, she closed her eyes and she kissed the finger that lay across her lips.

He did not put her down until they were far from the dormitory and in the upper levels of the stables. There she clung about his neck. The distant noises echoed up the cavernous passageways towards them. He could feel her breathing quicken. He put his arm under her waistcoat and his hand against her heart.

'Does it frighten you down here?' he asked.

She shook her head bravely but stared around with frightened eyes. Then she nodded, swallowing but not speaking.

'With me you shall come to no harm.' His hand cradled her lovely breast then slipped deeper, under her arm.

'Do not – do not put me to the riders,' she pleaded in a heavy Farbesian whisper. Even her voice was darkly beautiful. She had not listened to his words, or perhaps

74

she had not believed them. So he led her a little further down the ramp to where the sounds were more distinct. And she turned to him, wanting to be lifted, pleading.

The more he reasoned with her, the more frightened she became that he meant to do exactly what she most feared. He took her by the hand. They entered the tiered hay lofts of the stables proper. There were people gathered, mostly artisans and commoners, who were spectators, normally permitted to take no part. They would never dare to touch her. But the Farbesian was frightened of them. She seemed ignorant of the existence of this division. Or perhaps it was simply that she knew only too well on which side of the divide she belonged. So when a spirited group of tanners approached she became distraught. Words were useless; the Chamberlain relented. Yet as soon as he lifted her up again he could feel it in the way she clung – her dependency, the fervent sublimation of her will to his, as if her display of distress had been a last stand against her fear and now she acquiesced. 'Kiss,' he whispered. Her lips felt warm and moistly sensual. He carried her down the ramp and closer to the scene of the action. A low wooden partition overlooked a part of the stables laid out like the pit of a miniature theatre, with tiers of hushed spectators around it in a ragged circle. Quietly he lowered the Farbesian's feet on to the hay.

She was shaking. 'Shhh. Trust me.' The sliding of her body down his cassock had made the cotton band draw up tightly between her legs. He turned her to face the partition so she could watch and he placed her hands on the rail. Then he stood beside her with one hand resting lightly against her, one finger under her cotton band, just brushing the fine hairs in the small of her back gently upwards and testing her response.

The girl in the stall was in harness and on her knees. She was blindfold. Her wrists were secured behind her to a studded body-belt. Her hair was tied back in a

75

ponytail. Her ankles were fastened by short chains to rings on the body-belt, so she could move only by shuffling across the hay on her knees. But she could make love with her mouth and fingers and such avenues between her legs as her riders might select. She could not know for sure the full number of her suitors. Some leant against the staving, their thongs undone in readiness, their penises stiffly waiting while others directed her by taking hold of her head or breasts or buttocks and manoeuvring them into place. For the most part they kept silent until the grunts and moans she induced in them refused to be restrained. They drank philtres as aids to excitement and to help postpone completion. When close to climax, a rider would therefore withdraw and walk round, penis swaggering wetly while another took his place. And with hungry vigour she would take into her mouth or sex the new penis. Her erect breasts were grasped by their harness and wetted, slapped and nipped. And on withdrawal of the gulping moist penis from her sex, her hands, still fastened behind her at the wrist, took the slippy head of it between her fingers and played with it, trying to make it ejaculate while her nose and lips and tongue searched blindly between the other's thighs for the ripeness of his bursting penis.

Suddenly her fingertips reached down and back between the rider's legs. He arched his back and shuddered until his toes crawled out across the hay. The fingers clutched and probed the mouth of his anus and the rider almost came.

Under the Chamberlain's gently stroking finger, the Farbesian's backbone gave a sudden sexual tremble. She was like a bowstring that had been overtightened. 'Lean against the rail,' he whispered. He drew her hands along it at each side. 'Spread your legs.' Very swiftly from behind, he drew aside her cotton band and put just the pad of his finger against her anus and vibrated it very quickly. The pressure of her pushing forced her buttonless yellow waistcoat open; her breasts alone were placed within the arena; some of the spectators turned to look up at them. Her cheeks flushed dark with colour. 'There, you see,' he whispered, drawing the flaps of her waistcoat aside as her breasts thrust out over the rail and her heels lifted and her anus avidly sought indecency on the goading tip of his finger. Her back was deeply hollowed. There was something very special, very softly beautiful and waxy about her anal skin.

The rider's balls were in the girl's fingers; she reached back again, rubbing nervously between his buttocks with her finger, and the semen jetted out of him in an arc against her back. The other penis was already spurting when it came out of her mouth. Blindfold she could not recapture it.

The Chamberlain allowed the cotton band to slip back tightly into the Farbesian's crease. But there was now a bulge there – her stimulated anus like a firm little cratered burl. His hand slid upwards, under her waistcoat, between her shoulders, then gently down the hollow of her spine. When he turned her round and drew the cotton band up between her thighs, a small dark patch of her lubricant was already visible in the middle. He picked her up. 'Kiss – with your tongue,' he murmured. As he took that warm slippery honeyed instrument of pleasure between his lips, he twisted a finger under the cord round her waist to keep the band of cotton tight.

He took her further down into the stables, to where the scent of semen was almost stronger than the scent of hay. It was a broad, low-ceilinged corridor. A girl attended by a lady was in the middle, draped along a bale of hay. Collars round her knees were suspended from the ceiling. One rider had just finished. His penis, hovering above the girl, dripped the last of its semen on to her breasts. Another was rubbing and slapping her between the legs. Her lady was directing. The girl was moaning; her legs were trembling; her nipples, quite erect, were coated in the running semen. Other riders were standing by. The lady, now kneeling on the hay, moved from one to the other, sucking their balls and masturbating their heavy swaying penises in her fist. A commoner could never lay claim upon a lady but a lady could condescend.

The Chamberlain took the Farbesian closer. He asked the lady if his charge might touch the riders. The Farbesian clung to him, but her dilated eyes were fixed upon the penises, which the lady was still masturbating briskly.

From where the Chamberlain now stood, watching his charge standing so incongruously with the heavy ball sac in both her hands, he could see a second girl a little way along the corridor. She had been suspended from a beam by her widely spaced ankles. Her torso had been lifted upright between them and her wrists strapped tightly to her ankles. Pivoted at these two points her exposed body was free to swing. Across her belly were red stripes of punishment. Her sex had stayed open after her rider had withdrawn. He now crouched before it, his fingers toying with it, then his tongue extended to lick inside. Her breasts heaved; her belly pushed; she moaned into her gag. Another rider decided to join in. He stood behind the suspended girl and held her breasts up while the first one spanked them. Then he drew the spanked breasts alternately round to the side to suck them while his mate sucked between her legs. She became so excited that she had to have her clitoris taped. Then the two of them went inside her, one in front and one behind, riding so deeply that their ball sacs, shiny with her lubricant, smacked against each other wetly.

The Chamberlain detached the Farbesian's fingers from the rider's scrotum. He took her to the girl on the hay. The lady was developing the girl's clitoris through a wad of semen that had spilled. The Chamberlain put the Farbesian down, but held her cloth band tight into her crease. And at the front, across the taut bulge of her sex in the cotton, an oily droplet was expressed upon his fingers. He offered them to her lips. Trembling, she took them in her mouth and sucked. His other hand wormed a finger up between her buttocks, under the cotton, up into the crease, to find the cratered bulge of waxy skin which felt hotter than before. When the fingertip vibrated there, she hunched forward, stiff-legged and open, and the girl, reaching with her lips, took suck upon the Farbesian nipple. His fingertip continued its nervous shakes. The Farbesian collapsed, cheek upon the girl's belly; her nostrils flared, drinking in the scent of fresh warm semen being spread around the exposed clitoris by the lady's smoothing fingers. And the lady watched her with a glittering gaze.

After this the Chamberlain took the Farbesian aside to a quiet part of the stables to examine her. In some quarters simple sexual examination was underrated as a pleasure. Its rewards, coming slowly, were thrice-blessed. Her frame was small; her breasts were disproportionately large. He began by standing behind her with them in his hands.

There was a noise from the direction of one of the wooden archways and she gave a frightened start. He glimpsed two figures but when he looked up only one, a young man, was standing in the archway.

'No. Please, oh nooo ... Not here,' she begged, for the young man was now watching. And gradually he moved closer until he was standing in front of her. The Chamberlain gripped the cord about her waist and continued to draw it upwards until he could feel all the details of her nude sex through the stretched cotton sheath. She wanted to close her legs. 'Stay still. Stay open. Kiss.' Her face twisted obediently round to meet him. His fingers squeezed her through the cotton. She moaned against his mouth. And for the first time the inner lips had erupted through the outer ones, like a flower about to burst. And the fullness made the ensuing flow of lubricant difficult to control. Soon her sex would be entirely visible through an opalescent sheath. But at the top of her sex was what made her Farbesian. He could feel it coming alive in his fingers.

Nearby was a short stone pedestal positioned by the wall. The Chamberlain carried her to it. The young man followed. The Chamberlain beckoned him closer once he had set her down standing on the pedestal. Her eyes darted from the young man to the archway, fearful that others might be coming. The Chamberlain proceeded slowly.

He asked her to lean her hands against the wall behind her. She seemed apprehensive of the short gap and moved unsteadily, edging apart her feet. When she was almost still, he lifted the wet cotton band aside so it sprang into the gap at the top of her leg and her sex was intimately exposed. The young man gasped in awe.

The Chamberlain smiled. 'She is a Farbesian. Do you wish to touch it?' He saw the tremble in her legs when he made that offer. Gently he held her belly and drew the band fully to the side. The soft bronze pouting flesh was moistly nude, inviting to the touch. But at the top of her sex was the thing that made her so distinctive – an erect clitoris as protrusive as an upturned claw. It bore a knob-end like a tiny penis. When he drew the hood fully back, this instrument of sexual interplay extended nearly an inch. The shaft glistened with its waxy protective liquid. The young man took it reverently between his fingertips. The Chamberlain kept the hood back and held the wet cotton band aside. His middle finger reached across and tapped inside the open mouth of her sex, where she was slippy. A cloudy droplet swelled at the lower junction of the inner lips. As the young man's fingertips rubbed the waxy shaft of the clitoris, the droplet, breaking free, splashed darkly upon the pedestal. Her knob-end was almost spherical, not angled like the cap of a penis. The shaft was cylindrical; there was no tube slung beneath it, no hole at the tip. But it bounced and throbbed and held an erection exactly like a tiny penis. But at climax, if the Chamberlain were to let that come – at climax, she was Farbesian. No man could ever witness its progress and not be moved.

'Let her sit now,' the Chamberlain whispered. But the young man seemed unwilling to release her fleshy toy. He kept stroking it as the Chamberlain, still holding the band drawn to the side, lifted her slowly down so she could sit on the edge of the pedestal. Her toes were in the hay. Her feet were arched. Her knees trembled open. He made the young man stand back and he made her lean back on her hands. Her seersucker waistcoat fell open. Her back hollowed and her breasts protruded. Her sex was open. Her clitoris poked up. The Chamberlain eased her lovely haunches apart. The twisted fabric band was trapped in the crease of her buttocks. He drew it out, rolling it over the tightness of the cheek. Her bare bottom touched the stone pedestal. He spread her haunches wider, inducing the stretching feeling across the mouth of her bottom. She gasped. Her little fleshy sexual shaft stood up harder. When he knelt before her, he could see the join between her sex and bottom bulging because she was so stretched. Taking this bulge between thumb and finger, he squeezed it. At the same time, he put a finger inside her sex, rubbing upwards, searching the front wall behind the root of the clitoris. When he touched the special place, the Farbesian moaned in pleasure; her knees jerked open. He touched it again, rubbed it. 'Mmmh! Oooo!' she keened, arms atremble, tight jerky opening movements coming to her thighs.

There were two small bumps inside her, now hard and

smooth as ivory, and made of firm erectile tissue. It was as if her tiny clitoris had miniature balls bedded at the root. These glands swelled when she was aroused; pleasure could be precipitated there by massage with the tip of a finger.

'Stand up.' He took her left hand and wrapped the fingers round the wet rolled-up cotton band traversing her belly, instructing her to keep the band drawn open, to keep her clitoris exposed for him. And at the back, the cotton was twisted across her buttock-cheek. The cleft itself was quite free and open. The cheeks moved individually when he made her walk.

At the entrance to the lower stables, she stopped and turned, frightened to go on like this and wanting to cover her sex so no one would see she was aroused. The Chamberlain unfastened the cord from her waist, pulled the wet band free and left her completely naked between the legs, naked from the midriff down.

Then he saw the apprentice-girl Danime. She was glancing over her shoulder at them. Suddenly suspicious, he asked the young man: 'Was she with you?'

'Not exactly, my lord: she pointed you out.'

'Me?'

'She pointed out the girl.'

When he looked again, Danime had disappeared. A crowd had gathered; he edged through with the Farbesian.

Then he realised what had drawn so large a crowd: in their midst was Leah. Danime was at the front beside the Princess Janna, who was urging the riders on. Tethered close by the princess were two nude erect slaves.

Leah lay on her side. A cord was round her breasts. One leg was over a rider's shoulder. He had gone in this way to achieve depth of anal penetration. His sac was loose from hot exertion and his balls rolled back and forth across her inner thigh. Her back was deeply hollowed by the force of penetration; it shook her whole body; it made her little chained sex protrude nakedly under her tight smooth belly. Her mouth clutched hungrily the thick shaft of a swallowed penis. With each deep thrust her lips splayed wider about the flared base of the shaft.

Danime's eyes gleamed. The princess cried instructions to the riders. The Farbesian clung to the Chamberlain, hiding her naked pleading belly against his thigh. He spread his hands under her buttocks and gently lifted. He could feel her erection poking against him. When he tried to put her down again, her legs buckled. 'No –' she pleaded. When he looked again, the princess was preparing to depart with her team of stiff erections.

The young man was again beside him. The Chamberlain, staring at Danime, whispered a message into his ear. The young man's eyes sparkled eagerly.

It was a small hay loft. The Farbesian had to be carried up to it. And in a curious way this calmed her. It was quiet. The apprentice-girl was already leaning against the wall. The Farbesian seemed to recognise her.

The Chamberlain said: 'I did not know our bright-smith was party to the princess's private games.'

'She is not invited,' said the young man. But her eyes told that here in this hay loft was where she craved to be.

The Chamberlain laid the subject on the hay. 'Kiss,' he whispered. She bit his tongue, swiftly, softly, then she sucked it. At first her fingertips reached searchingly for him through the cassock. Then he moved away. She never called after him.

'Wait,' he instructed. The young man was eager.

Hanging in the corner on the wall were various articles of saddlery and other devices. The Chamberlain selected an anal stirrup. He put it into the Farbesian quickly and efficiently. She had never had one in her.

There was no need even to move it. Its presence was enough. When he looked up, the young man was naked and his erection was bone hard, and Danime was watching – Danime whom he had told could never have the girl. She had taken off her leather jacket; her folded arms enveloped her lovely breasts, clasped between the straps of her braces; her pert young nipples pointed upwards just as they had done above the workbench.

The Farbesian was so aroused by the stirrup that her fear was set aside. She wanted to suck the young man. She lay on the hay with just the bulb of his penis in her mouth, her head gyrating gently, stirring the root of the penis, while the tip of her wetted middle finger, up behind his balls, rubbed slipperily over the knotted surface of his anus. Slower and more gently she went, clearly wishing to prolong it. 'The sweet gift of lechery,' the Chamberlain murmured. She surely possessed it. Had he misjudged her?

Danime, cheeks flushed, head half turned away as though unconcerned, was nevertheless watching every rise and gentle fall of those balls, every rub of the wetted finger, every soft gyration of the captive head of the penis, waiting for the moment as tensely and excitedly as if it would be her own spurts of oily come which would soften to silkiness the Farbesian's thick deep-throated whisper.

The young man was groaning, his backbone hollowed like Leah's had been. The Farbesian had stopped rubbing him. His balls were retracted tightly against his penis. Danime now crossed the hay. She dropped to her knees behind him. Her tongue poked, tube-like, and blew a slug of spittle hard against his anus and the young man came, pumping glob upon glob of semen through the Farbesian's sucking lips. So copious was his yield that he was still pumping when Danime took hold upon him by the root of his penis, forced him aside and took over, kissing hungrily the Farbesian's semen-coated lips, drawing her own shoulder-straps down, her trousers to her knees and slotting her liquid labia to the miniature penis. This organ she had so deftly measured for the fitting of the jewels was now provoking her. And beneath Danime's tight nude buttocks riding up and down, the Chamberlain could see a gold split ring through the skin between her sex and anus.

When Danime was satisfied, the Chamberlain took the Farbesian in his arms. She wanted to be kissed – extended deep kisses with her tongue in his mouth. And she now seemed unconcerned about clothing her sex other than with his hand; her slippery clitoris poked through his fingers. He sat her on his knee to take the stirrup out of her. Then he showed her the phial of Sianon's breast-milk. He let her taste a little. Danime, watching, went quiet. Her eyebrows knitted.

He dripped small droplets of milk between the Farbesian's legs. She watched them running down her clitoris and into her sex. Her eyes flashed dark sexuality as the droplets tickled; her lips opened softly; her tongue pushed out. He dripped milk upon her lovely sex. 'The hour is nigh – my lord will wish to see you,' he whispered. Perhaps she did not fully understand. But when he picked her up and carried her, she wanted his finger inside her, up against the two small glands.

6

The Magus

That evening two attendants came to collect Sianon from the subterranean chambers. They fed and bathed her, groomed her, massaged aromatic oils into her skin then carried her naked, kneeling like a sacrificial offering with her arms held behind her and her breasts before her, swollen, shaking. Through tunnels and up stairways they hurried, ever onwards and upwards, out into the twilight, along dizzy parapets then over a narrow bridge across a black abyss to reach a beautiful tiled garden perched on a rocky pillar. At its far corner was a terraced villa built around a short tower. Intersecting grassy pathways wove through the tiled monoliths. She glimpsed nude figures running through the dusk and she heard cries of pursuit. Ignoring them, the attendants carried her up the steps of the villa and through to an inner suite.

Still kneeling, she was placed on a small elegant polished table. The attendants placed her hands behind her, on her heels. She had never been in a suite more luxurious nor more strangely equipped. It was brightly lit by chandeliers. A pure white fur carpet snaked across the marble floor towards two giant decorated blue vases. Ivory tusks projected from the wall. On one of the fur couches was an ornamental saddle. There were marble sculptures and oddly shaped vessels resting on a long curved table. But on the carpet was a naked very

beautiful girl. She had been bound with brightly coloured scarves. Rooted next to her like an empty watch-
tower was a very tall gold and ebony stool.

Three broad steps led up to a balcony overlooking the
garden. And on the balcony, between two kneeling
female attendants, stood a majestic grey figure whose
robe of ermine shone like snow.

The attendants waited. The grey master did not move.
His face, half turned away, watched expressionlessly the
activities in the garden below. The sounds were now
more distinct; there was a woman's laughter and male
voices groaning. The master shook his head. From
below came the sounds of a keen whipping then more
laughter. The master's thin lips moved.

'She was plighted to me young; and now she flexes her
wings; I cannot deny her these small diversions.'

He was speaking to Sianon, and now staring at her
with passive eyes. He walked slowly down the steps,
hesitating at the naked girl. 'Youth . . . What fount runs
more precious?' His nostrils flared, his eyes sank shut. A
trance-like expression transformed his upturned face,
made paler by the bright chandelier. The female attendants watched as if expecting to be summoned to the girl.
For there was this air of sexuality pervading the room,
as if some ritual was in progress which Sianon's arrival
had punctuated but not truncated. And now she would
become a part of it. She looked to the balcony; the
groans of wrested pleasure continued invisibly in the
garden. She tried to picture the young wife of this serene
master; she tried to visualise the whipping. And suddenly she thought of Josef, imagined him there being
sexually whipped by a woman, a mistress, perhaps a
mistress like her former mistress who used to bind and
whip Sianon's breasts.

'Look at me.' The grey master stood before Sianon.
Around his wrist was an opal amulet shaped like a giant
teardrop on a gold chain.

His eyes locked on to hers. She felt as if she were sinking into tiredness but could not close her eyes. She fought it, tried to wrench her gaze away. His wrist moved.

Suddenly the room jarred: there was a roaring in her ears; she could not breathe; she was pinned against a wall of blackest night. Tendrils of velvet pressure moved through her paralysed body, searching. Sianon struggled within herself. She heard his voice chanting strange soothing words. Then the tendrils of pressure turned to pleasure and she acquiesced. The weight lifted. Sianon floated. Then she was back in the room.

The opal stone was wet. Sianon's knees were open. Her sex ached gently. He closed its lips and held them as if to seal the pleasure-aches up inside her. Then he took hold of her breasts, weighing them in his fingers.

'You loved your mistress?' He must have read her mind.

She shivered; her nipples came up to firm thick points.

'You see – we have a good, tall stool for the milking.' He even knew the things her former master used to do with her. She was fearful of raising her eyes lest he might now discover all her thoughts. 'Janna uses it for her young men.' She could feel his stare upon her yet she could not stop the thought: Josef sprang to the front of her mind. She closed her eyes. The master said nothing. But when her eyes reopened he was holding up a black ring for her to see. It bore the Tormunite cross.

'Do you recognise this ring?' he asked.

She shook her head.

'The male slave with you never wore it?'

Her heart surged. 'I don't think so,' she said weakly.

He stared quizzically at her.

'I never saw him with it.'

Again he took gentle hold of her sex lips, stirring tendrils of unwanted pleasure. Then nodding as if satisfied she had told the truth he replaced the ring very carefully in its velvet pouch and returned it to the inner pocket of his robe.

He now removed the opal amulet from his wrist and placed it between her legs on the polished tabletop. Holding it firmly by the chain he rubbed the opal gently with a soft cloth. And the colours in the crystal brightened and shimmered as if the very crystal were alive. Then the ritual began.

The master nodded; the male attendant's arms closed round Sianon from behind. His hands reached down between her legs. She wanted to escape. He held her thighs wide. 'Still and steady,' crooned the master. 'Let her take it through the clitoris.' His narrow fingers rubbed the crystal. The colour scintillated red and green. He proffered it to her body. And Sianon's clitoris, defiant to her will, protruded strongly, shinily. It touched the glass-smooth surface of the crystal exactly as the colour fired green. It drained the colour and the feeling through her knob was so intense and sweet, like a fine twin tube of pleasure pushed up into her belly and splaying out through her nipples and then a silken cord being threaded through and knotted at her knob and nipples. The feeling of exquisite tension was still there when the amulet, its colours now subdued, was pulled away.

'Such a strong reaction,' the master whispered appreciatively. 'Our Chamberlain selected well. And see – the route is through the breasts.' He touched them gently. They were tender but the caresses felt good. 'With some girls it comes through the tongue, with others through the anus. The ley lines of pleasure can be trained, enhanced. Tonight we shall be well content with breast.'

The other male attendant had lit a candle and was warming a small gold cup against it. 'And now – a toast to your special beauty,' the master said, walking round the table, displacing the man who had held Sianon.

From behind, the master's bared forearm slid around her; it rested above her breasts, its grey hairs tickling her naked skin, with the hand coolly cupping and the forearm pressing gently down. The fingers of his other hand made a mouth around the base of her nipple.

When the first liquid came the attendant pressed the lip of the warmed gold cup below her nipple; the master trapped the nipple against the inside of the lip. She murmured in pleasure as the fine milky spray collected into droplets in the polished bottom of the cup. The master returned to the front and raised the cup. 'I shall keep you in milk,' he promised, sipping the warm contents as if they were nectar.

Then he put his hand between Sianon's legs; he played with her sheathed clitoris until her breathing turned irregular. Then he trapped her nipple against the lip of the cup and milked it again. 'The connection is good,' he whispered, for the spray was fuller. Between the milking of her nipple and the squeezing of her clitoris, the level in the cup rose until her nipple was immersed in milk. The male attendant watching became erect. It excited Sianon, to see a man's erection coming while she was giving milk.

A murmur issued from a little distance along the floor. The master's placid gaze turned gently in that direction. As he sipped Sianon's milk from the cup, his plaything reclined on the snowy carpet, her arms stretched across a thick yellow cushion, her cheek upon the plush. About each wrist was a soft cuff of orange velvet. Deep-blue silk scarves secured her legs at her knees and ankles. A dark indolence of sexual arousal dwelt in her eyes. Her lord had allowed her rest; now he would begin again.

He left Sianon with the male attendant, saying: 'Keep her breasts up so I see them drip.'

Sianon watched the master take the girl by the slender shoulders, then reach down under her arms to lift her, to readjust her so her ribcage swelled, her breasts moved and her fastened knees slid over to one side. Below them, the light now fell upon the place between her legs.

The attendant whispered to Sianon: 'His pleasure is to keep fulfilment just beyond her reach.'

The girl's clitoris had subsided but the lips were swollen, moist from prolonged stimulation. Already her breathing had quickened and her eyes had closed in readiness. But her mouth remained open.

Her lord swooped slowly down and kissed it, gently licking it. He whispered to her; her tongue slid out moistly through her lips.

Toying with her nipples, he whispered again; her tongue poked further. Her nipples had swelled hard; tiny goose-bumps covered the flesh of her breasts. He pushed her knees gently up to her belly; her clitoris protruded. It was still small. The first unwilling gasp of near-pleasure came with his touching her in this position. Then her lord drew her to her feet and made her stand shakily before him with her legs still tied together, her sex now buried between them. To front and back he slid his fingers down, searching for the two key places. The last remaining stiffness ebbed from her body. The master stood like a bird of prey above her slowly collapsing figure, supporting her, it seemed, only at these two precious points. Any movement back or forward she might make could only help precipitate the feelings. The only way that she could move was downwards; the slow collapse was her body's soft pleading for sexual release.

Her aroma had begun to drift across the room. All her liquid which earlier must have dried upon her was now taking to the air.

The master unfastened her ties and made her spread to show her clitoris. Then he spanked her bottom as she stood, legs wide, in the centre of the room. When she showed again, her clitoris was enlarged. He made her crouch on a tiny polished metal stool while he put gold tassels through piercings in her nipples. Then he began to touch her anus. This touching was possible because the stool was so small. Her sex was open on the polished convex surface. The gold tassels on her nipples shook. When she was made to stand again and show herself, her musk was seeping down her right leg. The master spanked her bottom to keep this fluid coming. He placed her in various poses and in different parts of the room. He precipitated her first climax by dint of over-zealous use of his fingers while she was marching on the spot. Her tears flowed freely – tears of failure. But her lord explained to her that he would forgive this one transgression, and that perfection must of necessity be sought before it could be achieved. Thereafter, each time it seemed she might yield to climax, she begged repeatedly then he allowed her to rest, slumped in a chair or on the white fur carpet, but always with her legs drawn up, so her clitoris could be seen and monitored. Each time it subsided he would begin again. Most of the soft parts of the furnishings became imbued with her musk.

The attendant's arms were round Sianon from behind. He had held her breasts up while the girl was being played with. Now his fingers clutched them. Sianon moaned. Small squirts of milk ran over his fingers.

The master was staring at the beautiful girl who lay collapsed on the floor. Her look of listless submission had deepened, as though the very interruptions of pleasure were becoming pleasure too.

The two female attendants had begun to disrobe their master. He stood proudly, with legs spread as one of them knelt behind him. Her fingers gently opened his buttocks; her tongue paid gentle homage to the entrance. As she licked, the other attendant tightened an ornamented thong about the root of the master's penis, which stood up between his legs like an engorged muscle and stayed thus as the girl's punishment recommenced, swaying stiffly as he walked, as he now swung the leather. She remained closely aware of its state; her mouth looked small as it tried to fit over the crown. He kept checking her clitoris and stretching her sex open to keep her in this state of high arousal while he attended to those other sexual places – nipple-whipping with a fine crop, close whipping of the anus and precisely focused strokes between the toes.

The kneeling girl was again being made to take the penis. At the moment it thrust between her pouted lips, the female attendant stretched the girl's wet sex open from behind. A soft gasp of pleasure escaped around the penis. It became a moan as the swollen penis sank deeper.

Her lord had hold of her head, controlling the depth of penetration as he pleased. And it pleased him to go very slowly. Her nostrils flared. The tips of the woman's fingers were moving ever further into her. The little finger, hanging down, brushed the erect clitoris poking from its sheath. The girl gurgled and tried to open out her legs. But they had been refastened at the knees and ankles. The fingers slotted deeper. The girl gasped aloud. 'Quickly,' said the master. 'Help her up. I need to spank her.' His heavy wetted penis slid from her lips. She was fraught with overdue pleasure as she was lifted. The plateau had been reached – her feelings raced across it. Every tiny movement of her body propelled her nearer to the sweet abyss. 'Gently – let her bend from the hips. Let her sex swell out behind her.' Its wet full folds slipped between her tied-together thighs.

'The spanking might finish her or it might slow her,' the male attendant whispered into Sianon's ear. 'There is no sure way of telling. If she's spanked on the buttocks, then stretched open, but if she's spanked on the backs of the thighs . . .'

The first smack struck her bare bottom and the girl

had to be supported: the master clasped his hands under her belly and lifted her on to her toes. Her legs, despite their bindings, tried to spread for the female attendant's hands approaching from behind. The fingers, steering clear of the sex, spread the cheeks of the bottom and rubbed the anus – two fingers, in a persistent circular motion. For as long as the fingers cared to rub, the cries of pleasure resounded through the room.

Suddenly the door burst open. A breathless woman crashed through, dragging two naked young men. Sianon froze; her flow of milk abruptly stopped.

The woman was of about thirty years, with beaded blonde hair gathered at the back in a short pony tail. She was semi-naked, leather-clad like a hunter. She bore a jewelled crop. Her captives were erect but clearly terrified of her.

'A good evening's sport, Janna?' the master asked. He had donned his robe.

The woman smiled mockingly. 'My lord, the pace is scarce above a canter.' She opened a cupboard and selected a marble dildo.

The master shook his head, muttering: 'No – one cannot forbid my princess these small excesses.'

Her gaze moved leisurely between the young men. They stared balefully back like captive animals. They were mesmerised; each time her gaze alighted, a penis twitched. Her fingers toyed with the instrument. Then she handed it to one of the female attendants. 'Put it on ice. For they have become hot there from the handling, so much handling.' Then she said defiantly: 'But they need it, my lord, how deeply they need it from me.' Her eyes burned with sexual fervour.

The master left the girl to be bathed by the attendants and he returned to Sianon. He gave her a cup of rich and bitter liquid to drink. 'It will help the milk come thickly,' he said simply. His fingers, softened by the girl's moisture, gently worked Sianon's engorged nipples. 'Sit back.' She watched his pale eyes staring at her breasts; she watched the young men's penises coming more erect with every little provocation Janna uttered.

One had been made to sit on the tall stool. The other was against the wall.

The master turned to the male attendant. 'Refill the cup. We want them full to bursting.' He lifted Sianon's chin and stared into her eyes. 'We want to see the sweet milk running out with no one touching them. Shall your breasts permit us this?' he whispered, and Sianon murmured feebly.

Princess Janna seemed agitated by the master's attention to Sianon. 'She must give the proper signal of assent,' she said firmly.

'Go on – head back, mouth open,' the master coaxed. He moved to Sianon's side.

Janna came closer; her fingers were twitching, her gaze was fixed on Sianon. A peculiar look was in her eye.

'Now – tongue out, curved up – nicely for your mistress.' At those last three words a soft shudder went through Sianon. The master observed it. 'Oh look at her, my dear – so yearning. Come then, nicely for your mistress.' And Sianon, tongue extended, shuddered again.

As the master now put the cup to Sianon's open lips, his hand gently supported her head, and her breasts pushed up towards the pastel frescoed ceiling. She knelt with thighs wide open; the spread lips of her sex reflected in the polished surface of the small round table. The bitter-sweet liquid gushed around Sianon's tongue; she swallowed every living drop; the thirst lay with her, though the cup was dry. She licked inside it, her tongue curving, pointing, searching. Her breasts throbbed. Then the drawing feeling came again inside them, fuller and more sweetly keen.

The master took the velvet flesh below Sianon's right nipple between his thumb and forefinger and twisted it, so her nipple stood out hard. Janna stood watching. He twisted the flesh till Sianon moaned. Then he did the same to her left nipple. And by degrees he spread her knees until her belly pushed out and her buttocks separated. Then he walked round her, leaving Janna alone in front of her. With one hand he drew her arms up and back behind her, so her breasts stood out from her ribcage. With the other hand he softly caressed her lower back.

Janna now approached Sianon very closely. There was fervour in her eyes.

'My lord, let me put her through her paces?'

'You have your young men.'

'Then let her help me.' She stared at him with those fervid eyes. Sianon felt the fingertips bestowing one last soft caress. Then the master stood aside.

The attendants were unfolding one of the fur couches to make a divan bed. Janna put a soft leather collar around Sianon's neck. Then she slipped her fingers underneath it, at the side of Sianon's throat. This first contact with the mistress felt to Sianon as intimate as if the fingers were performing a sexual examination. Fine goose-flesh coated Sianon's breasts. Janna held her by the collar and toyed with them. Then she drew her off the table to the floor.

'Stay kneeling. You like cock?' She grasped Sianon by the hair and yanked her head back. Sianon's jaw fell open. 'Oh yes, you surely do.' The tips of her fingers traced the line of Sianon's open lips. They tapped little messages of arousal upon Sianon's swollen upturned nipples. 'Show me.' Janna bowed down. She wore no perfume; her scent was athletic, overlain by the smell of new leather. Her thighs were taut; her breasts were small. And now her tongue was in Sianon's mouth, arching like a hot erect penis. Sianon sucked it, tried to push her lips down to the base. She made Janna's breath come through her nose. The beaded strands of hair tickled Sianon's ear and neck.

Janna drew back to unfasten the thong from between her legs. Sianon thought that she meant to perch astride Sianon's face and ride her open mouth. But she turned to the naked young man by the wall. Dragging Sianon with her, she made him stand facing the wall. And with her thong dangling, swaying between the firm cheeks of her buttocks, she mated with him from behind without any instrument of insertion, spreading his buttock-cheeks as wide as they would go and rubbing her sex between them. Sianon had never seen a woman use a man so. It excited her. She wondered whether there was true contact, and what it felt like. His palms were spread against the wall and he was groaning just as if he were experiencing penetration. The quickness of erection suggested that this was a renewal of interrupted pleasure for the man. She wondered what had happened in the garden: Janna had spoken of the hotness in his anus. There were whip-marks on his thighs.

Janna made him lie face down and spread-legged on the fur-covered bed. She spoke of the suitability of the male anus for sucking the female glans. Then she mounted him again. He became powerfully excited by the resumption of the act: his erection burgeoned thickly. She turned him on his side and began stimulating his anus with her fingers. He begged to be allowed to come. She ordered him to stay still. Then she placed Sianon in charge of his penis. 'Hold it – use two hands. Suck it or smack it should you wish. If he spills more than a licking he shall pay dearly.' It felt hot, and thick and so alive as Sianon clasped it in her fingers.

She watched as the second young man was made to bend over the stool and was subjected to vigorous anal spanking. The smacks avoided the buttocks completely. Sianon could feel her charge's penis swelling in sympathy. Janna masturbated the other penis as it projected under the stool. Then she put the ice-cold dildo into him. She made him sit on the stool with the dildo inside him. Then one of the women ministered to him with her mouth. His erection had come very hard as a result of the distension of his anus and the presence of the hard balls of the dildo on which he was forced to sit.

Sianon kissed the penis that was so near to bursting in her fingers. She sucked it under the hot tip. When she drew away, a fine sticky thread adhered to her lips. She could feel the pulse of a contraction through her fingers clasping his balls.

'Off the stool,' said Janna. 'On your knees, my man. Come here.' She tied a leash around the balls of the dildo inside him. 'Now crawl across the room.' She led him to one of the ivory tusks projecting from the wall. It had been carved to the shape of a phallus. 'Suck it.' As his lips slid down it, Janna gently tugged his leash. He gasped. 'No, no. Keep sucking.' His cock trembled as she tugged. He groaned when she urged apart his knees. His cock made a thick curved muscle. 'Only by chance did I discover the efficacy of making them suck. They come more copiously.' The attendant handed her a globular silver cup. 'And if the phallus is tinctured by use . . .' He shuddered in the throes of pleasure. Janna slipped her hand around his cock and drew it like a lever, back and up between his legs, until his balls pressed against the balls of the dildo and his toes curled up. His ejaculate jetted in a fine constricted stream into the globular cup. It flowed for many seconds, making a soft liquid ringing sound against the inside of the vessel. When Janna had finished drinking, it coated her lips like clear lacquer. She dragged him away and directed that the other young man be slotted to the phallus.

The master watched impassively. But Sianon was consumed by the sexuality of what she saw, the young man so defenceless, his sex so erect, his body sinking ever deeper upon the claw of pleasure with only one possible outcome, which he could not control. Janna caned inside his thighs. A partial emission occurred. She had gone too far. It ran down his penis. Janna chased it with her tongue-tip down the seam between his balls. She licked it from the rim stretched round the phallus.

The balls clung closely to the stem; his toes were giving way. Then his anus suddenly gripped the phallus tightly.

'It is a kind of spasm, another warning that he wants to come,' the master whispered to Sianon. He took her hand and drew her from the bed. He placed her kneeling between the legs of the young man. 'Kiss and touch it. Press your lips against the base of his shaft. But ease away each time that spasm comes – he will continue making his liquid; there will be that much more to drink.'

The master stroked Sianon's hair. The attendants carefully lifted the young man most of the way off the phallus. The ivory was hot when Sianon clasped her fingers round it.

'Hold it tightly,' said the master. 'Put your thumb like so.' He nodded to the attendants, who released the young man. His anus, coming tighter through the friction, slowly slid back down the ivory shaft. He groaned with pleasure as Sianon's thumb slid inescapably tightly up inside him. Her thumb was trapped and he was gasping on account of the distension and the sexuality of the living contact with her knuckle. And the master toyed with Sianon's sex lips from behind.

Janna had extracted the dildo from the young man on the floor. 'Kneel on all fours.' His erection started to come again when she said to the attendant: 'Bring my saddle.' It had a projection curving down from the back which was shaped like a stylised phallus. This instrument looked like polished ebony but it behaved like very stiff leather in Janna's hand. It was clear where it was meant to go once the saddle was fitted. 'Better than any riding bit, it gives me full control.' It differed in shape from a true phallus by having a thick annular bulge above the base of the shaft, whose purpose could only be to prevent expulsion during the exertions of the ride. And it had metal rings where the balls would have been. Attached to these were stirrups which would facilitate deep insertion. Lastly there was an adjustable leather choker for the genitals of her human mount. These attachments Janna applied progressively. The ride began with the instrument partially inserted: it was much thicker than a dildo, so time was needed for the anus to distend. And during this time, Janna was riding him round the room and stimulating his genitals by whipping. Once the root was bedded, the choker was secured; anal provocation was transmitted by her feet in the stirrups. A tubular gold cup on a chain had been fitted round his penis to capture his discharge. Janna rode him out into the garden.

The young man on the wall had again been lifted that Sianon might retrieve her thumb. Again she watched him sinking down upon the smooth shaft. 'More depth,' the master requested. The young man's knees were tied up against the wall so all the weight was taken through the anus. His cock projected, stiff as a bone. 'Masturbate him with your mouth and breasts.' She sucked his balls and belly. She tried to reach for his nipples. His shaft slipped between her breasts. Her nipples rubbed his balls. Her milk began to come. The master stimulated it to spurt. He directed the spray on the glans of the penis, on the balls, then on the place where the phallus entered. The young man's semen spouted straight up then slid thickly down his shaft. The girl was brought to drink the mixed emissions.

Sianon was still lactating when the master drew her back. He dried her breasts. 'The restraints,' the master said. He fitted linked waxed leather loops around her breasts, tightly, so her breasts bulged through. When her leakage was under control he gave her more of the bitter liquid to drink. Her breasts hurt. The loops were too small; as the liquid continued to work upon her body, the tightness made her murmur. He manipulated her nipples with a gentle drawing action. 'We must make a good bulb, a teat, for sucking.' He continued to stimulate her breasts but instructed her not to let the milk come – explaining that he wanted to explore the pathways using opal.

While her breasts were filling up, he demonstrated the use of an opal dildo to explore the anal pathway in the girl. The instrument fired, red and gold and blue. The girl tried to hold her anus open to take it. 'The slighter the contact, skin to vibrant surface, the keener the feeling.' The master held the hood of her clitoris back and slipped the nose of the instrument partly inside her. Her bottom baulked; the opal was expelled. Even before her knob had slowed its pulsing he was already repolishing the instrument. 'We really need something to prevent her closing. It will be easier if the two of them are taken to my study.'

The Chamberlain picked his way quietly through the tiled garden under a high moon which lavished silver braiding on the night-black cypresses. The Farbesian was in his arms. At the foot of a crag he halted: he heard voices. There was a gathering above. He felt the Farbesian's grip around his neck tighten as he stealthily ascended the steps to reach the rear of a grassy plateau backed by pines and drenched in moonlight.

She had nought to fear yet it took her some while to realise this. But once curiosity had taken hold he was able to put her down. He hung back a little, content to watch her lovely upturned inquiring face, her mouth half-open with a question which her lips would never dare to frame. She was like a sylph at the edge of the wood, staring at those women of a very different breed and wondering at the plight of their young captives.

The Princess Janna, becoming aware of her, brought her forward, inviting her to turn the screw. She had not sufficient strength to do it. There were saddled slaves, slaves in bridles, ladies immersed in punishing, bare-armed ladies awaiting a spillage of the sap of love. The Farbesian was now on the ground between the suspended slave's legs. Janna, behind him, turned the screw; the dilation caused ejaculation, like silver streaks of distilled moonlight. The Chamberlain watched the way the Farbesian's leg drew open to expose her sex to their warm caresses; the way her face turned modestly to the side as the jetting came more strongly. In that first brief spell, an evanescent mist rose like warm breath from the miltings on her belly. Then Janna chased the runny liquid with her tongue, leaving silvery sexual slicks across her skin.

The trails were long dry when he carried the Farbesian over the threshold of his master's private study, up inside the little tower attached to the villa. When she saw the girl Sianon stretched up in that position, she hid her face shyly against his breast. She did not even notice the other girl, asleep, stretched face down on the bed. He whispered: 'We must wait until he calls for you.'

Two blue silk bands which stretched down from the ceiling had been wrapped around Sianon's arms. They took her weight: no effort on her part was required. Her hands hung limply from the wrists. Her legs were open, her ankles fastened up to stump-like ivory posts. Only her toes touched the floor. Her breasts were heavy, sexually heavy with retained milk. The Magus stood before her in his cloak of ermine.

At his right hand, a large clear ball of vibrant opal rested heavily on a velvet-covered pedestal. Captured in its unflawed crystal was the toy reflection of his special room, with its tiers of candles supporting tiny star-like spangles. The sweet scent of the pastille-burner hung in the air. All around, amongst the resplendent mouldings and drapes, were arranged his precious talismans and instruments of sexual love. There were many artefacts carved from vibrant opal and from resin of Carne. He had used them on Sianon; she was drowsy from the pleasures of their pettings.

A lock of hair had fallen across the Farbesian's face. One sweet dark eye gazed anxiously up at the Chamberlain. He drew away the dark soft lock and kissed her very gently on the lips. She seemed reassured by the fact that he was allowed to do this in the presence of the Magus. But the Chamberlain's prime duty was to make her ready. He put his hand between her legs and comforted her and kissed her again. Her long clitoris, coming alive again, tickled the palm of his hand. Her smooth young fingers clasped the back of his neck. He could gladly have waited with her forever.

Taking her to a chair he sat her on his lap. Gradually, her tense gaze succumbed to gentle curiosity. She stared shyly at the nude male attendants. And she put one hand on his wrist as he continued to play with her, as if she feared their noticing how erect she was becoming. Yet as the scene with Sianon progressed and two of the watching attendants stiffened between the legs, her fingertips upon his wrist turned more caressive, moving upwards, tickling the hairs on his bare forearm then gripping him with a longer reach, in the hollow of his elbow as he masturbated her more visibly. Her head sank back against his shoulder and she gazed heavy-lidded.

The Magus picked up the ball of opal in his gloved fingers, the glove embroidered with the star of Torinth. One of the nude attendants lifted the velvet-covered pedestal and placed it directly beneath Sianon's spread legs. She moaned in anticipation as the Magus, taking a matt-black cloth, began very softly to polish the opal. A note resonated on the lowest threshold of hearing. And as if by magic the colour suddenly fired within the crystal; curtains of shimmering neon-red funnelled into vivid yellow-green streamers feeding shifting pools of electric-blue.

The nude attendant lifted Sianon by her buttocks until her ankles were straining at their tethers. Then the Magus set the ball on its velvet-covered pedestal. The colours were darkening, fading like the sound. He waited as her open sex was gently lowered on to the ball.

The Farbesian shivered sexually in the Chamberlain's hands; her fully erect clitoris was poised between his fingers. She had never seen vibrant opal in use for sexual pleasure.

Sianon's overfull breasts were trembling. It was as if her body was pivoted on the ball, which the Magus was re-rubbing gently with the matt-black cloth. Even before the resonances were audible, she began moaning in pleasure, pushing her tongue out. He wasn't touching her. The smooth ball was stretching her sex gently open; its upper surface was partially inside her. And the play of colours meant that it was vibrating, gently, unpredictably, rapidly, keenly. 'Listen,' the Chamberlain whispered. The deep thrumming sound could just be heard; the Farbesian's eyes stood wide. Snaking ribbons of colour grounded every time Sianon's little pulsing knot of erectile tissue kissed the glassy surface. And suddenly her trembling breasts began yielding opalescent droplets, deliciously sexual droplets of living, loving milk.

The Magus placed the cloth down. The colours in the ball again darkened and dissolved; Sianon shuddered gently as her flow stopped. He drew the pedestal and ball away to leave her suspended and spread. 'Put the Farbesian on the couch,' he said. 'Bring the fobs and circlet.' The Chamberlain felt her little sex tighten exquisitely around his searching middle finger. It remained thus as he carried her; and her erection did not go away. Then he left her to the Magus, sublimating his will as surely as she must do.

The Magus removed his glove and let her hold it. The Chamberlain watched his master's fingers moving between her lovely legs, watched his master's gaze caress her innocent eyes, listened to his coaxings and her murmurs. There is something profoundly moving about the slow masturbation of a receptive girl; her gradual descent through aching pleasure to the delicious depths of lewdness. The master was now anointing her nipples with the liquid from between her open thighs.

The circlet was said to be after a Farbesian design, but her expression told that she had never seen the finished article. It was a miniature ring in two halves; when pressed together they would click and seal; after that they could not be reopened. The inside surface of the circlet was of amber, the outer was of gold. It had minute points of attachment for the fine gold chains. The purpose of the circlet was to ring the clitoral shaft; once fitted, it would stimulate pleasure by sliding up and down but escape would be prevented by the head. The clitoris could then be tethered, sucked or masturbated exactly like a collared penis. And with appropriate instruments, vibrations could be induced in the ring.

There was also a tiny gold clitoral sheath which would be held in place by a full erection. The Magus began by filling this with oil, for the Farbesian was well-erect. He made her kneel up, bottom in the air, knees tucked closely to her breasts so her sex protruded behind her and her clitoris was accessible. He squeezed the nugget-like fleshy surround. The knobbed shaft extended pinkly, curving down. Her legs trembled. The Chamberlain watched her face – she was looking at him with eyes so sexually wide and dark. She wanted it this way. 'Ohhh . . .' she murmured. He offered his hand. She kissed it, sucked his fingers. Her belly was shaking but she was trying to keep her legs stiff, her sex still, so the tubular gold sleeve could be fitted – so her little sexual knob could slide up inside it to the very tip. 'Mmmh . . .' her tongue was searching between his fingers. He took hold of it. She groaned and shuddered. The expelled oil suddenly squirted on her belly; the sheath was fitted. He released her tongue. The Magus turned her on her side then began to tap the sheath and play with it. And she was watching the Chamberlain with those beautifully sexual eyes. She kept watching him as the master's finger went inside her sex to stimulate her glands. The Chamberlain went to the tethered girl.

Sianon's body made the shape of a cross. Her clitoris too was out. Unlike the Farbesian's it comprised but a tiny bulb. But her labia were much wider open. She was more used to being opened and her labia had been conditioned by this special form of masturbation with the opal pleasure ball. He examined her tight, split buttocks. They were a bright, even red from spanking. They were hot to the hand. Fitting his thumbs between them, against the more velvet and as yet unspanked anal skin, the Chamberlain placed under tension this wrinkled vortex of delight. Her thighs stiffened. The vortex tightened. The Chamberlain pinched it. Then he stroked it. Then he flicked it with his fingernail. Then again he stretched it with his thumbs – for a few seconds – before he pinched it again, stroked it, flicked it. Each contrasting stimulation forced a separate involuntary pulsing squeeze. She was open, tied by her arms and legs. There was nothing she could do save enjoy the anal flickings and the strokings, the tappings and the gentle stretchings. A girl could be brought to climax in this very way, once she had been made susceptible by prolonged masturbation. But this girl could experience the added pleasure of giving milk.

'Chamberlain . . .' The Magus now required assistance. The Farbesian was across his lap, belly up and breathing quickly. The gold sheath had been removed from her clitoris. The Chamberlain took her wrists in one hand, stretching her body gently. She moaned. Her belly bulged to meet the masturbating fingers. Her breasts rolled. The nipples pointed up. Fine beads of sweat were under her arms. The scent was of ripe beeswax. He massaged her arms and breasts and belly, pumped her turgid nipples gently in his fingers. She was looking at him, upside down and open-mouthed. But her eyes were glazing over – her climax was near. Could the ring be fitted before it came? Would the fitting trigger it?

The Chamberlain stared at the beautiful bulging belly, the thick sweet vee of the aroused labia, the hood drawn fully back, the clitoris so proudly erect. 'Hold her open.' The Magus wanted her sex to be stretched at the moment of fitting. The Chamberlain reached over and put his fingers gently in. She started to gasp. The Magus stroked back her hood. The shaft of her clitoris was trembling like a penis about to pump. When the split ring began to close around it, she turned rigid – legs straight, toes curled, fingers clenched. Gently the Chamberlain eased her leg to one side. Again he held her sex stretched open. And the ring suddenly clicked – so finally – sealed itself around her shaft. The fit was tighter than anticipated; this was because she was so aroused. Her clitoris stood with this gold band seemingly welded around its middle. For several seconds nothing happened. Then as she moved slightly, the wave of feeling must have struck. She wanted to sit up to climax – wanting to move towards it, to have her sex down between her legs, perhaps to sit on her climax, to have her ringed knob poke down between her sex lips and rub the master's ermine robe. The Chamberlain held her shoulders down. Her back arched. Her buttocks tightened. Her knob stood up. The Magus pushed a fingertip underneath the hood, pushing back, pushing up. He rubbed another fingertip horizontally against her labia just below the root of her shaft. She started coming on – as a normal girl might come, mouth wide, breathing deeply, legs and belly shaking. Then it happened.

Her eyes turned languid. All the stiffness and tightness seeped out of her muscles. She sank back limply in a swoon. The first faintness had come. But she remained erect. The Magus lifted her gently to a sitting position. She lay against him as limply as if her body was filled with heavy liquid. Her head lay against his neck. Slowly her eyes fluttered open. And it was a curious feature of the Farbesian faintness, that it did not assuage any of the desire. It left the victim more demanding of pleasure. Her lips looked fuller and softer. She tongued the master's neck and ear. She tongued his mouth. His erect penis stood up between her thighs. She lightly squeezed the extreme tip between her fingers.

'A little lubricant, Chamberlain.'

And a little while later, she was gasping again, head back, body rising and falling. Her knees were tucked up underneath her arms. Her collared clitoris protruded quite uncaressed. Her anus, slippy but tight, was opening and closing in luscious spasms around the knob of her master's penis.

The Chamberlain went over to the spread-eagled Sianon and masturbated her anus while she watched the Farbesian. Her anus responded. He used only the tips of his fingers, but several fingers, just inside. She stiffened when the Farbesian again began to pass out with pleasure. Sianon's nipples were lovely, almost bursting again. He could feel the muscle of her anus pulse and tighten. He put his fingers gently deeper. Then he held her belly, held her knob, which had become wet and slippy. Her bloated breasts trembled deliciously.

And he recalled the Farbesian's first investigation by

the Magi – how she had lain spread-legged on the bed and they had made her masturbate repeatedly to the point of faintness. Each time, she had awoken more aroused. But no true climax had ever seemed to come. After the fourth time the Magi could take no more and the order was given that she be turned over, belly down and that her ankles be tied to the corners of the bed, and that the lubricant be brought.

The Chamberlain suddenly felt Sianon's knob pulse quickly and her bottom tighten round his fingers; without realising it, he had been stimulating her too thoroughly. He let her knob slip gently free and slid his hand up to her taut full swaying breasts. Her nipples, still waxy from previous spills of milk, turned slippy from her wetness on his fingers.

'Bring her here.' The attendants unfastened her. The Magus wanted her to suck the Farbesian, who was slowly coming round. He had never allowed her knees to come down; even while she was in the faint, he had held them tucked under her arms, so her sex had remained exposed and the distension of her anus by his penis could clearly be seen. Sianon now knelt on the floor, licking the balls clinging like soft limpets to his shaft, licking the thick tube where it entered the Farbesian.

The Farbesian tried to lift her knees up higher to give the tongue freer access, and the penis slipped out. Sianon reinserted it. The Farbesian moaned and opened out and sank down it to the balls. She took Sianon's head in her hands. Sianon licked her open sex, licked the ringed shaft of her clitoris, sucked it like a tiny penis, tried to pull the collar off it with her teeth. The Farbesian's belly arched between her tucked-up legs, her bottom pivoted on the penis; her breasts poked out; she gasped, turned, tongue out, offering it for sucking, gluing her lips to the Magus's mouth. She passed out while she was still kissing.

The Chamberlain, drawing himself away, moved to the window. The provings of the young men were still under way on the terrace. Princess Janna attended them; the provings would be protracted. The penises were in polished erection. He turned back; the Magus too was making ready. The little guide chains – reins – were being fastened to the gold and amber collar around the erect clitoris. The Magus called him back.

The Chamberlain unbuttoned his cassock and strode across the room. The Magus was again inside her. Her back was arched like a bow in tension; her hands were reaching up behind the master's neck; her chained clitoris stood out. Her sex was moist. It smelt deliciously of beeswax. The Chamberlain, crouching, slipped his penis up inside her, shared her with his master, shared her little body in its throes of passion, until she passed out. And once his master had tired for the present, the Chamberlain, now sitting on the couch, remained inside her, with her draped against his body, facing him, his stiffly swollen wet erection aching pleasantly from the desire to spill inside her sex, a desire which he would resist, if only to feel her liquid running down him while she slept, if only to feel her opened anus with his gently curling fingers, if only to feel her soft lips sealed moistly to his neck.

7

In Ladyseer

Josef woke from his dream. There was no palatial room, no beautiful chained seductress beside him. He lay upon a simple bed. Yet everything had seemed so real. He felt a surge of relief. But there was a curious pang of disappointment too, at the thought that his dream girl had never existed.

He closed his eyes and he could still see her. Then the feeling came inside him, deep down, the slow sure reawakening of sensations that had only been held at bay while he was engulfed by heavy slumber. It had not been a dream. Gingerly he sat up.

When the seed is sown, the body knows; a womb knows when the embryo is planted. The seed of sexual craving had been sown inside him. And now it was taking root.

He must have been in this room for some long while: dimly he now recalled the leather-clad female guards coming in at intervals to examine him and to feed him a sweet fragrant liquid. He had felt drugged; yet still he had experienced a peculiar pleasure at the intimacies of their workaday attentions. He did not know that his lady had been waiting in uneasy patience for this moment wherein desire and growth were refreshed by sleep.

The door opened and Lady Belangaria walked in, flanked by her Seerguards, who took up positions at each side of his bed while she went directly to a point opposite his bed where there was a lectern bearing a large open book. Lady Belangaria's pale visage faced rigidly ahead as her eyes stared down at the page. Her fingertips touched it. Her lips moved as she chanted the words. For a few seconds her eyes closed. When they reopened they were looking straight at him. They were calm and knowing eyes but they belonged to a creature a station apart. The tailoring of her emerald gown was immaculate. At her throat was a blue pearl choker. Her hair was powdered and surmounted by a tiny velvet cap.

When Josef was very young, in his own country, at some grand function he had been presented to a lady, a dowager – a woman in a way like a mother or aunt, yet a world apart in nature. He remembered that powdery dustiness, her scent of cloves, and the strange sensation of her caked skin against his lips when she had turned her cheek away as he had reached to kiss her. This woman had the same expression but in her gaze there was this difference: they spoke of ownership not dispassion. She had said that she would be his mentor. To the child that he had been, his dowager had not possessed the qualities of warmth and kindness; nor did Lady Belangaria, in her eyes. But in her eyes was kindled something else. It had not crossed his mind that a woman with powdered hair might harbour, other than fleetingly or academically, thoughts of the flesh, let alone that she might wish to procure such feelings in others.

He could smell her perfume, which was of gardenia, suffocatingly sweet.

'Josef, do not be afraid, for you are chosen.' Her voice had emphasised the last word. Her eyes were uplifted, ecstatic.

'My lady,' he ventured respectfully, 'I am a nonentity in this land. How could I be "chosen"?'

She shook her head as if he were teasing. 'You of all my creatures cannot sense it?' She raised her hands as if divining the augury from the very air. 'I cannot believe that you were given no sign.'

His unease deepened. 'Chosen for what?' he whispered.

The first hint of uncertainty misted her eyes. 'There is disagreement on that point. But your destiny is here with us – with me. Your arrival has been long awaited.' She turned the pages of the book. 'It is decreed here that "in the Ninth Reaping there shall be a stranger, not of you, not of us ..."' She stared at him. 'You said the word yourself.'

'I said "nonentity".'

She turned the pages again. 'And here, that "their breasts shall know him by their bounty." I understand there is a girl ...'

His heart began thumping. 'Sianon. But that was done to her in the Abbey.'

She shook her head, then closed the book. 'The Perquisitors were briefed to be vigilant. And Quislan searched you out.'

'But she left me for dead.'

'She is short-tempered and is ill-disposed towards men. When she sent back for you –'

'She did?' The revelation shocked him.

'You had disappeared. When I heard you had reached the Abbey I asked her to ensure that you arrived here safely.'

He laughed hollowly. 'She wanted me drowned.'

'She is easily annoyed. And you did not drown, Josef.' And once again he was surprised to hear her say his name. 'Now that you are replenished and rested, your lady wishes to look upon you. Josef, oh Josef, my plans for you are great indeed.'

She smiled possessively. She nodded to one of the leather-clad Seerguards then held her arms forward while the guard slipped over her emerald gown a pure white full-sleeved lawn blouse which fastened with ties at the back. She intended to examine him. The second guard drew back the sheet.

His penis lolled heavily against his leg. The gold penile ring was still missing; the clamp which had been put around his genitals must have been removed while he was asleep. The sinking feeling was there at the base of his penis: he could feel the blood vessels dilating. His lady mentor sat lightly by his side upon the bed. Her scent was subdued by the dry starched aroma of her blouse which had billowed around her. Her figure was in flimsy contrast to the power she exuded. She had great dignity: the guards hung upon her every slight movement, every lift of her finely drawn eyebrows.

Josef was in a half-sitting position, leaning back on his arms. Her gaze moved calmly and unshyly down his person. Then her hands followed; the small fingers extended, touching his chest lightly, reading his form like a blind woman's fingers might, exploring under his arms where the sweat had dried as a salty coating on the hairs, then returning to his chest and touching his nipples, gently pinching them. His erection had come on hard; a clear liquid was of its own accord already being expressed from the tip of his penis. He ached inside. The ache was pleasurable. She smiled knowingly.

'I have many young suitors – as you shall see,' she teased. 'But none so special.' Resting her hand upon Josef's belly she glanced at her guards, who stared inscrutably at his gently leaking penis. 'Can you not yet smell that it is different?' she asked them. She brushed her finger up his stem then held the shiny finger up. She shook her head. 'They are not attuned.' She sucked her finger. And her expression was ecstatic. Her eyes re-opened and stared at Josef. 'Nor are you?' Though the feeling inside him was very strong he could smell only starch and gardenia. 'In time you shall be introduced to some who are very much attuned and who will wish to drink their fill. Lie down.'

He did as she instructed.

'Bend your knees. Take no heed of my Seerguards. It is you and your mentor. Your mentor desires to explore.' After a short while and his first clear moan she said: 'A little aromatic oil for my fingers. He is a little shy of being distended.'

His balls were in her hand; she was drawing them up, keeping the skin behind them stretched and smooth; and the tips of two lubricated fingers were pressing upwards just inside the anal rim. It was clinically precise and slow, as if she were taking a pulse there with her fingers. Clear liquid was oozing very slowly from his penis and hanging in a thick droplet from a shiny thread. 'His nipples are up. But he is afraid to close his eyes for fear of what I might do. Josef – I do it anyway. Your gaze could never stay my hand.' She leant forward, her blouse brushing the insides of his thighs. 'My plans for you are comprehensive. It is only the beginning.' And so saying, she pushed her fingers gently deeper, until their pads found and pressed once, just once, against the place where the Succubus had been, and the pleasure came so swiftly and intensely that Josef tried to get away from it. He saw the look of obsessive exultancy in his lady's eye. 'Lie down. He has not climaxed but the gland is very full. We may yet train him.' She wiped her fingers on the cloth the guard offered.

While she was speaking, Josef lay there with the place inside him aching with the expectation of pleasure. He could see something of that expectation now in his mentor's eyes.

'He needs a ball-strap.' She applied it quickly, expertly, tightly. It was a thin leather band with a captive metal ball near one end. The ball was placed against the underside of the base of his penis; the strap was wound tightly round. His erection came harder. The pressure of the ball sealed his tube. His mentor dried the earlier leakage from his penis. So hard was he that the mouth of his penis protruded open and the veins stood out but there was no more leakage. 'Hold him down. More lubricant.'

One guard climbed on top, pinning his shoulders. The hot thong between her legs went in his mouth. The moist lips opened to his tongue. His mentor's fingers slipped inside his anus, against the gland, seeking it, kneading. His ejaculation began cascading with no ready escape. His constricted penis bucked a first time, open-mouthed, gasping, sucking, slowing, gathering momentum. His scrotum tightened to his penis, then it came again, painful pleasure, hard pleasure, so deep inside, and the feelings as if her fingertips were plucking at the very whipcord of his spine. 'Come,' his mentor whispered, 'Come, for me. See how it gapes its little mouth.' She buried her fingers so very hard into the gland that he thought that he would die with pleasure. His semen spurted in a fine endless jet, past the constriction and through the gasping glans of his penis. The guard's sex descended again, grinding ever deeper into his mouth, forcing renewed spurts of semen from his twitching penis.

It was still twitching when his mentor wiped her fingers again and the guard got off his face. The strap was left on him, the sensation of incompletion was still with him and he could do nothing to shake it free.

'Turn him over.' They brought a small cushion. His mentor explained to him how he was required to lie in order to avoid direct stimulation of the frenum of the penis. 'We must encourage the inner gland.' Even the experience of being turned over, the shifting of his weight, had produced sexual feelings inside him because the gland was enlarging again. When they were finished, his legs were open and his erect curved penis pointed awkwardly down towards the foot of the bed. The cushion raised his pubes. His balls were exposed, his buttocks open.

She stood up. 'Proceed.'

A shaped, long slim glass vessel was slipped over his erect penis. The constriction was now removed from the base of his penis; drops of fluid began to leak into the glass. There were straps at each corner of the bed and one in the middle. Being lowered from the ceiling was a chain. Josef, spread-eagled face down, was now strapped to the bed, with his penis sheathed in the glass. When the body-strap was drawn tight around the base of his spine, the pleasure was accentuated. She pressed her fingers up under his balls. His penis in its glass was straining against the bed.

A trolley was brought and placed where he could see and begin to guess what was going to be done. On its top shelf was a range of solid metal balls, each joined by a link to a separate rod. At the end of each rod was a large eyelet crowned by a hook. Lady Belangaria lifted the first and smallest ball, which was about the size of an apple. It was steel grey and very smooth and shiny. But it was so heavy that it required both her hands to hold it steadily. 'Oil him,' Belangaria whispered.

He was already strapped down; his legs were already strapped open; there was nothing he could do to move. She explained that it would not always be so; that sometimes she would want him untethered yet willingly yielding. The feeling was one of falling, constant falling, a sinking in the pit of the stomach and below. He might have cried out in protest but he uttered only gasps of pleasure. He was being opened so much more fully than had happened with her fingers. Against the resistance of the resilient muscle were these intensely pleasurable feelings of being naked on a bed, spread open, quite powerless, while three woman oiled and spread his anus with the heavy metal ball which was hooked to the chain dangling from the ceiling. In a peculiar way, his gasps of pleasure rendered him an accomplice to this perverse action. When he was at his most vulnerable, with the full width of the ball spreading him so tautly, his lady paused. Bending close to his face, she kissed and bit his lip, held it tightly in her teeth while the sweet scent of gardenia filled his throat. Then the ball slipped down inside him, very coldly. Josef moaned. When its weight began to press against his gland, the feeling turned exquisite – intense, unquenchable. He wanted to ejaculate again. His lady's tongue-tip pressed against his own. He felt the glass tightly sheathing his penis. His lady's fingertips caressed the nape of his neck until the full weight of the sinking ball was taken. His penis had made some spillage but the pleasure was still there. The coldness of the metal slowly drained the heat from inside him, causing a sweet numbness that made the flesh upon his back and buttocks shiver.

Lady Belangaria drew away to consult her mystical book, leaving Josef to her Seerguards. They massaged his shoulders, slapped his buttocks, opened him, poured oil down the guide-rod attached to the metal ball.

'His balls must be developed. I need to see them poking proud,' said his lady. A leather string was fastened so tightly in a figure of eight around his scrotum that the skin shone and the balls stood out. Belangaria stood behind him, watching. 'Turn the guide-rod,' she whispered. A wooden bar was inserted through the eyelet below the hook; with it, the metal rod fastened to the ball inside him was slowly twisted round. The feeling came in the two places – the anal ring, through which the rod was being twisted, and the gland inside him, against which the smoothly polished ball was sliding. And again he felt as if he wanted to ejaculate but it did not come fully, though he experienced pleasure through the partial flow. And the weight of fluid kept building. He was being milked slowly; each new turn of the instrument stimulated the swollen gland in some small measure to overflow.

The guards twisted the rod progressively until the

chain above it locked. 'Hold the bar steady.' Lady Belangaria again approached Josef. One of her guards now held a large mirror angled so Josef could see his back and buttocks and everything his mentor would do.

Lady Belangaria grasped the metal guide-rod between the ends of her bare fingers. 'Look at me.' Through the mirror he could see her intent face, and her hand. She tugged the rod. He moaned. She held her head high but her eyes were staring down at Josef's face in the mirror. Her hand, fingers first, began sliding down the length of the metal rod. Her fingers touched his anus. Her gaze was diverted. 'Your balls, Josef. Your balls – so tight and beautiful in their bindings. Shall I ever allow them to relax?' Her fingers kept coming, sliding down the rod; her nails felt cooler than the metal had been. 'Your balls, my darling.' One by one she tested them in the fingers of her other hand, squeezed them like fruits. He wanted to come. 'So tense – relax . . .' The fingers went deeper. Her thumb rubbed slowly the hard bridge of flesh between his anus and his scrotum. He could feel the running drip of fluid spilling from the end of his penis into the glass. He knew that she would want to drink it. Her hand slipped gently out to join with the other and enclose both balls. She told him: 'I shall whip them,' and she nodded to the guard, who quickly pulled the wooden bar from the eyelet.

The oiled rod untwisted; the turning pleasure came inside the ring of Josef's anus; the smooth rotating ball pressed against his gland; she squeezed his bulging scrotum as if it bore two fragile eggs that she would now eradicate. His ejaculation was full and prolonged. He felt the glass being drawn slowly and wetly and tightly down his penis, pulling the liquid out of him.

As she sipped his semi-clear fluid from the glass, she said: 'The girth of the metal weight must gradually be increased in order to improve his yield; the anus will adapt by stretching.' When she explained about the ladies he would be required to please, the feeling was still there inside him and his body was still making copious liquid.

Over the next several days Josef discovered what took place in the quaint-looking houses clustered round the garden lake that he had seen from the window of the palatial room. For this was Ladyseer – the secluded place where lived the select coterie of mature ladies who would put him to the proof. In idiosyncratic suites of rooms, on elegant verandahs, in hidden flowered arbours he was introduced naked to a succession of graceful ladies, each one in her temporary way as demanding as his mentor, each one keen to monitor his erectile capacity and to stimulate his flow. But despite Lady Belangaria's promulgations, he remained peripheral to their attentions: they had their own entourages of males. But they were solicitous of what his gland produced: in this circle the male fluid was evaluated with discernment and finesse. It was drunk or eaten as a delicacy with chopped herbs; the ladies were connoisseurs of its various consistencies and applications. It was taken *al fresco* from the living vessel, or from a warmed glass, or it would be stored and served on ice. And it was used on the face and neck and breasts as a veil against aging.

The trysts would take place in privacy where the ladies might lay aside decorum and yield to abandon with their victims. Sometimes they wished only to penetrate him. More usually they required him to please them. On such occasions he would be fitted with a sheath. The ladies would wear spurs or other inducements with which to urge him on. Then each night with Lady Belangaria he would be subjected to the ball and chain. Each night a heavier one was used, 'the better to exercise the gland.' The flows would be copious and the leaks never truly stopped. When in the daytime the ladies did not particularly require him, Belangaria used on him the spur – a pure gold instrument which clasped the base of his genitals and bore a stoutly curved extension which went up inside him and was crowned by a bulbous pad which pressed against the gland. She would make him walk with it inserted. She would take him on to her terrace and milk him to completion with the instrument still inside.

Josef's reward for bearing such flagrant acts of sexual degradation was a form of pleasure more pervasive and continuous than anything he had known. At the sight of the spur his erection came. When she was putting it into him with the Seerguards watching, the feeling would be there, the nearness of spillage. And she would caress, kiss and coax his bloated penis. So whenever he was summoned to a lady's chamber, his sex was over-ready for whatever she might have a mind to do.

One such lady was Postrina; she wore gowns in lilac and her hair was dyed ebony black; she occupied the first level of a house which cantilevered out over the lake. In the early-evening sun she used to sit him on the floor with his head supported on a small purple cushion on her couch. The gold spur would still be inside him. She would remove her lower garments then kneel astride and ride his face. Her sex, small, virginal and pink, softly wrinkled, sea-salty, fringed by the dyed-black hair, would force its way into his mouth. Her rocking would stimulate his body to move against the spur inside him. She would check at intervals that his erection was curving upwards like polished bone, a smooth fat obelisk to Postrina's pleasure. Then clasping his head lovingly in her hands she would drive her sex fully and deeply into his mouth until she hunched in pleasure, her lilac earrings dangling freely and her narrow high forehead touching the back of the couch. The first time she did him this way, Josef climaxed. His lady had not been expecting it to happen. She had been touching his penis every little while, and she heard his groans but at her moment of abandon she was too far forward, too deep in her own throes of pleasure, too tightly clutching his head, too focused upon dripping her own virginal nectar down his young throat. His penis bubbled over; all was wasted. She admonished him, then lovingly rubbed it in until it dried upon his balls.

Other ladies preferred the penetrative route. On occasion they would work him in pairs. It might happen in leafage by the stream. His gold spur would be taken out only to be substituted, after adequate foreplay and deep kissing of the glans, by the closer intimacy of a naked fist. They would take turns. Gloves would be shunned; skin contact was needed – fingertip, palm, knuckle and nails. When the insertion of the hand was complete the lady would toy with him as in foreplay but now from within. Her accomplice might watch, or smack his penis, or bring water from the stream to cool it. In time the fist would bunch and very slowly twist inside him with its angled thumb-joint rubbing back and forth across his bloated gland. These ladies had long experience of such methods. With each individual rub a small measure of his fluid – clear fluid, like watered honey – welled and overflowed. By pressing her lips against the frenum of the penis the accomplice could drink the trickles. By this means he could be milked continuously. And when they tired of him he would be equally as hard and unsatisfied as when they started.

One such penetrative lady was the Marquise. She did not reside in Ladyseer but appeared at one of the gatherings. Her breasts were still voluptuous. Her hair was softly curled, her voice silken. The hostess kept two girl-slaves who were not permitted contact with the males. The lady guests would watch the girls masturbate while they, the ladies, were working the males. The Marquise kept Josef erect and producing milt throughout the night. By applying cooling poultices she was able to postpone his first true ejaculation for several hours. At the height of his arousal, the Marquise placed him across her knee with his head on a pillow and she trapped his penis between her bare thighs. Her oiled fingers progressed inside him. There were other nude males being penetrated, either standing or prone. The girl on a nearby stool was masturbating with some beads. She sat with feet pressed sole to sole to keep herself open. The Marquise stroked inside Josef, provoking the slow flow of hot fluid. He felt its warm wetness between her clamping thighs. When the girl on the stool came to climax, Josef started to climax too. His lady captured his ejaculate in a lipped globular glass which lacked a stem and therefore could not balance unaided. The girl immediately scurried forwards and doubled over on the floor in front of the couch where Josef lay. She was on her back with her bottom in the air and her feet behind her ears.

'They have the agility we have lost,' said the Marquise. One of the ladies oiled the girl's anus. Then the glass of milt was inserted until her anus gripped it under the lip without spillage. 'Our vessel of love – her body shall keep the chrism warm.' Thereafter, any ejaculating penis not required to feed a lady from its living spout was directed into the mouth of the buried glass. The girl's sex was kept excited by progressive insertion and withdrawal of the beads. At intervals the warm fluid was decanted; their cups replenished, the ladies drank.

The Marquise's hand, progressing ever deeper into Josef, passed the point beyond which it could not easily be released. He could feel her fingers and thumb exploring, squeezing, pressing in tempo with the exertions of the other ladies' males.

One was passive; while the penetration by a strap-on dildo was under way his lady steered him by a strap looped round his genitals; as she adjusted her position to attain greater and deeper rampancy, his erection

123

came and went. Then curiously, for no obvious reason other than the prolonged penetration – unless it was the angle of the dildo, which was very steep now – the penis stiffened very hard; the lady rider began thrusting more slowly, yet firmly; and the erection really bulged.

'He has reached the heavenly point,' the Marquise said. And Josef, groaning, was reaching it too. The male being ridden began to pump thick semen through the lady's fingers and on to the floor. The Marquise with her hand still inside Josef turned him; his anus twisted about her wrist; her thumb-joint pressed firmly up against his gland, and with his weight now supported on that one swollen sexual place, his cock poked out and up, reaching for her open soft lips, which warmly engulfed it, sliding down and down until they pressed against his pubes, sealing his whole shaft inside her mouth. He felt his ejaculate pumping and pumping as if it would never stop. With each pump the glans of his penis, expanding, was constrained by the warm soft squeezing girdle of his lady's loving throat.

After that first meeting the Marquise used him often, but always at one of the other ladies' abodes. Sometimes her preference was to place him face down on a bed with his genitals on a hard cushion and his erect unsheathed penis pointing backwards. His legs would be drawn wide apart. Then with hot labia open the Marquise would ride the upturned undersurface, which would turn slippy with her exudations. Every so often she would stop to knead his balls or to pry apart his buttock-cheeks and to play with his anus while his shaft was trapped between her labia. He would feel her clitoris like a plump pip pressing down against the back of his tube. If she decided to bring him on in this position, she would place a dish on the bed underneath his upturned penis. Then she would take a fat clyster. He would feel the curved nozzle going in, then the cold lotion filling him. The nozzle was curved so she could ride the back of his penis during filling. 'I want you full to the brim. Do not come before I tell you.' Her demands were great. The nozzle was never held steady; it made little jerks and suffered small interruptions in the pressure while she slid along his shaft. He would feel her legs spreading and her weight descending so her bare breasts touched his back and her plump pip pressed so intimately against him it almost closed his tube. And the cold cream was still filling him.

Lady Belangaria would sometimes assist the Marquise. She would come to Josef and kiss him, touching the place where the nozzle entered, and biting his lip. The Marquise having climbed off, might suck one of Josef's balls into her mouth. Belangaria would continue to pump into him the lotion until the clyster required recharging. He would beg to be allowed to come. Belangaria would caress him, for his state would give her pleasure. The Marquise would charge the clyster very full and show him the thin crop preferred for this specific usage. She would oil it between her legs. Then with her liquid she would oil the hard curved place below his anus. She would draw his legs apart indeed. His balls would retreat. Belangaria would cautiously reinsert the nozzle and watch his anus contract involuntarily tightly round it. The Marquise would now begin whipping the hard curved place to stimulate ejaculation. She would count the strokes. Belangaria would be pressing the plunger to drive the climax from within. Josef would feel the exquisite cold pressure of lotion flowing inside him past his gland. Belangaria would bite his lip and the Marquise would hold steady the barrel of the clyster as Belangaria depressed the plunger. The crop-strokes, one by one, would keep pressing shut his dilated feeder tube where it strained inside his body just below the skin. And his semen would come in long spurts, discretely interrupted by the rhythm of the strokes. The two ladies would drink it.

125

Such were the ladies' individual trysts with Josef. They loved him like the fount of youth; they drank of him just as freely. On the tenth day Belangaria decreed that he should be formally displayed.

The grand reception was held in the Lady Seer's palace. The guests exclusively were ladies, the slaves young males. Public inhibitions were suspended. Novel cocktails were tasted. At table, epicurean pleasures intertwined with servile love. Slaves were draped naked across the board. Shaved balls garnished plates of shrimp consommé. Strawberries were dressed with cream whipped freshly from the slave and chilled by crushed ice put inside him. After dinner came the more intimate games, with two or three ladies to a slave. Then the party descended to the basement suite.

The whipping room was circular and was tiled from floor to ceiling; every whisper of the ladies could be heard. They drifted between the adjoining rooms whence Josef could hear the moans of the other young men. The ladies became ever more demanding. Seerguards performed the heavy lifting. Lady Belangaria was determined to put her new acquisition through his paces.

'Yoke him.' A heavy wooden bar was thrust under Josef's arms and behind his shoulders. His arms were fastened to it. Then his knees were drawn up and open and fastened to it too. The yoke was suspended from the ceiling by two rings. Cloth strips were used for the bindings, which took the strain but did not bite. Placed strategically around the room were tables of refreshments, and chairs, should any of the ladies tire. So open was Josef held that his knees were level with his chin. His belly thrust out, his penis projected; his balls hung freely down – the sac was loose; it was warm. All the key parts – the genitals, the anus – were to hand.

Lady Belangaria whipped his balls using an instrument that was long but not heavy – a thin flexible slippy whalebone band on an ivory handle. It was strong enough to punish the balls but not to harm them. The sound of the swish through the air was distinctive – it wavered because the whalebone vibrated. Its music drew the ladies from the adjacent rooms. They gathered round to listen and watch. Against the underside of the erect penis it would make a snapping sound, against the balls a dull slap, and under them a loud smack. But how it could numb them, how they could ache. And this ache was quite different from a penile ache: it was deeper and pervasive. All the while that she was whipping them, even when she stopped to stare up into his face, the sexual feelings were there inside him, and there in his leaking penis, and the whipping melded all these feelings into one.

She whipped his balls from the front, near the join with the penis. Then she whipped them from the sides. Because his legs were drawn up, nothing interfered; there was no obstruction that might mitigate the blows. His balls hung down like hot pears. The ladies now took turns to gather each one separately in the cup of a palm, for they had expanded. So hot were they that the ladies reacted as though the delicate skin of their palms was burnt by the contact. Belangaria called for ice-water in a jug. She held Josef's erect penis while his balls were dipped inside it. Then she whipped them wet, until the wrinkled skin relaxed and filled out and they were hot again in her fingers.

Belangaria then instructed that Josef be shaved. 'I do not want your juices running to waste in all this brush.' His erection never softened while the shaving was under way. The suds mixed with his slow emissions and dripped on the tiled floor. The Seerguard's fingers kept slipping up his anus, wanting to explore the place where he was swollen. The soapiness made a burning sensation come inside him. Belangaria asked her guards to explore the possibility that his anus might be kept open while some device as yet undefined was put inside which might be used to flick or slap him internally, for she considered the idea of internal slapping potently eductive. 'I could use it on my girls, to spank inside their flesh and I could use it inside you to spank your gland.' The guards were drying Josef's balls; the shaved skin, soft and heavy, was sticking to their fingers; one of the ladies wanted to kiss these newly shaven places. The pressure from inside him was a slowly pulsing ache that felt as if it would never recede.

His lady squeezed just the knob of his penis. A drop of clear fluid exuded. It was part of the steady welling which would not abate. He glimpsed in the adjacent room a young man sitting stiffly erect on a table. Another was draped across a chair. A lady was choosing a dildo.

And he could hear in the greater distance, enthusiastic laughter and the deep hollow groans as of some unearthly creature being baited. Then a group of ladies arrived from that direction greedily licking juice from their fingers. Lady Belangaria coyly smiled.

There were various instruments hanging from a rack near Josef. Several were of the same type, having four to six metal balls on a fine chain. The handgrip of the chain was shaped to take three fingers. Lady Belangaria selected a chain with five medium-sized silver balls arranged along its length. She dipped it into a long glass cylinder of silky opalescent lubricant. 'You do not recognise it?' Immediately it touched his skin he knew what it was: it felt slippy at first, turning sticky as it started to dry. She began to feed the lubricated balls up his anus. His flow increased to a partial trickle.

But there was an interruption: the corridor door opened. Josef's anus tightened. The guard who walked in had with her a girl. And the girl was Leah.

She caught her breath when she saw Josef. His heart

stopped. His lady proceeded with the insertion until only the handgrip was left dangling. His tightness was expelling the rich lubricant over her fingers. Josef closed his eyes. 'Open them,' Belangaria whispered keenly.

She took Leah from the guard. Then she announced to the ladies: 'She was with him in Servulan. Tell them, my child.'

'He was given the freedom of the Abbey,' Leah whispered.

'Tell them why.'

Leah's eyes glittered. 'He wore the Talisur ring.'

There were gasps around the room.

Lady Belangaria stared at her assembly. 'Can you now doubt that he is special?' All eyes were upon Josef. 'The proving must continue.' And taking hold of the handgrip she pulled the chain quickly out of him.

'Look at it,' she said. His penis was trembling, very tight. The procedure was interrupted for several ladies wishing to kiss it in this state.

Then the insertions recommenced. And seeing Leah still looking at him made the shiver come inside Josef and the flow of fluid from his penis correspondingly increased. Belangaria allowed her to suck her coated fingers. Then she lubricated the chain with semen from the cylinder, inserted the chain into Josef and slowly drew it out with an upward pull so the metal balls rubbed past his gland inside. He almost climaxed. Belangaria started to feed the balls back inside him too quickly for him to be able to cope. Josef groaned; she slowed the insertion and the pulsing subsided. She toyed with his bursting penis. But then the feeling of her fingers beginning again, pushing each cold lubricated ball up into him was overwhelming. Through half-open eyes he saw one of the ladies doing things to Leah as she stood there, urging her with whispered provocations and her fingers splayed round Leah's sexual chain.

And soon, Leah was clambering on to a stool and

biting Josef's nipples. Her little pearl-like teeth were sharp; the sensation was excruciating. His knob end was brushing her sweet round belly, leaving a trail there. She half mounted him, but her labia could not spread about the upper side of his penis on account of her chain. But briefly he felt her small erect clitoris pressing against him where he had been shaved.

Belangaria played with Leah on the stool then had her moved away for the lady to resume her pettings. Belangaria's fingers went up inside Josef alongside the partially inserted chain and pressed one of the silver balls against his gland. The pressing caused a back-pressure to travel up his penis. The head swelled. She now pressed rhythmically inside him. She instructed him not to come, stating that she wanted him kept on the brink. She kept playing with his anus. His balls hung down in their stretched shaved pouch.

'I love you for your balls,' she murmured. She fingered them, found the tubes inside them, referring to the 'special pain – like when your finger goes a little too deep inside an inexperienced girl and presses to the side of her womb. I have heard that it is like that.' She applied narrow, spring-driven clips that were strong enough to clamp the tubes and small enough to stay in place. They made the tubes hurt, with a dull ache. 'It will excite the flow,' she said. Josef hung there with these two metal instruments of sexual torture projecting from his balls. 'Spread wide.' The chain was still inside him. She pulled it quickly out. The small clamps attached to his scrotum lifted and fell, lifted and fell. She wetted the chain in the glass of semen and started feeding the string of balls back inside him. Again the feeling of her fingers, freshly slippery with cold semen, was exquisitely arousing. He started to come, his anus opening and closing round her fingers, trapping one of the balls. 'Hold back.' She pressed a glass container to the root of his stem. 'Let it run, not jump.' And she continued with the insertion as the ejaculate poured from the wide open mouth of his straining penis and ran into the glass.

'Leave him with it inside for now.' She looked at Leah being cared for by the lady. 'Would you like one inside you too?' she teased. And she examined the bodily place where Leah was sexually used. 'You have something in common, you two.' She tipped the glass until Josef's semen ran into her fingers. Then she anointed Leah's anus with it as Leah reclined with knees up on the lady's lap. The anointing and the pouring of the fluid semen down Belangaria's fingers, pushed just a little way into Leah's lovely anus, caused an erection to come to Leah. And Josef's erection re-stiffened as he watched. 'You have something very much in common – soul mates. Let us then explore this commonality. Unyoke him and bring the two of them.'

It was her inner sanctum: an environment of male slaves all around her. Leah was the one exception. Even the female guards were debarred from such sessions. Belangaria felt particularly excited in this world of strange creatures whom she could control by whispered commands. There was the all-present smell of maleness – warmth, new sweat, ripened half-dried escaped seminal fluid on their bodies, up between their buttocks, matting the hairs of their bellies and legs where they were left unshaven. She moved among them, brushing against them, kissing their upper bodies, allowing her hand to slip below, touching, gripping – penis, balls – her fingers sliding part way up the creases.

She called the device the mounting block. It was a sturdy quilted bar supported at each end on a frame. Its level was such that the male slaves could lean or crouch across it while they were being entered. It sufficed for girl slaves too, as long as they were being used like men. This was Belangaria's one proviso. It enhanced the eroticism of the encounter, to do to the girls only those things that could be done to men. This was why Leah had been admitted.

Tonight was to be Josef's turn. Belangaria wished to see how her protégé would respond to the penis. 'Put him to the block,' she whispered.

She watched as his legs were being opened and his belly was pressed against the beam. His penis hung heavily through the repeated stimulation: when a penis was thus treated, the weight would always sink towards the tip; the scrotum would soften and extend. He stopped breathing when she took hold of his balls and detached the clamps from the tubes of gristle that led up inside him. When she squeezed these tubes between thumbs and fingers, though he moaned, his erection started.

Moving away from Josef, Belangaria waited until his erection lolled to the point where the bulb of his penis sank below the horizontal. She signalled to the slave who had been waiting. He spat on his hand and rubbed it quickly round the cap of his penis. And Belangaria returned to the front. Her intention was to watch with Leah. But as Josef's penis started to stand up as the slave started hunching, Belangaria could not resist gently lifting Josef's chin, encouraging him up on his toes. She eased his balls up on to the quilted bar then pressed the thin stem of the crop against them, keeping them trapped, shiny and bulging, all the long while the slave was pumping. The bulb of Josef's stiffly curving penis swayed and bobbed. Clear fluid trickled down the underside of the stem. When the slave withdrew, spent, the crop was wet with the exudations from Josef's penis. A thick drop of milkiness was running down inside Josef's leg. Belangaria had him removed from the block and held by two slaves in a sitting position with his legs wide open. When she stood behind him, she saw his balls hanging heavily down below his buttocks. But it took a good long time for his erection to begin to go down. All that time, his penis was leaking. Belangaria chose another stud. 'To the block,' she whispered.

This time, she had him placed sitting, as was sometimes done with girls: the girl would sit with her bottom overhanging. With girls, the slaves would sometimes try discreetly to miss the anus and slip instead inside the slit. Belangaria would without exception prevent it. Even in a girl, she found the stretching of the anus so much more arousing: the girl's legs would be over the bar. Her sex would be hanging down, open, peeping as Belangaria played with it from the front. So it was with Josef: his genitals were suspended below the bar. Already his penis was returning to erection, to provide this sweet separation – penis standing up, moulded under the curve of the bar; balls exposed, dangling.

When the stud went inside, Josef's penis curved so stiffly that its shaft partly buried itself up against the cushioning of the bar. Belangaria, walking round behind them, put her fingers up inside the stud and masturbated his inner gland. He was well used to his ejaculation being triggered by direct finger-pressure to the gland. At the precious moment, his body froze, the gland made a hard ball under Belangaria's teasing fingers; his anus wanted to tighten. 'Stay open,' Belangaria murmured. She released the gland and rimmed the open anus with the soft wet pad of her middle finger in little rubbing strokes all the way round the perimeter. Then she twisted all four fingers slowly back inside. 'Open,' she coaxed. He moaned; ejaculation followed swiftly. Her other hand monitored his penile pulse – heavy beats in the tube below the stem distending Josef's anus. Belangaria continued until the pulse had stopped, the penis had softened, and her fingers now moved freely inside him. A soft wet slipping sound was made when his cock was expelled.

With the third one, Josef's erection came on quickly, at the first touch of the penis. But because the

133

penetration continued long, there were times when it partially subsided. And this somehow made the vision all the more erotic – to see a half-soft cock brought repeatedly back to hard erection by persistent penetration. Belangaria encouraged the stud to take good deep strokes. His cock was shiny with the semen that the previous two had left inside. She closed her hand around it, letting her thumb ride up inside Josef with every forward stroke. And that extra distension, combined with the change of anal shape, made him really rigid. She took her thumb out. 'Lift him back. Now – deeper with your penis.' She went to the front. It was an exquisite sight; the stud's cock was fully up inside. Josef's penis arched rigidly up and was trapped under the bar. His balls hung down.

Belangaria whipped them in stages – the tubes, then the balls, then the underside of the base of his penis. And as she did so, she recalled those sessions with the girls, whipping their labia, rubbing their clitorises with the crop, while they were being penetrated anally. She never touched Josef's penis; his spendings, slipping like warm cream, much thicker than they had been of late, came by reason of the other penis, as it beat the existing semen inside him to a foam, which emerged at intervals, squeezed round the thick girth of the stud's shaft, salty to the taste, like scuds of spume on some wild thrashing sea. She made the stud pull out for his creaming. Belangaria, nostrils flared, drinking in the heady scent, held the two bubbling penises squeezed together, smearing the slippy new semen round and round their lengths as fast as it emerged.

And when she looked at Leah. Leah was really very excited, and subsequently very responsive. She had her taken into the corner where Josef could not see what was being done to her, but could surely hear, to judge by the force of erection returning in his penis.

Belangaria called upon her sculptor to capture the

essence of this special moment. And she had two requirements in her sculptor – that he be kept naked and sexually stimulated while he worked, so the muse of eroticism was all-pervasive, and that he work rapidly, as becomes a true artist. To that end she specified that he must complete the work before he yielded up his seminal flow, declaring: 'Once the yield has come, the driving force is gone and the artist turns to sluggard.'

While the sculptor was working and Leah was moaning from the intimacies of the two strong attendant penises, Belangaria coated her fingers in the thick clay slurry. She took his erect penis in her fingers and wormed her other hand inside him. The sculptor began to wriggle in a little sexual dance. The veins on his penis stood out. Belangaria took stiffer clay and coated him, plugging the mouth of the tube and continued masturbating him, continued working the softer slurry deep inside his anus. She felt his climax beginning in the internal flesh which was being smeared by her slippy hand. She watched his semen squirting through the soft clay plug in the mouth of his penis; she folded its oily strands like egg white into chocolate. And when she looked at the sculpture it was complete, and urgent, vibrant, evocative, and the real Leah with her two anal lovers was not even finished.

Belangaria wiped her hands then went to Josef, who was still held facing away and unable to see Leah. And while she was refitting the clamps to the tubes of his balls, and he was presenting himself – his sex, so vulnerable – for her to deal with as she wished, and Leah was moaning in the throes of muffled climax, and the clamps were turning slippy from the penile leakage as Josef's anus was being opened by the slow turn of the muscle-stretcher, Belangaria was assuaged by a wave of tenderness for these two creatures, who were like favoured toys, content in the love of their mistress and acquiescent in their fate.

135

8

Leah's Tale

It was a strange reunion. Leah sat propped at the head of the great bed, her arms folded across her knees, her large perfect eyes staring at Josef with an expression he could not fathom. A curious bond now existed between them: she had once thought him influential; she seen his fall from grace; she had witnessed his degradation. And she was his one link to Sianon. But when he mentioned Sianon again Leah's gaze wandered to the statuary and the other trappings of opulence in the room.

'Leah – when you saw her was she all right?' he asked.

'Sianon?'

'*Yes*.' He stretched along the bed towards her.

'She is safe,' she muttered. Then she stared straight at him. 'I think her master means to keep her for her milk.' And now Josef's gaze fell.

He felt the tips of her small fingers brush his naked shoulder comfortingly. 'It is our destiny – to use our talents for the greater pleasure of our masters.' Her eyes sparkled. 'It gives us pleasure too.'

'But the harsh way they used you – you especially – in the Abbey . . .'

'My lord, I saw you watch my pleasure coming. I remember that. Did that not please you?'

'I was never a lord,' he said bleakly.

'I did not know it then.'

'You mean you would have suffered such things at my behest?'

'Some of them were done because you were there. It did not take away my pleasure. It added to it. I wanted to please you, as Commissioner. I know I must have: you wanted to take me to your cell that night.'

She had said it all. He looked at her and could not deny it. In the Abbey, she had seemed so vulnerable – a virgin. How could he ever forget what he had seen?

Her little gold chain extended between two studs, two-thirds the way down her inner lips. The chain had five jewelled links – he knew the exact count – each one with a small inset ruby. The chaining of her sex symbolised that this access was to be considered closed. She still wore the chain. Yet now she seemed so worldly-wise.

Amongst the collection of statuary in bronze was a new addition. Though small, it took pride of place in an alcove just above the bed. So deeply arousing was this work that it made the heartbeat quicken. And the subject was before him in the flesh.

Leah again lifted the statue down: she loved it. Again she looked at it with proud wide eyes. She was so beautiful and so proud of her sexuality. Again she wanted Josef to touch and to admire her statue. She handed it to him; his hands were weak. And she watched him with glittering eyes as he stared at it. The feeling in the pit of Josef's belly was one of exquisite yearning for her. The two men – their bodies – were somehow subdued, incomplete, merged into the rough-finished base. There was an urgency in the rendition of Leah: as she lay back, her little breasts were gathered up to thick uneven unfinished points; her chain had been selectively buffed to make it glimmer. But most achingly provocative was the captured sexual act, the puncturing of her swollen aroused body by the penises – the puncturing of her protruding anus and the puncturing of her pouting mouth. Josef looked at the statue and recalled the soft gasping sounds that he had heard, of Leah gagging on the pumping penis as she came to pleasure.

Leah had now got off the bed and begun to examine the other bronzes in the room. Her fingers selectively searched out the erect penises; she kept closing her hand protectively around the balls. Josef's erection was coming; the tip was beginning to weep; he half turned against the bed to hide it. Leah returned with a bronze cast of a large erect penis. She sat on the bed playing with it, taking the heavy balls in her fingers.

'Were you never a Commissioner?' she asked him.

'No.'

'Not even before you came to the Abbey?'

'No.' It was as if she still wanted to believe that he was. When he looked at her he almost wanted to believe it too. One knee was slowly slipping open and those early memories of her flooded back as her chained sex stood revealed. For Leah had a sex so lovely that it invited exploration. The piercing points made by the studs were now slightly inflamed from the repeated touching by enquiring fingers and repeated stretching of the chain: that much was different. He remembered that when she was made to stand or kneel, with her inner lips safely inside the smooth split bare shield of the outer ones, and the chain tucked up – pushed gently up – inside her, no trace of gold or jewel could be seen. Then as she became aroused, her sex would lubricate. Any movement of her thighs or buttocks – if perchance her anus were being examined or stimulated – would cause the chain to slip a little, until by degrees, it would dangle. And its pulling would cause her outer lips to split like the wings of a beetle and the inner lips to bulge down. The entrance to her sex was narrow – it might accommodate a female forefinger or the little finger of a man. In the Abbey there must have befallen many such

138

explorations. Josef now imagined the scene, with Leah lying with her little sex spread to the limits of its chain and the pad of a nun's finger probing for the mouth of Leah's womb, exerting a pressure so sublime that Leah would reach up and kiss her lover and squeeze herself around the finger. Her little knob would be extended like a red shiny blister from its hood and the nun would tease it with the finger newly moistened from inside.

But Leah's very treasure was her anus – enlarged and made sensitive by repeated stretching. Leah had been taught to crave such stimulation. The Abbess had been training her to satiate the soldiers' perverse lust. But no monk attending her had been able to resist. Their flesh, by dictum denied access to her sex, sought solace in her bottom.

Without Josef's realising it Leah had moved closer. Now she snuggled up. 'Why do men have two hearts?' she whispered. He frowned at her and she smiled back. Her fingertips were idly brushing his shaved belly. 'When the boat-women punished you . . .' And as if it were the most natural thing to do, she took hold of his naked balls and squeezed them gently. All he could do was close his eyes and listen to her words. He could not prevent the erection burgeoning. It appeared she thought it neither strange nor untoward. 'On the deck, when it was coming, when this heart was pumping out its love . . .' She squeezed his balls again. 'I wanted to kiss it then. And I wanted to kiss it when the Lady Belangaria put those clamps on it; I wanted to kiss it when it was hurting. The monks would never let me drink their juices, not properly. Look – you are leaking.' She licked his penis quickly, suggestively. 'Sometimes, when they lay on top of me, I could feel their first heart beating against my back – so tense, they were. Then I would feel this other heart that only a man has, so close against my bottom, as if it too were trying to get inside me. And then it would start pumping like the first heart, but harder, and I would feel their juices soaking through the sheath.'

Josef was transfixed by her frankness. Her eyes sparkled sweet wantonness. 'But that first time, in the training cloister, when you were watching, I knew I had pleased my lord.' Head tilted to one side she stared at him.

He nodded weakly.

'Because my breasts were small I had been taken to the Abbess to see what might be done. It was while she was examining me that she found my – my anus, to be so responsive. She said it was a talent that must be nurtured. She used her finger in me. I wanted the funny feeling to come. But it would not quite come, not that way, not at first. But it was still lovely.'

Hearing her speak of such practices made him ache gently inside. He could not hide his erection. She seemed to think it the natural way for a man to be. His quietness prompted her to continue:

'She put things into me, many different kinds of things. She used powders to make me itch. I could not keep still. It is such a peculiar feeling. While it was happening, she held my legs open and Sister Sutrice sucked me here.' She showed him. 'And the pleasure came – hard.' With her eyes closed, she shook her head very gently from side to side. 'Oh – so hard. And it was lovely. Then they told me that my bottom would be trained. They had me fitted with my chain. The Abbess said my sex was so beautiful that it must never be opened by a cock.'

'There were many suitors for you, among the monks?' One look at her again and Josef knew the answer.

'I liked it,' Leah murmured. 'There was one special young monk who was very kind. When we were alone he used to kiss me – so gently – and whisper to me. Sometimes he would hold my wrists. He used to touch my love-button. He once kissed it.' She put one hand to it, exposing her clitoris. Her other hand reached back between her legs as if caressing something invisible. 'I used to hold his other heart while it was pumping. I liked him more than the others.' Josef watched her lying on her side, her legs scissored, her hand between them, her fingers clutching rhythmically at the air. The cheeks of her bottom were open and he could see the place which had been the subject of this close training. The tender tissues bore the signs. But even in its swelling it was beautiful. He had the urge to kiss it. Leah gazed over her shoulder at him. He lay closer, encompassing her perfect belly in his hand. She gave a little shiver. Her breasts were small.

'At night, after my training by the monks, the Abbess and Sutrice would share me. They used a dildo of matted horsehair which Sutrice had had specially fashioned. One of them would use it on me while the other was sucking. Just before my pleasure came they would stop sucking. Then the rubbing of the dildo would be enough to bring me on.'

Leah spared no detail in her explanation, interspersing her account with sexual postures and gestures and unabashed advances. She had turned to face him. 'It makes a feeling in your bottom, like an ache, but nice,' she murmured. Her eyes were fixed on Josef's erect penis. 'The monks were forced to wear sheaths but yours is bare, like the soldiers' were – I could feel their warm skin against me when they were inside, and feel them going slippy when they squirted. But only the first one or two; after that it was slippy all the time. Yours will already be slippy because it is leaking.'

His thumb was under her chain; it was caressing her sheathed clitoris very slowly; her labia were already soft. She was finding it harder and harder to concentrate on what she was saying. He asked about the soldiers. Each time his little finger touched her anus, it responded by expanding like a soft thick-lipped mouth seeking to suck the fingertip.

'At first I was frightened,' she began.

Gently he took hold of her knees, tucking them up. 'Tell me what happened,' he whispered, continuing to touch her. Dearly would he have loved to go further.

'The marshal said he wanted to watch me please his men. He took me into the garden.'

'How many soldiers?'

'Five or six. No, six it was. I counted.' Never did a tale spur such arousal in a man. She whispered: 'I liked it – the taste; they called their love-juice "spunk". The monks were always sheathed. With the soldiers it was good, for theirs were naked: I could feel it coming out and I could taste it. With the monks, only their hearts were naked between their legs. They sometimes let me take their love-hearts in my mouth. And I would feel them beating – when the love-juice came. Or when they were on top of me I would feel the love-tube pumping up my bottom. But I would never feel the squirt inside for they were sheathed. With the soldiers it was different.'

She licked her lips. And how he wanted to slide above her so her reaching lips could sip the fluid from his leaking penis.

'Were they harsh with you?'

'They were so ... so urgent. Not steady like the monks. And they never played with me properly, like the monks would. I wanted it but they did not seem to know to do it. And that just made me crave it even more. When one of them would spunk inside my mouth or up my bottom, the funny feeling would come inside my belly – like a hurt, but not a hurt – like an ache, but very sweet. They carried me out on to the grass ...'

She broke off, looking away, reliving it. Then suddenly she arched up, reaching for his penis as he knelt above her, grasping it with her two hands round the base. Falling back, she held her lips wide. Clear drops of his fluid – one, two, three – fell down into Leah's lovely mouth. He kissed her. She told him that the soldiers' juice was stronger. He sucked her between the legs then tickled her labia, pulled the chain, gave little wet smacks to her clitoris, which excited her greatly. 'Now,' he said, 'tell me everything your soldiers did.'

'The first one did me without my feet ever touching the ground.' When she spoke in detail of the penetration, Josef opened her anus, making her moan, and he held it thus, with three fingers a little way inside it, gently stretching it for her.

'The others were in front of me, watching,' she whispered. 'When they lifted me off his tube it was still hard but it had a slippy cream, like soft-boiled egg white, under the rim. They made me suck it clean. One put his fingers up my bottom. Then he went inside from underneath while the next one did it in my mouth. He showed me how to pump his tube.'

Josef stared at the bronze statue and pictured Leah on her back now, lying on the soldier, one cock inside her bottom, the other, fat, stretching her mouth, her small fingers round it, pumping, her other hand between her legs, clasping the heart-shaped balls.

She made an open sucking gesture with her lips. 'They showed me how to love them deeply with my mouth. It is a funny feeling – inside your throat; if it comes when it is too deep you cannot taste it but you can still feel it going down. And because you are sucking so deeply it makes you want to open your bottom very wide so you can feel the love-heart beating against you. When they were feeding me this way, I wanted them to play with me. But it was still nice. The marshal told me I am the most beautiful creature he has known.'

Josef did not doubt it. Again he rose above her, took her feet in his hands and spread her open. His rigid penis, searching, probed between her legs, touched the naked hot lips then slipped between them under her chain. Pressing gently he oiled his leaking glans in the cup of her sex. Then he put it to her bottom. 'Oh, God . . .' he groaned.

Her chain stretched wide. Her little knob stood out. Her cheek was turned away. Her beautiful kissable anus was expanding very slowly, softly sucking his penis in. Inside she felt oily and red hot. Her bottom held just the bulb and it squeezed. And she looked at him sidelong while softly squeezing. Then she put out her tongue for him to kiss. He sank very slowly up inside her. She caught her breath, but her tongue still protruded. His penis was right in. Her bottom felt so hot. And because he was above her, his balls were dangling; their smooth skin pressed against the velvet surround of her anus. Then his shaved pubes touched her open sex.

She moaned, thrusting gently, rotating her hips. He sucked her tongue once – she had to reach. He was still holding her small soft feet. Now he sucked her middle toe. He could feel her knob against his pubic bone and her chain impressed into her open sex lips. He sank deeper into the delicious hotness; she gasped; he rose above her, pinned her feet against the bed and took slow deep strokes inside her bottom. 'Let me suck it,' she moaned. As he drew out, her mouth reached up between her legs, took one testing lick of his leaking glans – 'Mmmm – it's stronger now,' she murmured – then her lips locked round it like a limpet.

He pulled out and slid it far back inside her upturned bottom. 'Oh! It went deep that one,' she gasped, reaching up to kiss his face. 'Let me ride,' she begged. When she was on top, she faced away. He reached around and rubbed the jewelled chain gently against her clitoris and pushed a finger inside. She started to come, so he eased the touching, made it very gentle but kept his finger in her.

Her bottom kept squeezing. Her fingers slipped down underneath and clasped his balls, like a heart that would soon begin beating. She massaged this heart urgently, her fingers pressing into it, seeking. And she lay back against him, so his penis slid a short way out, and her anus clutched in spasms the sensitive glans until he could not hold back. Her fingertips must have felt the climax coming from deep behind his balls. 'It's beating,' she murmured, 'Oh, quickly ... Please ...' Trembling, she pulled his penis out and pointed it up between her thighs, trying to crouch forwards to reach it with her mouth. She was already shuddering as the semen started to spurt. It arced above her belly and splashed into her open mouth. It was on her face and neck and breast and still coming. He could feel her shudders through his fingers round her knob.

She turned her head and kissed him, the sticky salt fluid hot and astringent on her tongue. Then she smiled triumphantly – she had made him spill his heart, that tight, pumping, tender heart that dangled under his penis between his legs – he had spilled his heart for her.

Leah snuggled up against him. He kissed her. He wiped the semen from her cheek. She put her head against his breast. In a few minutes she was in a deep sleep. He looked at her lovely face. Then he kissed her eyebrows. She did not notice. When he turned, his mentor was in the room.

'Had we anticipated that you would have plumbed her depths with such alacrity, we might first have fitted you with your ring, that her experience be that much more piquant and that she might not fall asleep.' Lady Belangaria raised a finger. The door opened and two female guards came in. She pointed to Leah, who remained half asleep, innocently unfrightened, when they lifted her off him. Lady Belangaria then sat beside him on the bed. 'But there is this interesting difference for a girl – that exhaustion is no bar to pleasure; it merely makes its throes more protracted, its methods more exacting of the lover; and for the orchestrator, the culmination more satisfyingly complete.' She turned to

145

him. 'In the male the requirement is fortitude. And my protégés are not exempt. Turn over.'

He gasped when his cheeks were opened. It felt as if her two fingers, sliding up into him, were coated in liquid pleasure. 'It is a small preparation which serves to stimulate the gland.' Only after she had had him secured did the stimulation begin to work in earnest. He was on his back, 'so no relief may come through contact with the penis.' His mentor sat with him and Leah watched his penis straining in its skin. 'And all of this is a salute to you, my dear,' Lady Belangaria told Leah. 'Fear not, none of it shall be wasted.' She turned to her guard. 'Have the love-seat made ready for their nuptials in the conservatory.'

Under glass the summer evening's heat had been captured and softened by the night; dawn had broken; the re-warming was just beginning; the light was already good. And light was so important in the subtleties of pleasure.

Lady Belangaria watched her charge's penis stand yet further from his body as the guards lowered him on to the thick, ingrained wooden phallus of the love-seat. Leah was being masturbated standing. Her eyes were black with sexual excitement as she looked upon the bulging penis kept hard by the deep stimulation of the wooden phallus. 'Sit her on him,' Belangaria instructed. 'And bring my chair. The intimacies of love are nectar for the mind.'

In anal coitus there are two pleasure-points for the girl – the head of the penis fitting to the place deep inside her where her cavity begins to narrow, and the stretching of the anal mouth about the widening at the penis base. When the latter is augmented by external pressure from the male pubic mound, this pleasure-point is the more potent.

'Go deeper. Get it deeper up inside her,' she directed.

For the watcher, this viewpoint from between the girl's legs – of her breasts and belly, sex and opened anus – reigns supreme. Leah grunted softly when the pressure of full deep contact came, with Josef's smooth pubic mound against the stretched rim of her anus. Her knees were up beside her breasts, her armpits were quite naked, shaved. Josef's hands were stretched round her thighs, supporting her like a bundle, a soft pale sexual bundle gently impaled upon his bulging stake. His fingertips now gripped clasp-like upon her outer pubic lips and pulled them, causing her inner lips to peel open to the limit of their chain. The sexual shiver travelled up her belly, up the mid-line, to her breasts, which trembled separately in the shaft of sunlight. The fingertips continued to pull her even though she could not open any wider, on account of her chain. But her sexual knob, coaxed by the stroking of a finger, suddenly extruded fully from its hood, causing a gentle gasp, causing her slim white hands to reach for his wrists. But they did not try to stop him. They just held his wrists while his fingers eased, then prised, her hood ever more fully back and the skin around her knob inverted from the force of her erection. The Seerguard now applied a little dab of the anal stimulant to her naked clitoris. Her labia tried to close but could not.

Because of the stretching, the light now fell inside the lovely hollow of her sex. She was a virgin but the various fingers of sexual enquiry must have languished over-long. The lower part of the back wall was visible, deep red, shiny moist – kissably so, if one's lips could but reach it – tight and curving, blatantly stretched by the pressure of the penis from behind.

'Lift her,' said Belangaria. 'Slowly – and nicely.' Amid Leah's gently quickened breathing, the pink anal skin was drawn down by suction through the continuous pull of the shaft. This slowness of drawing made her anus want to close – a quite involuntary reaction which

147

could be cured by training. Belangaria, with gentle admonishments, soft strokings of Leah's underarms and gathered breasts, light squeezings of her aroused nipples, encouraged her anus to relax. The shape of the rim of Josef's glans inside her was visible through the drawn skin just before the head was yielded. The hot, newly emerged shaft was laid against her open-lipped sex. Her fingers immediately slid across and took the penis, rubbing the streaks of love-oil and moisture, rendering even her embarrassment a highly sexual gesture.

'I want your body to weep its pleasure like honey from a wounded comb,' Belangaria whispered. And she took Leah's fingertips into her mouth, sucking while Leah shivered, open-sexed. When Belangaria drew aside the penis, Leah, understanding what was wanted, twisted to one side. Then Belangaria's fingers were up her bottom, delving amongst the moist stretched aromatic folds, while Leah with one hand held her sex half open, her knob projecting for her mistress.

Stimulation ever deepening, layer upon layer of desire peeled back: this was Belangaria's purpose – to keep that female knob projecting and potent; to channel all the abstract tender-hearted female passions into overpowering lust.

To this end, she fitted to Josef's penis a special instrument, a cockscomb sheath. Leah moaned when she realised it was intended to stretch and stimulate the very place that Belangaria's fingers had just vacated. The sheath was open-ended, so Josef's glans erupted like a bursting succulent mushroom through the narrow mouth of leather. Care was needed, for ejaculation might come about by this straightjacketing of the swelling glans during fitting of the sheath. The supple leather clung to the penis like a tight second skin. But slung under its head was the cockscomb – three one-inch balls of shot, individually encased in leather and arranged as a vertical column. Belangaria stroked his rigid penis. She rubbed its captive balls of shot. They moved independently and to a degree freely, from side to side and up and down. Prolonged use was the secret – prolonged use inside receptive nubile bodies had made the leather soft. So there existed this contrast, the suppleness of the clinging leather, the firmness of the shot.

Belangaria looked at Leah. 'Be brave, my little one ...' Leah shivered and lifted high. And Lady Belangaria, moved with sudden love, held aside the penis and bestowed deep sucking kisses upon Leah's fleshy anal ring. And because her lady was kissing her there, in so rude and sensitive and sexual a place, Leah shuddered and closed her eyes and spread her legs so wide that the gape between her sex lips threatened scission of their little chain. Belangaria now guided the bulging bare-headed penis into the place she had so wetted with kisses. 'Oh – so beautiful, you are,' said Belangaria. Leah was looking at her longingly and moaning gently, with her tongue now extended and her sweet pink anus stretching, contracting, trembling, trying to spread. Suddenly she groaned: her anus opened like a blossom and ingested the swollen head. The muscle temporarily locked around the rim of the glans. 'Oh yes, so beautiful ...' Her slim white legs were trembling. Her belly bulged up. Belangaria licked its tight umbilicus. She thought how she would like it pierced – with a tiny gold ball pushed under the skin, so the umbilicus projected, so Belangaria might look at it, touch it, kiss it, suck it, while Leah was being slowly masturbated with her legs tied open and her hands behind her head.

Drawing back, Belangaria massaged the shiny hard bridge of flesh above Leah's stretched plugged bottom. She put her fingers inside the tight young sex to test the progress of the insertion. She could feel just the head of the penis through the wall of skin. She could not get a

149

firm grip because the inside of Leah's sex was weeping oil. Leah murmured, open-mouthed. 'Do you like it when I squeeze you here?' Again she touched the buried head of Josef's penis, which was unduly swollen, spilling through the constriction of its sheath. Again Leah murmured. 'Let your lovely body open. It want to feel his cock-end sliding in.' Leah gasped and spread her knees. She drew them up beside her breasts. And the penis started coming into her, slipping deeper. The first part of the sheath slid through the entrance. Its leather had a waxy surface from repeated sexual oilings. It slid more easily. 'Stay,' Belangaria whispered. For she wished to look upon her in this very sexual pose, knees tucked up beside her breasts, arms now cast back, armpits naked, sex wide open, anus half swallowing the leather-clad penis, the lovely bridge of shiny flesh above it bisected by a fine dark line which any tongue would wish to lick. And the cockscomb, shaking under Belangaria's teasing fingers, was poised to be pushed inside.

The first leather-coated ball, impinging against the front of Leah's anus, twisted. The penis pushed but the ball resisted. Leah pleaded softly. She was yet small despite her training. 'Oil –' said Belangaria. 'A little oil here. Drip it!'

'Ahh!' Leah cried out gently.

'Pant, my darling . . .' said Belangaria. 'Pant.' As the sweet breasts rose and fell, Belangaria supported her. 'Sit on it – sit up. More oil.'

'Ahhh!'

'Oh – sweet creature. There. Take it, sweetheart, take all of it inside you.' And she masturbated Leah's knob with pure fresh spittle while the sliding cockscomb distended Leah's bottom, ball by oily ball.

As Leah sat hunched upon Josef's penis, Belangaria put two fingers inside her sex to feel the cockscomb lodged behind. One by one she rubbed the balls from side to side. 'Oh for lips that could reach inside you like a snout,' she murmured. For they could suck the glans of Josef's penis with its cockscomb moulded through the wall of skin. She pressed her fingers down inside towards the rim and she could feel the penis thrusting in and out. 'Have you a mirror? Did you think to bring one?' she asked her guards. One was found. She made Leah hold her sex open while she showed her the bumps of the cockscomb so prominent inside. Then she masturbated her to the point where her body turned soft, her little nipples fat, her belly yielding, and the flush of sweat was under her arms. Then she made her lift right off the penis, letting her watch in the mirror how her anus expanded and tightened as each ball was being shed. Afterwards it felt hot and soft and beautiful to Belangaria's searching fingers. 'Put your fingers up your cunt.' Leah found it difficult because of her chain. 'Now – fingertips touching mine . . .' Leah trembled gently with her fingers inside her sex, with Belangaria's tongue inside her mouth and Belangaria's fingers up her bottom, pressed against hers through her inner skin.

'Lemon oil, this time,' said Belangaria. 'Shhh . . . It is better, more stingy, now your bottom is well stretched.' And sting it did. This time Leah could not keep still on the penis. 'Ride the itch.' Belangaria could not keep hold upon the cockscomb up inside. 'Lie her back,' she said at last. 'Hold her open. Hold her quite still.' The bumps were just visible inside her. What to put there, up inside her sex, to help to bring her on? Could she smack it, with a thin leather? Could such a leather be directed precisely through the opening to strike against the back wall far enough inside? And what of irrigation, with a fine jet playing only on this inside skin? Or a feather simply put inside and twirled?

Leah's knob stood out so hard that her contractions were beginning unassisted. And Belangaria still could not decide. 'Quickly – draw the seat back. Lie it down.' Josef, still bedded to the chair, was on his back. Leah lay on top, slipping backwards down his sloping belly, sliding up his chest. She was supported only by the grip of her anus round his penis, and by Belangaria's playing with her, wetting her proud clitoris, her belly button, her breasts, drawing her hood further back, licking her lovely knob which projected like a stubby penis. Between each hard and beautiful contraction of her bottom, its muscle could not hold her. Her anus slid ball by ball along the penis, finally shedding the glans, which began spurting up her body in powerful jets as Belangaria smacked beneath its balls. Leah was still coming, her knees up, her breasts above her face, her tongue seeking semen dripping from her nipples, when her lady's fingers swept back up her bottom, scratching all the itchy skin inside to make the itching worse.

9

Minette

Belangaria, leading her special slave by the leash attached to the simple clasp around the roots of his genitals, stepped out on to the highest terrace of the gardens of Ladyseer. Josef squinted against the daylight. The sun was half high – a good time of day, a time of fragrant promise. Colours were vibrant; early warmth suffused the air. In the heat of the afternoon there would always be the pools, rills and fountains wherein the fire of lubricity might be tempered and the rites of love extended. For in this garden there were girls as well as young naked men. And there were well-equipped ladies in discreet attendance. As Josef started to notice these trysts, his sex began involuntarily straining at its leash.

When she pulled upon the leash, his balls were drawn forward; he knew to follow. She strolled with him through graceful pergolas of damask rose and oleander. They came upon an open place in which a beautiful girl was being treed. She still had the toes of one foot on the ground. The smooth brown multi-stranded branches seemed to clasp her lovely body and squeeze it. Her lady's servant was watering the tree. 'Its fleshy nodes seek moisture and warmth; they are not truly sentient but behave as though they were. Its growth is sure enough for her to feel it. The sap is an aphrodisiac.' Even as they watched, the sparse leaves were twitching, readjusting. One of the nodes was inside her. Her labia stretched around it as if it were a soft tusk. 'Once inside it continues expanding through the hours until we choose to detach it.' A second fleshy node like a fig was weeping nectar by her cheek.

Suddenly the girl moaned and sucked the aphrodisiacal nectar from the node. Her lady examined her enlarged clitoris intimately. The nectar was exuding from her where the stem of the fruit protruded.

Belangaria tethered Josef to a trellis and tested his anus. Because of the girl – her moans, her lady's touchings – he was doubly susceptible to the attentions of his mentor's fingers. He was becoming attuned to these little messages of bare-fisted love put up inside him by every little rotation of her naked knuckle, every tiny scratch of her nails. She wanted to be able to speak to his soul through these small loving gestures.

She squeezed some nectar from the love-tree and rubbed it behind his balls. It would absorb slowly through his skin, engendering pleasurable feelings.

She waited with him until the fleshy node inside the girl had swelled so much that it was in need of detachment. But the lady was still playing with her. She was pleading. Her clitoris was pushed out by the force of the swelling. As the lady took hold of the engorged emergent stem the girl began to squirm. The lady snapped the stem cleanly. The girl's leg went rigid. Then her climax began in earnest with the fleshy fruit still inside her, stretching her, still exuding its nectar. And with swift, repeated upward cupping strokes, the lady smacked the glutted sex lips, spanking aphrodisiacal sap over thighs and belly with a force that shook the breasts, until all the pent-up sexual cravings in that taut sweet belly had been squandered in the lady's cupping fingers.

Belangaria detached Josef's penile leash from the trellis. She led him onwards. At the edge of the terrace, cascades of yellow broom and flame nasturtium tumbled from beneath her feet. The sweet mélange of perfumes filled her nostrils. Scattered through the garden were the secret bowers. She knew them, every one.

Descending the steps, detouring around a giant tree rhododendron, crossing a tight bridge over a verdant ravine, she lighted upon the special place. The arbour faced full south, the warmth of trapped sun verged pleasurably on the oppressive, inducing tiredness. All movement was slow, all sounds softened, all eyelids sleepy. Bibulous bees flustered deep in velvet-throated flowers. There were two ladies with the girl. She had been lifted from the love-tree. Sip by sip they were feeding her its sweet decoction to keep her sex awake. Her sex was swollen though it had not been entered by the love-tusk. She now faced forward, belly bulging, legs astride, her split buttocks nestled in the stud's lap, her soft pink anus stretched wantonly about his thick black shaft.

One of the ladies took a shine to Josef. She said she would be good to him. He was taken aside.

The sun beat down upon the backs of the girl's thighs. The penis looked purple-black, the balls matt. Josef's clasp had been removed from his genitals. His balls were being re-shaved. His lady had made him sit upon a marble balustrade. Close shaving of the genitals was good for sensitivity. It would enhance the effect of the nectar when it was reapplied. He had a good strong erection even now, even without the clasp; perhaps it was the cool marble against him; perhaps it was because he kept glancing sidelong at the girl, whom Belangaria was now attending.

The other two ladies were ministering to Josef. He was now sitting astride the stone balustrade. They made him sit forwards, keeping the pressure under the base of his penis, squeezing the balls out to each side. His sex was weeping clear honeydew which ran slowly down the underside.

155

In the bushes was a girl watching him. He had first glimpsed her a few minutes earlier. And now the rustlings had approached a little closer. None of the ladies spoke to her. They ignored her as if they did not want to frighten her away. One of the ladies was starting to feed a stiffened waxed cord of oiled, fine gold beads through the piercing in his glans. He could not stop his penis twitching. The end of the cord emerged through the mouth. The other lady attached to this a small gold globule which her fingers could grip. Between them, the two ladies began to draw the beads upwards through the piercing and the sensitive tube at the end of his penis. Josef wanted to lift. It felt like the imminence of an ejaculation centred at the tip. He moaned and writhed. The ladies kept drawing the fine beads through him. One lady held his balls down, the other lady pulled. His head twisted to the side. From the bushes he heard a gasp of concern. The last bead was deliberately too large to pass the piercing. The lady holding the globular weight drew the string of beads tight. The other lady held the pierced plum of Josef's penis. Her finger and thumb rubbed its mouth around the beads. His clear liquid was running through her fingers. The first one relinquished her hold upon the weight. She made him kneel on the balustrade, with his head down, his cheek upon the stone. He could hear the rustle in the bushes. He could feel his erection angled down, the heavy globule dangling from the beaded cord drawn through the mouth of his penis. He could not see what they were doing to him but he could feel something cold being inserted inside him. There was a delay before it took effect.

They had made him climb down from the balustrade and walk. The weight on its beaded cord was swinging from his standing penis. Suddenly he felt his knees collapsing and the feeling of impending climax starting deep inside him. One of the ladies wanted to hold his penis. He had to kneel, head down. He felt her hands turning slippery with his issue. It ran like warm oil. She smeared it on his back and balls and belly. And still he felt as if his climax had not truly come, but he wanted it to, how he wanted it. And he could sense the shy gaze of the mysterious girl.

Lady Belangaria had now rejoined them. 'Minette is interested,' whispered one lady as she removed his beads. Josef's mentor smiled. 'Then you should take him to the palm house, where there are some shady places.'

At first he forgot about the mysterious Minette: his ladies saw to that. That afternoon, a succession of admirers came to the palm house. Some desired only to watch. Some desired to whip him and to masturbate him with objects put inside him. Others desired to see him kept restrained and erect, with the sexual feelings just below the surface, so the scratchings of the finger-nails or the probings of the tongue might at any stage unleash the flood. In a way that he did not fully understand he looked forward to their cruel attentions. Each new face or body – for some would strip naked while they whipped him – in a perverse way he almost thought of as a conquest. And when their praises were bestowed in lavish terms, the throb of pride would surge inside his breast more keenly than the ache of pleasure inside him.

Then came the time of Josef's first assignation with Minette. It was a conquest that Josef was to find more deeply moving than all the rest.

He was being whipped, hanging high against the wall. The lady punishing him had stopped to give him more water, for it was warm in the palm house. The lady was forced to use a stool in order to reach him. A little of the drink spilled; it was then that Josef glimpsed the vague form in the shadows. Then the lady began using

157

her crop across his naked belly. And his erection, which had earlier subsided, came on intensely, perhaps aided by the quantity of fluid he had drunk. She increased the steepness of the crop-strokes, wishing to avoid direct whipping of his penis. Then his ejaculate started to come. And it was copious. It was on her hand, on her wrist, before she had managed to grasp his penis and put it into her mouth. And while it was still flooding and she was murmuring greedily, Minette emerged from the shadows to obtain a clearer view. The Seerguard ignored her. The ladies discreetly left.

Immediately he knew her to be the watcher from the garden. Yet she was collared. Her stance was uneven. She had very silky pale-brown hair, and a narrow face, beautiful in its way. One lip was drawn down at the corner. Her eyes were radiant.

Minette cautiously approached him. Her lips opened nervously as though to speak. Instead her head bowed shyly. Then she glanced towards the door.

The guard came across and began pouring more water. Minette's gaze crept back. Then she whispered: 'Oh . . .'

Josef watched her take the stout wooden pegs in her fingers and push them into the sockets in the wall, that his feet might take the weight from his wrists. The guard reached up to him with the drink. He shook his head.

'She wants you to drink. You ought not to refuse her.'

Josef looked down at the innocent eyes staring up at him. The young woman had never spoken to the guard; there must have been some prior arrangement between them.

'Just drink,' said the guard. 'She will attend you.'

Minette began gently sponging his penis; water trickled down his leg. She stopped, stared at it then looked up at him, holding up the sponge absent-mindedly until he quaffed the contents of the mug the guard was holding, and the sleeve of Minette's gown was wet. She glanced beseechingly at the guard, who replaced the mug on the table, walked to the door and bolted it. Minette put the sponge down and retreated into the shadows. A short time later she re-emerged wearing only a vest. It drew attention to her slim long-limbedness and it draped over her full breasts. She returned to the table and poured a drink. She held it up to him. Josef shook his head.

'I shall attend you,' Minette whispered soulfully. She stood on the stool. Her large attractive eyes stared at him and he could feel her quick, excited breathing. Her lip turned down very slightly at one side, as though as a child she had been smitten. She reached up and kissed him very gently on the lips. She did it as though she were inexperienced in kissing but it was a very slow and deliberate kiss which had a profound effect upon him. She made it clear she wanted him to drink. But already he felt overfull. She kissed him again: bending her head, she kissed his nipple with that slow deliberate kiss. Immediately, his erection came. It stayed there as she fed him the liquid. Then she stood down.

And she simply knelt on the floor in front of him, waiting with hands clasped, staring up with limpid eyes at his erection. He had to close his eyes and try to make his mind go blank, so that this painful erection might subside. But it was very difficult to do; he could not shun the image of her before him naked but for her vest. The front of it stood away from her belly on account of the fullness of her breasts, whilst at the back the hem hovered just above the swell of her buttocks. It brought to mind the sexual practices he had witnessed amongst the novices in the cellars of the Abbey; perhaps this girl was a follower. But she had not drunk any liquid; she was waiting for him; his bladder was full to aching.

At length he felt the heavy throbbing weight of his penis begin sinking. It was then that her love play

159

began. He felt her moist lips tugging gently at his shaved balls, her tongue exploring wetly the crease at the top of his thigh. She began to bathe his genitals with her spittle, distributing it all over his penis, over his naked balls, underneath them. The evaporation of this spittle made his genitals cool. Her fingertips now pressed firmly into his bladder. She knew exactly where to press to make him gasp. He heard her breathing quicken in anticipation. She took his half-erect penis in her hand; she balanced his balls on the tip of her tongue; she masturbated him slowly and pushed the tips of two fingers under the base of the shaft. He moaned, almost unable to contain himself. The pleasure was there, a peculiar feeling; and his erection did not come though she was masturbating him gently. She put the head of his penis in her mouth, just holding it there and waiting as she stroked her cool wet fingers behind his balls. He could feel her lithe body moving, gyrating slowly, sexually, pivoted about her pouted lips sealed softly about the head of his half firm shaft.

'Oh, no . . .' he moaned. 'Don't do this. No . . .' The first spurt of urine came and he was still inside her mouth. She gave a little shudder of pleasure. The flow stopped. Wretchedly he looked down. But her eyes were softly closed in anticipation; her hand and mouth were sealed around his penis; her other hand was between her legs; he could see her nipples poking through her vest; he could feel her tongue dancing, coaxing the tip of his penis. It spurted again, and oh, the feeling of sinking and of her sweet caressive tongue dancing in the stilted stream was exquisite. Then her mouth pulled away and his flow was again interrupted; his reaction had been automatic.

'Don't stop,' she begged. 'I want it. I want you to wet me, bathe me with it. I want to feel its softness on my skin. Don't waste a single drop.' Her lips were wet. There were dribbles on her vest. She kissed the droplets from his penis then ran her fingers through her hair. All trace of her former reticence had disappeared. She sank back on to her knees, legs open and she exposed her breasts. She gathered them between her arms then began to stroke her nipples with her fingers. Her head sank back, baring her collared throat. When she opened her eyes, his erection was already restored.

'You cannot do it with it hard? I know some can.' She jumped to her feet and stood beneath him, against his leg and facing out from the wall. 'This way it is good for us both.' His balls were beside her ear. She drew her hair aside to make the skin contact with them. Her arm was raised across her breasts, lifting the vest; her hand was gently round the base of his penis. And after a few seconds' silence, he realised that she was masturbating herself. She murmured gently, turned and kissed his balls. 'Now,' she whispered, 'Please . . .?' Her thumb pressed under the base of his penis. It started to subside. 'Oh – please . . .' Her tongue-tip danced against the end. He tried to make it come. She pumped it from the base. He groaned with the sinking shivering feeling. A fine spray was emitted from his penis. He kept pushing, squeezing. She moaned in pleasure; the spray descended in a weak arc jetting from the hand-pumped penis, coming stronger, spraying the front of her half-lifted vest, spraying her breasts while the heavier droplets fell directly on to her shoulders. She kept turning, licking, kissing the tip of the penis, capturing the flow in her mouth and squeezing her legs together to intercept the warm trickles running down her belly. Then she turned to face him with her vest fully lifted, her hand round his genitals, twisting them from side to side to direct the flow upon her nipples and underneath her arms. As soon as the flow began to abate, she took his penis deeply in her mouth. He could hear her moaning as she played with herself while she swallowed; her sucking quickly caused his flow to stop and brought him to a stiff erection.

She stood before him, her breasts dripping, the wet vest draped over them, sticking to her skin. He could see between her legs the lips of her sex swollen with arousal and her brown bush sparkling with the droplets that his penis had emitted. She untied him from the wall and made him drink. As he was drinking she knelt squarely on the floor and sucked him as he stood there, until the flow was stimulated. Then she held his half-stiff penis against the side of her neck beneath her ear; the flow sprayed under her hair, on her collar, under her vest at the back and down the middle of her spine. Her sex was still dripping when he lifted her kneeling on to the wrought-iron table. He placed her facing him with knees splayed open. Her made her hold her vest up and hold her sex lips open. Her clitoris protruded. Josef stood between her legs and sprayed. When her wet breasts touched him and her sticky-drying cold nipples clung to his skin, his erection started to come and the flow abated to a fine intermittent stream which he kept directing against her open sex. He felt for her clitoris with his fingers, mating it to the mouth of his penis, spraying it until the stiff rigidity of her tongue inside his mouth caused his flow to break, then masturbating her gently until his penis softened enough for the flow to resume.

She pulled away, wanting her breasts rewetting. When the pressure would not suffice to make the jet reach, she lay on her side, took hold of his penis, sucking it hard then playing with herself until it softened and began to spurt again, then redirecting it according to her will. Her climax came with her lying across the table, her head overhanging. His balls were in her mouth and she was sucking them and moaning and he was spraying a very fine jet over her belly and between his fingers which were holding her sex lips open. Her clitoris was jumping like fish in the fine cascading stream.

Her hair and neck were wet. The saturated vest was

rolled up under her arms. Her breasts stood out, misted with fine droplets. Josef lifted her, drew her wet vest over her head and still she wanted his penis.

'Harlot!' a voice cried. Minette froze. Josef swivelled round. Glaring at them was a young scantily clad girl with long blonde hair and piercing blue eyes. Balanced in her fingers was a crop.

'Mistress . . .' Minette tumbled from the table and on to her knees on the floor.

'Who let her in here with him? Seerguard?' Jealousy burned in those cold blue eyes.

The guard advanced, pale-faced and chastened. The girl raised the crop; the guard flinched. The girl grasped Minette by her wet collar. 'Take her to my private rooms. Don't let her dress. I shall deal with her directly.' The blue eyes threw a single stinging glare at Josef. Then the girl was gone.

'What thought you of our new Empress?' Lady Belangaria searched Josef's face.

'Empress . . .?' His mind raced. Lady Belangaria smiled wryly. He had seen her so briefly he knew not what to say. 'She looks very young,' he finally answered.

His mentor's eyes lit up. 'Too young, yes, for such responsibilities and too enmeshed in silly games. A wiser head was what was wanted.' She paced the floor then turned. 'You have been summoned to her private apartments tonight.'

He knew Minette must be at the heart of this summons. He acquiesced when Lady Belangaria prepared him with Leah watching. Thoughts of Minette filled his mind as his mentor put two fingers into him and expertly rubbed the sexual gland.

The guard opened the door, which was quilted in polished leather. The door closed behind him; the guard had not entered. It was not the sort of room Josef had

163

expected. It looked like a man's study, far more opulent than his own study which he had long ago left behind. The wooden surfaces were dark and richly polished, reflecting the warm light of the lamps and candles. The floor was waxed. There was a heavy writing desk and a mirror-like table. There were chairs and couches covered in the quilted leather. The room was warm; he could feel the warmth on the naked soles of his feet; a fire glowed in the grate. On the sideboard there were tall jugs and decanters of pale cordials; there were fluffy white towels and fine-pored sponges; and there were instruments in gold.

Minette was standing against the opposite wall. She was wearing a fresh white cotton vest and pure-white brief pants. Strips of cloth dangled from her wrists. She had been shaved; he could smell the soap; and he could see in intimate detail the shape of her sex through the clinging material. On a small table near to her rested a half-empty tumbler. Its lip was still moist; she must only just have put it down.

A little shiver moved up her legs; she glanced at the tumbler then looked at Josef; her gaze was desirous. He picked up the tumbler. The cordial was softly aromatic; it smelt sweet and herbal, faintly pungent. It was a scent that he would come to associate with this room and Minette and pleasure.

'I thought to find you with your mistress,' he ventured.

'It was I who wanted you here. If my mistress discovers I have arranged this tryst I shall be punished.'

'Then I trust she is far from here?'

'Are you in truth a slave? You are not like the others.' Her words took him aback. Her gaze was knowing. 'Are you under my lady's spell?'

He stared at her in a different light.

'You ask about my mistress. Come . . .' Minette took him by the hand. She led him into a gallery then up some stairs to a dark landing. She drew aside a small eye-level curtain in the wall. 'Sometimes I watch from here. They cannot hear us through the glass.' When he looked at her she was again the timid lovely creature with the smitten lip.

The window looked down into a beautiful boudoir. Two naked male slaves were fastened at the head of the bed with their feet behind their ears. Prostrate on her back with her head overhanging the foot of the bed was the beautiful blonde mistress. The big toe of each of her feet was inserted into each anus, stimulating the two erections. But she was sucking semen from a naked creature – a man yet not a man. His bronzed body had the accentuated musculature of a classical statue. He stood at the end of the bed leaning effortlessly over her face: one hand was clenched behind his deeply hollowed back; the other was caressing her. Her toes anally masturbated her slaves; her lips were round the creature's penis. For as long as she sucked him his semen kept coming; when she took breath it overflowed. She was drowsy eyed as if his fluid were a drug.

Josef looked to Minette.

'The Incubus – do you know of it?' she murmured desirously.

His eyes grew wide. 'I know of the Succubus.'

Minette nodded. 'The Succubus is under the jurisdiction of the Lady Seer. The Incubus is reserved for the Empress. It is decreed that this separation must exist. The Succubus bestows male prowess. The Incubus is for female pleasure. My mistress likes to drink.' She stared at Josef. 'Is not the purpose of male ejaculate to provide sensual pleasure for the recipient?'

'And your mistress, does she share the Incubus with you?' He remembered her remark about the ability to urinate while erect.

Minette nodded unabashed.

'Then what need have you of human men?'

'Perhaps for their uncertain moods.'

The unstated pact between himself and Minette was changing. While he was the helpless slave she was the halting girl who rescued him from the whipping. But her nature was more complex.

Josef stared through the window. When he turned again, Minette, poised to descend the stairs, was waiting, the cloth strips dangling sexually from her wrists.

In the study, he stood in front of her, took her gently by the chin. Her dark eyes were so beautiful. He kissed her smitten lip and felt within its trembles the image of the shy uncertain girl. He took the lead. 'Stand like this.' Her eyes acquiesced. He coaxed her right knee to bend until her foot arched and her thighs were half open. And looking at her thus, just looking at her lovely face and sheathed breasts, and her labia pouting through her briefs, and contemplating the things that she might allow him to do, he could not stop his erection. He turned, walked over to the sideboard and filled the tumbler to the brim.

On the wall above her head was a brass rail. He bound her wrists to it with the cloth strips. Then he fed her the cordial from the tumbler. He held one of the smaller towels under her chin. She drank greedily. The tumbler emptied. He refilled it. She drank rapidly the first half of this one, then the pace slowed. It took a few minutes for her to consume all the liquid. Then he refilled the tumbler. She managed another third of it. By now she wanted to close her legs. He brought a leather stool and placed the offending foot on it, resting on its toes. Then he fed her more liquid.

'Nnnn . . .' she murmured. The leg upon which she stood was trembling. Josef put the tumbler on the table. Then, looking around the room, he left Minette fastened to the wall, thereby abandoning her to one of the pleasures of this form of love, that the victim remains uncertain about what the dominator next intends to do.

No instruction had been given to Minette apart from the first directive about the position of her leg. Even from this distance, Josef could see that her shivers were making her nipples erect.

In one of the drawers of the writing desk he found prints of girls in bondage, with naked men punishing them. Some of the girls had gold inserts through their labia; in one case these were fastened to loops round the tops of her thighs, so when she was made to splay her legs, her sex opened too. In one print she was being whipped there. Josef took the prints to the table and spread them out. Minette was murmuring. He went back to her. There was no mark on her pure-white briefs. With one quick slide of his finger, he eased the gusset aside. Her sex poked out, pink and naked. Because of its recent shaving, the skin was soft and clinging to the touch. He wondered if the Empress had shaved it. He gathered it intimately into his hand and he could feel the first oiliness against the tip of his middle finger. Still holding her sex, he drew her vest upwards, up above her poking nipples, high up to expose her armpits. She had been shaved there too. He kissed this smooth, smooth skin, sucked it, squeezed her clinging sex lips between his fingers, licked under her nipples, left them wet, drew the loose vest up over her head, licked her armpits again, then kneeling down, he sucked her sex until all the scent of soap was gone and her clitoris stood out hard. Then he left her skin to dry.

When he came back her labia looked fatter and more wrinkled and were indeed dry and cool on the outside but when he pressed his fingers there, the little creases in them still retained trapped spittle. He dried them carefully in the soft loops of a towel then he returned them to the soft clutch of the gusset of her briefs. Then he again made her drink. She began to wriggle even as she was drinking. He then explained that no urine should express without permission. And amid her groans he proceeded to kiss her lips and put his hand down her briefs and touch her little pee-hole. Then he twisted her round against the wall and drew her briefs completely down and smacked her. Her vest was stretched across her shoulders. He smacked her soft sweet buttocks with his bare hand. Then he drew her briefs up and pulled the gusset to the side and masturbated her until she dangled from her arms and asked to be allowed to sit.

He unfastened her and carried her to the polished table. There he sat her on the very edge, with her briefs round her knees and her sex projecting. She clasped her arms imploringly about his neck. Her breasts were trembling. He moved her forwards until the head of his erect penis probed between her legs. Her open labia kissed then clasped it. He pressed the glans more firmly against her. Suddenly her feet tucked under the table, lifting her briefs out of the way. 'Oooh,' she groaned. It was coming. His penis pressed. She squirted. His glans felt warm and slippery. A little soft stream continued to run down to his balls. He drew away. Her flow stopped. 'Lean back.' He spread her aromatic liquid all over her naked pubes, into the creases of her thighs and up around her nipples. There was not enough to anoint her underarms. Josef refilled the tumbler and made her drink. She was a beautiful shameless sight leant back on the table, her vest drawn over her head, her briefs round her ankles, her belly distended and this smooth expanse of naked skin between her thighs and chin. Her scent, her warmth, her sexuality, were potently arousing.

Suddenly she leant over on one elbow, took his penis and plunged it into the tumbler. Then she sucked it dry.

'Lie back,' he told her. 'It's you who must receive.' He found her so beautifully sexual that he just wanted to keep giving it to her. He put two fingers up inside her, reaching forward, lifting. With the other hand he gently rubbed her knob; with the heel of his hand, he pressed down on her bladder.

168

'Ohh,' she gasped, tossing her head from side to side. 'Ohhh!' And a fine clear stream jetted straight into the air. Its droplets drew a trail up her belly. He smoothed them over her skin. They felt soft and slippery; the scent was herbal. Again he pressed from above and at the same time from inside; again she jetted. The droplets splashed her neck and hair and lovely lips. He kissed them. They tasted faintly bitter, but warm, sensual. While he was still sucking her tongue, his fingers were still inside her and he felt the warm ejecting spray splashing up his arm.

It took a long and gentle masturbation before the liquid was fully dried. Her skin felt softer; it smelt more arousing; her sex was making lubrication. Her bladder was still overfull. He could feel it from inside. She murmured a little protest as he lifted her off the table with his fingers still in her. He stood her in the middle of the floor and smacked her bare bottom with his bare hand. Then he drew her briefs up and smacked her through them until she started to pee. The wet briefs made the smacking more sonorous and effective. Once she felt them begin to soak she could not stop. He carried her to a leather armchair and sat her in it with her legs over the arms. Then he smacked her sex through her wet briefs. The smacks kept interrupting the flow. He pulled her briefs down and smacked. The smacking made the urine spray. His arms and chest, her breasts and face were covered in it. 'Make love to me,' she moaned, gripping his penis, drawing him forward until his balls were inside the wet briefs stretched between her thighs. Her sex was leaking over him. His penis was plunging in. When she felt his climax coming she drew his penis out and gripped it, pointing it and squeezing, controlling the flow, which came in hot thin jets against her knob until she cried out. Then all she wanted was to suck him until the hard jets came against her throat.

'Don't stop.' The young voice had come from behind him. The Empress now moved round and sidled behind the leather chair. Gone was all trace of her drowsiness; her eyes were brightly alert, her fingers nervous as she stroked Minette, whose head sank back. Josef watched the slim white fingers coating themselves in Minette's wetness. 'Your bed is made ready, my harlot. Dismiss this feeble creature and you shall have more male fluid than you can ever swallow. And your mistress shall be there to whip you slippy while you drink.'

Minette murmured. The Empress smiled like a cat.

When Lady Belangaria grilled Josef about what had happened there was a hard edge to her gaze, a jealousy whenever he mentioned Minette. He suspected his mentor saw her as an obstacle in her path to the Empress.

Whatever the reason, it goaded her to want to expunge those earlier pleasures and win him for herself. While Leah watched she put the gold spur inside him. Its pressure, the feelings of helpless arousal it induced in him, seemed to assuage her annoyance. The harder he became the more she enjoyed it. Later that night she drew Leah away from him and took the spur out and stared lovingly at him for a fleeting instant.

'My lady – what is it you want of me?' he whispered.

'Do not question. I want nothing that you cannot give.' She fitted the thick gold torc through his penis. The feeling of wanting to climax lingered just below the tip. Then she put her bare hand inside him as he lay upon his side upon her bed. His leakage steadily spilled around the metal. He could not set aside the haunting image of Minette being whipped by the young blonde Empress. When his lady moved her hand, it made him moan. The scent of gardenia flooded his nostrils. She pushed to the wrist and twisted. Her wristbone precipitated the powerful climax that squeezed the semen from the gland. Then as her hand squeezed up to make a fist inside him, the semen continued to pour out round the gold ring as a deep viscid expanding pool into Leah's cupped hand. Leah sat back, lifting her hand like an oyster to her lips. The white curds slid; her agile tongue caressed them; the colourless whey ran down her arm.

'I am so very pleased with you,' Lady Belangaria whispered to Josef. 'Tomorrow shall see you rewarded with the Kelthlings.'

Sceptics doubted that the Kelthlings could be made to breed. Time upon time their willing victims tried, pouring forth the lifeblood of their sexuality, dashing themselves like waves against the rocks of lust – all to no avail. This time it must be different.

10

The Muster

In the crisp dawn of the day of the muster, when Janna, her lips salty from the sexual dribblings of a slave, lay in debauched sleep, the Magus – sharp, acute, untired, hawk-like – took Sianon by the naked arms on to the black basalt balcony and down the polished granite steps to his garden suffused with pale dewy light. Her naked feet soundlessly kissed the smooth slabs. Her naked thighs slipped into the pool of still air. No leaflet murmured on the branch tips of the trees.

Her breasts were unnaturally enlarged; his attentions over the last few days had seen to that. Their skin was stretched, their areolae velvety and brown. Through long nights of measured pleasure, the bitter potion had been administered by mouth, intermingled with the slick effusions from the reddened glandes of penises rendered fat and hot by overlong punishment. Sianon now knew instinctively the hot soft feel of such a penis, the soft tiredness in the thick girth of its shaft, the scrotal pouch so thin it would cling to her like a second skin while the balls rolled freely inside it. Most of all she knew the gush of liquid: when semen sojourns overlong inside the body, when it is churned by punishment, it thins to hot water. Butter thickens, semen thins but stays sticky.

The Magus had watched and admired her, wanting to see her young mouth always filled, wanting to see her constantly drinking. He would put the cup of potion to her lips as sensuously as Janna would insert the rampant spilling penis from the slave that she was punishing. Sianon would be face upwards, her head on the seat of the couch, her legs open on the floor, with a girl slave simply holding her clitoris. To each side, her arms would lie limply spread, resting palms uppermost, isolated from her body, so her breasts in their heavy unsupported fullness would transmit every soft vibration as a jellied shake. The Magus would study their every sexual shudder, directing that nothing should touch them, that they should be free to swell, to bloat with milk and tighten. 'At the muster they shall shine,' he had said. But at dawn, restless, he had brought her out.

In the bottom of the dell the air was cold. The greenery was greyed. Sianon walked in front of him to the rocky bank on the far side. The way steepened and the path became steps, passing under rock bridges, circling ever upwards in a narrowing spiral towards an eyrie. On one side was the wall of rock, on the other the precipitous drop. Fear made her short of breath. The Magus deliberately remained several steps below her, watching her tortured progress. Her slim legs turned to heavy weights, uncontrollable, clumsy; her panicky fingertips ineptly clutched at tiny snags in the stone. She inched along, facing the wall of rock, terrified to look down. At long last, shaking and breathless, she crawled giddily on to the grassy top.

The pinnacle was only a few feet wide. Near its centre stood a forked stunted tree sprouting thin shoots from its base. On all sides the rock fell so precipitously that she felt as if she were on a disc of grass suspended in the sky with nothing but air between her and the mountains. She reached out for the security of the tree.

The Magus stepped on to the grassy platform and balanced on the edge. Sianon could hear footfalls on the steps below. The Magus waited, staring pensively at her.

Then another naked offering appeared above the edge of the disc. The Farbesian, though frightened, was secure in the Chamberlain's arms. He passed her to the Magus and she clung to him. The tiny sexual restraints glimmered between her legs.

The Chamberlain went to Sianon. He detached her fingers from the branch. The pale nudity of her skin was a magnet to the sparse light. He drew back her auburn hair, exposing the leather collar. He drew her arms back, away from her breasts, forcing them to lift. Her nipples pointed up. She saw the Magus's gaze upon them. She did not want to stand up without using her hands to steady herself. But the Chamberlain lifted her to her feet and led her quaking to the more exposed side of the tree. Balancing himself on the edge of the drop, he fastened her wrists individually, high against the branches of the fork which reached forwards and outwards into the air. He moved her legs so far apart that she was on her toes, her arms thrown forwards, her breasts overhanging, full, the brown teats swollen, extended. Then he pulled a long curved shoot from the base of the stunted tree. And as he waited, he tested it for flexibility.

The Magus took up his position with the Farbesian in his arms, his eloquent fingers between her legs, drawing back her tiny reins, flicking at the exposed tip of her collared clitoris. Little squirming wriggling movements began in the seat of her belly.

Wave upon wave of sexual expectancy travelled up Sianon's shaking legs, up between her buttocks, through her belly to her breasts, so distended, trembling, dangling into space. The Chamberlain's fingers searched between her buttocks to calm her. Her legs were wide open; his slippy fingers found the place. Her knob stood out untouched. Then the first beam of true sunlight burst through a gap in the mountains and the Chamberlain started whipping her breasts, whipping their fullness, with the tips of his fingers still twisting inside her. The pleasure came through her breasts and bottom at the same time; her poking clitoris was never touched. All the richly sexual feeding over many days was now deliciously rewarded. Her breast milk sputtered at first then spurted then sprayed, creamy golden in the first sunlight, arcing, shattering under the flashing whip-strokes into tiny star-like droplets plummeting into the grey depths far below. The Farbesian watched with desirous lips. The flow continued. The Chamberlain flung the whip aside and tried to grasp the teats in his fingers. The milk went everywhere.

The pleasure-trembles remained with Sianon when the Farbesian was put to her breast while Sianon was still in bondage against the tree. The Farbesian, reined between the legs, sucking, craving, and turning faint through continuous masturbation, could not cope with Sianon's flow. The milk from one breast spilled from her lips; from the other it sprayed over her sweet black hair, down her naked back, into the Magus's hand in which her open buttocks were sitting.

'The gathering is under way, my lord,' said the Chamberlain. He was balanced on the edge of the rock. Below, across the bridge, beyond the seclusion of this select garden, the preparations were beginning. Vessels were unloading in the harbour. The streets were filling with stalls. Clusters of people were gradually moving up the hill towards the great elliptical dome of the Mega-nopticon. It was the dawn of a day like no other; when lord would rub shoulders with commoner, when soldier would vie with peeress for a love-slave, and the baccha-nal would extend through the night.

By mid-morning, slaves from every quarter had been assembled. New blood was at a premium. Beauty took many forms – unusual physical or emotional traits; singular development of the sexual nodes; wanton promiscuity. Prior to the muster was a display of the choicest slaves. The viewing gallery, built of polished blocks of virgin marble, was a hundred paces long and thirty wide. It was open to daylight along its north side and its high ceiling sloped steeply away from this side to become the rear wall. The end walls, converging inwards, completed the effect of a funnel. The light was therefore all around, diffused by multiple reflections between the four pure-white surfaces and unscarred by the harsh contrasts of direct sunlight. A triple row of low cylindrical granite pedestals extended down the middle of the floor. Through the centre of each pedestal was slotted a black obsidian pole surmounted by an eyelet. The slaves dangled from silken ropes fed through the eyelets. Every rope was tied-in neatly; every stone surface was honed smooth; every edge was finely bevelled.

Presiding over the display, directing the positioning of the slaves and admitting selected viewers, was the Whip-master, bull-necked and tiny-eyed.

Sianon could hear footfalls and chattering voices coming from above, behind the sloping rear wall: a large group of people was assembling. There were other sounds too, echoing from deep below her feet. Halfway along the gallery on the inner side, two transverse trench-like slots cut in the floor sloped steeply downwards under the rear wall and into blackness. Following the path of each incline was an overhead metal bar.

The masters and mistresses in their finery moved amongst the slaves. There were many shades of skin and styles of hair and body adornment. The girl to one side of Sianon was long limbed and athletic; the next one had her head and body completely shaved and wore a gold ring through her top lip. A little further along was Leah. Another girl had been tethered tightly to the black shiny pillar by a gold twine threaded through her punctured labia. Others had been tethered by devices that slipped inside the anus then expanded to prevent retraction. They stood with buttocks pressed against the pillar and hands uneasy by their sides.

There were a few males who drew the attention of certain ladies, discreetly taunting and binding their erections.

Sianon's wrists were tethered back to back above her head. This pose by lifting her shoulders emphasised her breasts. The Whipmaster had drawn back her ankles to the sides of the pillar. It gave her the feeling of falling forwards. Her breasts hung outwards. All along the gallery she could see the naked beautiful girls and the Whipmaster moving amongst them, displaying them like succulent fruit for the visitors who might wish to taste.

Into the midst of these epicureans there loped a curious rider in a carriage surrounded by a retinue of guards. He looked old. His bath chair had little wheels; its sides tapered forwards to a cantilevered plank supporting his lifeless spindly legs, which lay like long twigs under the embroidered coverlet. The chair was fashioned of a lacquered horn-like substance; its lips were rounded. It resembled a chariot. It had a vertical pole which empathised with the black obsidian pillars to which the initiates were fastened. A small container swung from a hook on one side of the pole. The charioteer gripped the pole to steady himself. He was regally dressed, with a gold necklace on his barrel chest. There was a red rose pinned to his robe. He was grey but well-kempt, closely shaven.

His guards wheeled him slowly between the lines of lovely girls. His eyes sprang sharply this way and that. A little way beyond Sianon his retinue stopped. His gaze was on a girl tethered by her anus. He whispered to his closest guard, who stood in front of her. The Whipmaster moved behind her, loosened her tether then tugged it upwards. The girl, gasping, tried to move back and on to her toes, her legs automatically drawn open. The guard reached with a bare cupping hand between her thighs. Sianon could see his fingers gradually being taken up inside. The Whipmaster took the girl by the hair and held her head back against the pillar. Her masturbation continued for the grey sage's pleasure. Her breasts were responding. The guard drew from his belt a larrup. Her hands defensively moved up at first then sank passively and clung to the pillar. When he started to spank her sex with his hand still inside, her thighs tried to close. The Whipmaster corrected her. Her knees bent open. Her belly enjoyed deep intimacy with the investigating hand. The larrup lashed the creases of her thighs. The redness spilled in two broad bands up her belly. Her breasts bulged as if awaiting spanking. The Whipmaster's lips quelled her moans. The master in the chair watched without responding. Then his gaze began to rove. Again he whispered to his retinue and he was rolled along, leaving in his wake the continuing exhibition of masturbation and spanking.

The bath chair had come to rest in front of Leah. Reaching with a hooked cane the master slipped the hook under her chain. A guard unfastened her from the pillar but she did not know what to do. She just stood there, afraid, with the hook of the cane between her legs, pressing against her labia. The grey master's hand around the cane was large, not bony like his legs. But his other hand was gloved in a cloven mitten and Leah was looking at it fearfully. Awkwardly he beckoned with it as he drew the cane slowly towards him. Her belly protruded. She stood at the edge of the pedestal until the guard lifted her down.

With his good hand the master examined Leah's breasts and belly. Then he asked that she be turned round. This good hand – unusually large – spread open the cheeks and explored. It rapidly unveiled her secret passion. He called for a moist cloth, which he used to anoint her sex and anus. He examined so carefully the puffy pink skin that Leah began to become excited, which secured his deeper interest.

'Simple explorations are the sweetest,' he murmured in a gentle voice. 'They stimulate responses at the deepest level and the feelings they engender are profound.'

The guard lifted Leah across his master's lap. She could see the girl being larruped. Her own anus had been larruped at the Chamberlain's behest. Now it was the subject of a deeply sexual interest, a petting so intimate, prolonged and thorough that it verged on the obsessive.

She lay on her side, her back towards him – he had asked for her to be put that way – her leg now drawn up. Then he was trundled around, his thumb and finger pinch-stroking Leah's anus, Leah becoming more and more aroused. Quietly he removed his mitten from his other hand. But Leah, glimpsing it, twisted round. She gasped in shock: the hand was malformed, its skin livid pink as if broiled. The first two fingers were fused together and greatly enlarged. Leah stared in horror at them. Then compassion filled her lovely face. Her eyes gazed sadly up at him. Gently she took the damaged fingers and caressed them. Then she took them into her mouth as if they were the bravest penis. Her lips pouted sexually round them. And a strange expression crossed the master's face. His good hand lovingly stroked her perfect body. She kept the damaged hand close to her cheek and kept kissing it. Then she drew it down between her legs. She took a sudden breath through her nose. But the fused fingers were too large and cumbersome for her small chained sex. Undaunted, she directed them to her bottom. 'Wait,' he begged her. And he oiled the fused fingers in the container of lotion that hung from the pole of the chair.

When Leah's bottom opened, the lotion was pushed

down the length of the fused digits. The thumb slipped under her chain. Her eyes were wantonly wide. He called to the guard, who was well erect.

The grey charioteer now directed Leah's seeking lips around the guard's penis. She lay stretched across the bath chair, sucking penis, holding her sex open, moaning because of the fused fingers masturbating her bottom. Her sex was moving, seething because of the pressure and tightness as the double finger pushed. The guard pulled away: so keen were Leah's sucks that he had partially spilled. This fluid trickled from the corner of her mouth. Her charioteer kissed her. Her tongue was rampant. She moaned and tried to retain his double digit inside her even as he drew it out. He drew her legs up so her sex and stimulated anus protruded over the edge of the chair. The guard moved round. His penis opened Leah's bottom and slipped in as far as the balls.

The master's good hand prised her chained lips gently open. His little finger slid inside, pressing down to stimulate the penis in her bottom. The ejaculate started to stream inside her. She lifted her head and took the double finger in her mouth and bit it with her small pearly teeth. Sighing in pleasure he watched her anus expanding and contracting round the pumping penis.

Afterwards she snuggled up to her charioteer. They kissed. He introduced a moist absorbent cloth into her bottom to clean her. Then he took the rose from his gown and trimmed it with a knife: it had a node with branchlets below the head; these he shortened. He scraped the blade down the stem, which unfurled like a miniature umbrella. Then he pushed the stem up her bottom; the node and branchlets prevented its slipping directly out. The flower head was a broad red ball. The unfurled end tickled inside her whenever she moved her limbs. The guard lifted her down. 'In the pit,' said the master, 'run like the wind. Don't let them catch you. And keep this rosebud safe till your return.'

But when finally Leah would become available for return the scant petals of the rosebud would be crushed and bruised.

When the time came for the women to be sent down, the Whipmaster issued this warning: 'Those left in the compound – woe betide them. The Minatyr have boundless passion. And your flesh shall be baited.'

The guard handed him paint-stick about two inches wide. The salve was waxy smooth and red. 'Begin here with this one.' He had selected Toinile. 'Lift her up.' Two guards lifted open her freckled thighs. Her wrists were still manacled above her head and round the pillar. Her labia protruded. Her sex gaped. Its ruby stud caught the light. The Whipmaster rubbed the paint-stick very gently upwards inside Toinile's labia – allowing it to push them open, making them pout about it – then on the outside – turning the pink nude double ridge of flesh shiny crimson. Then back inside her it went, gently twisting. Soon Toinile started to murmur and to move. Her belly bulged between her drawn-up legs. Her tight sex sucked the paint stick. 'Gently now. Not too much,' the Whipmaster whispered, drawing the stick away.

Toinile began to writhe and moan, softly at first, intermittently, guardedly under her breath. When her head lolled back, one of the guards lifted her gently astride his thigh. His foot was on the pedestal, his bared thigh horizontal. Toinile's weight was now supported on her painted sex. His thigh muscle tensed, lifting her bodily on her sex; she moaned. Her manacled outstretched hands tried in vain to reach for him. 'Go gently with her,' said the Whipmaster. The guard clasped her round the ribcage, eased his thumbs up under her breasts and rubbed her nipples. And into the emergent gap between Toinile's legs went the Whipmaster's fingers. Toinile shivered with pleasure, started to gasp. 'Lift her off – quickly.' The Whipmaster wiped his fingers. On the guard's thigh was a moist red mark.

181

Toinile, taken down from the pedestal, was now held between the two guards in a sitting position with her legs open. The Whipmaster moved behind her. 'Your back, my darling – hollow it. Deeper . . .' Her belly bowed out; her haunches projected like large round balls behind her. The Whipmaster wanted a more sexual protrusion. 'The anus is designed for pleasure. Therefore let it pout.' The paint stick stood like a bright red penis. 'There . . .' Her rapid contractions made the tight cupped muscle repeatedly kiss it, dabbing coloured salve round the rim. Toinile moaned in resignation as her anus finally opened of its own accord to permit the sensitive inner skin to be smeared with salve. Squirming with arousal she was sat on the pedestal while her trembling nipples were turned into tight glistening crimson cones.

One by one the women were painted in the same places as Toinile. The spectators continued to move amongst them while the painting was under way. The Whipmaster moved down the line, administering the stimulant. Sianon awaited her turn. The feeling of heady faintness was already with her; the sweet tingling fullness was in her breasts and between her legs. The guards were watching her keenly. She kept looking at Toinile, now fastened up again, moaning gently, her body spread, her sex open. A guard was playing with it. The length of his middle finger was red. And Sianon looked at his penis standing starkly between his legs. His escaped liquid had crystallised to a twisted silvery ribbon round the stem. The Whipmaster was about to do Sianon.

'Wait,' said a decisive voice.

'My lord, they are due for dispatch,' the Whipmaster said. 'I cannot keep them waiting.'

The Magus came to her. 'I take responsibility.' He lifted her up and stared at her breasts. The faintest, softest oiliness was there in her nipples.

The Whipmaster hovered. Undaunted, the Magus stayed with Sianon, just staring at her breasts. Then he took the paint-stick from the Whipmaster. 'Unfasten her.'

Her back slid down the pillar. Her knees opened. 'Hold her – gently.' A deep sinking feeling came when he put the paint-stick into her bottom. The salve was waxy, like a candle, but smoother and much softer than a candle. The first kiss of it was cool and sexually sweet. She started to murmur, reaching for him, touching his cheek while he was doing it to her, just as she had touched him when he had fed the opal beads into her and made the pleasure come so strongly that her breasts had spilled.

Her fingers were turning weak. Her toes, curling, gripped the silk of his gown. He put the waxy stick deeper and gently twisted it, depositing a soft coating. The twisting made Sianon moan and caress his cheek and neck. Her eyes, half-closed, watched her master's strong erection poking through his gown. She wanted to hold the head of his penis and to stroke his balls, to soften his sac with her weeping milk.

He drew the paint-stick out of her. 'While you are in the ring, I will be watching,' he said. The feelings in her bottom were growing keener. She moaned, legs open. She wanted to come. He painted her sex lips and clitoris. The pleasure started while the lips were still being painted. It made her want to rub her sex against her master's skin, against his wrist and arm. There was leakage from her nipples. Her master rubbed them dry before he painted them. Everywhere the paint was smeared, it felt as if a cool moist drawing poultice was plastered to the sexual skin.

'Fasten her up again.'

'But she shall be needed,' protested the Whipmaster.

'Send her with the next batch.'

'But if the potency of the unction should wear off?'

'Apply more.'

The first of the initiates were standing in a line, their arms over their heads, their manacles slung over hooks attached to runners under the bars. The women were wriggling, trying to rub their legs together, to squeeze their bottom-cheeks, to shake their breasts. The Whipmaster kept spreading their legs. They began pleading for satiation. When Toinile was lifted on to a hook, she nearly climaxed. The Whipmaster whipped her legs. She could not keep her bottom still.

Sianon was now fastened facing the pillar. From the corner of her eye she glimpsed Toinile edging sideways, losing her footing, crying out and disappearing. While the others were being dispatched, her master, arms folded, moved around Sianon, just watching her. Her breasts were round the pillar, her nipples shiny. Her wrists were secured high above her head. 'Restrain her ankles,' he murmured. He donned a pair of pure-white gloves and a matching pure-white sheath. He took a thin white cloth in his gloved fingers. Then he climbed up on to the pedestal behind her.

Sianon sucked the black obsidian surface to suppress her moans. Her ankles trembled against the stone. Her nipples extruded milk through their shiny red coating. His white-gloved fingers milking her breasts were turning pink. Her open labia rode the thin cloth against the smoothness of the pillar. It turned slippery as the thrusts up her bottom were transmitted through her belly to the stone. The sheath, tight around his fatted penis, emerged streaked with bright salve then plunged in to the hem. His ball sac, high up between her thighs, slapped against the smooth black stone. 'More unction, up in here,' the Magus demanded. When he was done, the thumb and all four fingers of each glove were now stained pink with painted milk and the cloth and sheath were warm with discharged juices.

And in due course it was time. Then Sianon too was

lifted up, made to walk spread legged; then she was suspended. She could hear clamouring voices echoing up from the chute in the floor. She looked up at the hook and the runner. Then she heard a scream. One of the women had disappeared. The next was being edged towards the chute. The Whipmaster was encouraging her. Sianon fought the panic. 'Be brave,' Sianon whispered to herself, but she was terrified.

'Step forward my dear.' The Whipmaster's smile was evil. Sianon was on tiptoes, arms stretched tight. The floor shelved. It began to drop away beneath her feet. The wheels of the runner screeched. Her toes scrabbled for the floor then could not reach it. She saw the coffin-shaped tunnel approaching. Panic welled inside her. The runner bumped, then dropped. The scream was cut off in her throat. She plummeted down the blackness of the incline.

11

The Pit

Through the pitch dark came the rush of freezing earth-damp air against Sianon's face. The metal runners screamed above the roaring in her ears. The rail twisted and turned. She dangled helplessly as the runners bounced and lifted and dropped. With every bump came the fright of endless falling. At a tight bend her weight was flung outwards. She thought her naked legs would strike the wall; she thought the creaking strap between her wrists would snap. She heard a scream far ahead then a muffled roar. The rail was levelling out but she was moving ever faster. Flickers of light shot past on the walls; they grew stronger, brighter. She shut her eyes. Suddenly she was being hauled upwards – the rail was rising and the light was blinding. And with a terrible jerk, the strap suddenly snapped. She tumbled forwards on to straw and sand. The roar of the crowd was deafening.

She was in a cage with other women at one end of the pit of a vast oval amphitheatre beneath a high glass dome. In the middle, raised on a mound, was another cage. At the far end was a third one. These other cages looked empty. Narrow moving shafts of reflected sunlight crisscrossed the arena. The balcony was lined by hordes of excited masters and ladies in bright flowing robes. Behind them lay an enormous sea of spectators, milling, shouting, cheering, waving mir-

rors. People overhung the higher tiers, pointing, screaming.

At the foot of the central mound a gargantuan
phallus arched skywards from the sand. Clinging precariously to its steep veined shaft were at least five
naked girls. Others had fallen back to the sand only to
try again. Aided only by a thin leather rope flung round
the girth of the phallus, they hauled themselves up,
fighting, kicking, reaching for the meagre hand-holds
under the rim of the glans. Each time a climber would
gain the advantage, a volley of beams from the mirrors
would strike across to try to dazzle and dislodge her.
The contenders were vicious. The captives in the cages
could only stare open mouthed.

One of the climbers dangling from another's legs was
hauling herself inch by inch up the other's body, pausing to bite her on the neck – amid cheers – then pressing
onwards, upwards, dragging her rivals off the shaft until
at last, gaining a foothold under the glans, she grasped
the stopper in the mouth of the phallus. Suddenly, all
sounds from the crowd ceased as she clung to the head
of the glans, tugging with all her strength. Then the plug
came away and the fluid spurted then bubbled out,
drenching her. She lay back, holding on with one hand,
riding the gushing waves of mock semen cascading
down her athletic body. The stadium erupted: tier upon
tier of frenzied people with their arms in the air chanted
their heroine's name: 'Janna! Janna!'

In the cage the women stared around with terrified
eyes, as if they might at any second be plucked from the
refuge and immersed in the mayhem. Suddenly, a fan-
fare sounded. The contenders dispersed. The trium-
phant Janna slid down the shaft. Hair drenched and
plastered down like a blonde skullcap, she made one last
sweeping circuit of the base of the phallus then ran
across to the cage. Clutching the bars, her eyes wild with
excitement, she cried to the petrified women:

'Would that I could be with you when you face the Minatyr. My heart is.' The fluid glistened on her tautly muscled skin. 'And remember this: when you are out there – fight them! Do not take it lying down! See – the crowd love you if you make a stand.' She seemed to be staring at Sianon.

A group of leather-clad guards carrying short smooth batons emerged from an inconspicuous doorway beside a large gate in the middle of one of the long walls. They marched in unison to the centre line of the arena, bowed, then held the batons aloft. The crowd cheered, pointing at the caged women. Sianon shivered. Then the men broke ranks and ran to their stations around the arena. Two arrived at the women's cage.

'Do not rely on the keepers. Fend for yourselves!' shouted Janna.

The gate was unlocked. The keepers walked in. Janna followed but took no further part.

'Out! Come on!' the keepers cried. As the frightened women began to hurry past them, they threatened them with the batons. The tip of a baton touched a woman's buttocks. It barely touched her but she cried out and jumped away. The crowd roared and the women ran stumbling through the gate. As Sianon ran past with the others, she glimpsed the baton. It had a heavy ebony handle and a slim amber stem crowned by a small gold ball. A weak blue light drifted like mist inside the amber; there was a soft buzzing sound. The instrument was jabbed towards her. Sianon ran.

But once in the vastness of the arena, the women, fearful of what unknown terror might lie before them, stopped running. They clustered in groups, staring apprehensively around them. The phallus shone slickly in the sunlight. But the arena was otherwise empty. Sianon watched the people on the lowest balcony. An ominous quiet had fallen; they were waiting. She followed their collective gaze to the guarded large gate at the opposite end of the arena. The hush was almost tangible. Then the gate opened.

The creatures – the Minatyr – spilled out. Her mouth fell open in horror. Nothing had prepared her for this.

The crowd roared. The women in front of her swerved and turned back. The gate clanged shut behind her. She saw the fearless Janna clinging safely behind the bars. There was panic among the women. Instinctively Sianon crouched down. It gave her a second more to think.

They were like no earthly creatures she had ever seen – naked, small, grotesque, sub-human. They ran awkwardly on hind legs almost like a goat's but had the body of a man. And yet they stood endowed as no mortal man was. Their erect penises curved upwards, as thick and long and naked as forearms, bouncing as they ran. Their balls were as big as a ram's.

Drums sounded. The watchers jeered as the panicked women tripped in the sand and fell. The Minatyr were upon them. Sianon's eyes searched desperately for a means of escape. She scuttled crouching to the wall. It was vertical; the exit gates were fastened. The keepers stood before them, arms folded, batons at the ready. But the cage in the centre of the arena was open. Sianon suddenly understood – they had to run there for safety. This was the game.

She took a deep breath, then sprinted diagonally across the arena. A cheer went up. Her attempt had been spotted. There was a grunt behind her. A hairy hand half closed about her ankle. Sianon twisted. The creature went sprawling in the sand. She turned, dodging two others. They were ungainly in changing direction on the uneven sand. The crowd cheered her on. She tripped. A creature tried to pin her down. She felt his penis, thick and heavy, pushing up between her legs. Then the creature was knocked off her by another. Sianon struggled to her feet and ran with both of them pursuing her, growling. Her heart was bursting as she gained the mound. The open cage lay before her. There were a few women already safe inside. She flung herself at the gateway. But she fell short.

The creatures had her by the legs and were dragging her away. The women inside were too afraid to help. Sianon kicked. The tears came to her eyes. There was no escape. The keepers watched impassively. 'Please?' she begged them, stretching her arms imploringly. 'Please?' she moaned, her fingers clutching at the sand, her breath coming quickly, her breasts heaving. The keepers never moved to help.

Outside the cage, in every part of the arena, women were now being mounted by their ugly captors; few women had escaped. Some had been flung face up or face down on heaps of straw; some were being carried, others touched and fondled in the air. One or two were still running. But they could not get away because the walls were vertical. The excited watchers pointed out the participants and the practices that fired their zeal. Every level of society was represented in the crowd – elders, soldiers, servants, riders, slaves, magi. There were some who stayed aloof from the proceedings, and others of high station were screaming encouragement more loudly than the rest; their voices could be heard above the ravings of the Minatyr.

There was a young woman clad in suede, almost hanging over the balcony in her effort to get closer. Her flashing eyes were brimming with excitement; it almost seemed she was possessed. No longer able to contain herself, she ran round the periphery, pushing others out of the way. Below her, Sianon had broken free and taken brief flight.

The Chamberlain, watching from across the arena, understood this zeal. For this, most of all, was a time of choosing: opportunity must be grasped forthrightly or missed forever – unspoken troths adrift in the mind.

Every watcher had some mystic ideal against which these initiates were being measured. When the privileged had avowed their choice, the residue would be passed around or left to appease the Minatyr.

But this spirited girl in suede had taken an interest out of turn. She was a common artisan.

'No – don't stop her,' Janna told the officious keepers. 'The crowd like her.'

'The crowd don't give us orders.'

'Exactly.'

The keeper blanched. 'My princess . . .'

But events overtook them both.

Sianon glimpsed the slim figure dangling by the fingertips from the brim of the wall. Then the figure dropped to the sand and crumpled. For a second she was winded. Then she was up again, flying, kicking sand in the faces of the creatures. The crowd roared to its feet. Running to a keeper, she grabbed his stick, then fended the shrieking Minatyr off with it. She kicked one off Sianon and dragged her back to her feet, dragged her to the safety of the centre cage. The keepers wrenched the stick away from her and held her securely. She never took her eyes from Sianon. From a spiral stairwell in the floor other keepers appeared, then several annoyed officials. The Chamberlain hovered in the background.

An official strode forward. 'Who is she? The judges are livid. The girl must be punished.'

'You cannot,' the girl said defiantly. And she held up her ring finger, displaying a twisted gold and bronze torc. 'Ring-elant. You cannot touch me. Today I am a free-woman of the city.'

'Naive young girl. Chamberlain!'

He shook his grey head gravely. 'It is so, my lord, it is so. Provided she commits no crime. She may have bent the rules, but the crowd . . .'

The official glowered menacingly at the girl in leather. 'Who are you!'

She never quavered. 'Danime. And by this ring, I claim first call upon Brown-hair.'

'And is *that* the law?'

'Not law, my lord,' said the Chamberlain, 'but tradition dictates that where –'

'Then get rid of her.'

'But the crowd . . .?'

'Take her down. Release her later.'

Janna had now appeared. 'Keeper – give me that rod.' She tucked the handle through her belt. 'Open the gate. Open it! Let's see what the crowd makes of this,' she declared, grasping Sianon's wrist.

And a few seconds later they were in the midst of the arena surrounded by Minatyr. The tears were in Sianon's eyes as Janna, against the backdrop of the ecstatic crowd, stood there howling abuse which drove the creatures crazy. She kept taunting them with Sianon's breasts, dragging her at arm's length across the sand as if she were human bait. After the first time Janna used the rod, they were too afraid to tackle her. But she would deliberately leave hold of Sianon and allow the creatures to descend. Their penises were enormous, hot and completely naked. The scent was much stronger than from a human penis. They tried to push them up between her breasts, to make contact with her face. And they dragged her on to her belly; she could feel the hot length sliding down her back; the fat balls sinking against her. But her painted sex and anus were far too narrow for access. And every time they came close to trying to force an entry, Janna beat them back. And this taunting continued amid frenzied cheers while Sianon was dragged the remaining length of the arena.

'Open the gate!' Janna cried. Too late, the two excited creatures mauling Sianon realised Janna's intent. Spurning the rod, she grasped the two of them from behind by the necks of their balls. To wild clapping of the crowd, she conducted the captive Minatyr, now crouching on their haunches, backwards through the gate of the compound, with Sianon scurrying after her.

First she had them shackled. Then she tamed them with a sexual whipping. Sianon gradually became aware that these creatures, however grotesque of face or gargantuan of sexual parts were in spirit men, with very human responses to all the sexual stimuli that Janna provided. Their taming was as arousing to the female viewer as the sexual punishment of a male slave. But the scale of the reaction was fuller in every way. A number of privileged spectators – mainly female – had begun to drift in from the tunnel side of the compound. Sianon looked in vain for the girl in leather.

Janna was now so preoccupied with taming her Minatyr that she seemed indifferent to anyone else's presence. She called for instruments of dilation.

'She wants to force their erections even larger,' a voice whispered in Sianon's ear. She turned and faced the bars. The Chamberlain was on the other side. He had entered from the tunnel. His cool hand slipped through the bars and took her wrist; his fingers pressed against her pulse. At the sound of the whip, he stroked her hair. She wanted to look at what was being done; she knew her pulse was quickening. 'Close your eyes,' he whispered. 'There is no hurry; the ladies will be queuing up to take a turn.' Her forehead pressed against the bars. He squeezed her red nipples as a deep groan came from a Minatyr. 'Oh, so big his cock is becoming. He surely cannot hold out long.' With a cord he secured Sianon's wrist to the bar. 'Don't turn,' he said. Then he entered the compound. She could hear him whispering to Janna amid the intermittent metallic clicking of an instrument and the powerful sexual groans. She did not try to turn. She could imagine everything.

Two drifting ladies halted in front of Sianon. They stared at her wrist restraint then at her breasts. Then they stared past her into the compound. Moving close, they now stood, one to each side of Sianon, caressing her gently on the belly. They requested a moistened cloth with which to wipe the paint from between her legs. Then one hand from each lady worked her, opening her sex and teasing her knob as if it were a penis. Their efforts were embellished with remarks upon the progress of the dilation of the anal muscle in the Minatyr.

Along the tunnel complex came other sounds: girls' voices pleading; grunts of more Minatyr; ladies' chuckles. The focus of the action had begun to move out of the arena itself.

The ladies with Sianon had intertwined their fingers inside her. One of the ladies kissed her and Sianon could feel the lady's sexual arousal in the luscious movements of the lady's tongue. She could hear the Minatyr crying out in climax. 'They come in bucketfuls,' the other lady whispered. She took hold of Sianon's chin. Then the Chamberlain returned and the ladies moved along the tunnel.

He unfastened Sianon's wrist and led her from the compound. Then he stopped and looked with admiration at the place where she had been deeply explored. He was taller than Sianon by a head and shoulders. Her breasts came just above his navel. He had had to set her back against the wall to look at her sex. Some of the ladies were looking at him touching her. 'I can see your heartbeat in your lovely breast,' he whispered as he straightened up. In one hand he held the heavy metal instrument of dilation. It was dripping with seminal fluid from where the Minatyr had overflowed on to it. The ladies hinted that they wanted him to put it into her. With his free arm he drew her to his body. Her belly pressed against his thigh. Her toes lifted momentarily from the sand. And her breasts pressed against the serge of his cassock, depositing there a small quantity of pre-emission. His fingers nervously squeezed and slipped upon her teats, removing the last vestiges of paint. Then he slung the dilator to his belt and led her onwards.

It was a network of wide tunnels and chambers which must have extended underneath the great arena. It was well-lit from overhead by grille-covered shafts; Sianon could hear the cheers and screams as the games proceeded; soft showers of sand would occasionally descend. But down here were games of a more select and intimate order. Sianon was excited – deeply excited by the things that she saw. Naked, she could not conceal her excitement from the Chamberlain, who would touch her sex and anus so gently that the feeling would begin to come at the tops of her legs, around the front and up her belly like ascending fingers of pleasure even where he was not touching. Her legs would tremble and he would make her stand still, thighs open, feet planted in the sand while he watched her.

Then he came to her again and put his bared forearms around her nude body from behind. Droplets of heavy pre-milk were forming at the tips of her breasts. He took care now not to smear them. They pulled and tickled as she walked.

He stopped her at the entrance to a chamber where two ladies dressed in finery were with a collared Minatyr and a naked girl. The girl was in sexual union of a kind; he was far too large for consummation; but the act was no less arousing for the watchers even though it could not be completed. Under the direction of the ladies, other means were being explored. The intimacy was compelling. The Chamberlain sat Sianon on a table.

The Minatyr was on a leash but his handlers had clearly trained him. The Chamberlain went to examine the various instruments of stimulation hanging on the wall. The girl had been fastened by one wrist behind her head. Her other arm was left free to coax the giant penis poking out above her belly as the creature crouched astride her. There were empty goblets on the bed. One of the ladies had dark wavy hair. Her middle finger glistened wet. She kept touching the tip of the giant erect penis that the girl was clutching. The Minatyr kept murmuring. Then Sianon saw that the lady was pushing down into the penis her long pearl necklace. She was pushing the pearls with her middle finger, which was why it was so wet. Sometimes she used a smooth stick.

The Minatyr had narrow hips. His legs seemed wider apart than in a normal man, as if to accommodate the giant balls. The other lady was behind him and holding these in both hands, lifting them away from the girl's lower belly. Her sex was reddened and wide, as if he had repeatedly attempted entry. Her anus looked small by comparison as if the pressure from the front had forced it even more tightly shut.

The Chamberlain returned. He opened Sianon's sex as she was sitting on the table. He fitted weighted clamps to her labia. He played with her breasts but did not touch the nipples, taking the body of the breasts in his hands and shaking their firm gelatinous mounds. Her drops of pre-milk thickened and broke free, running over the web of skin between his thumb and forefinger. He kept shaking her breasts gently with her body turned sideways so she could see the girl masturbate the creature with her arm and broadly spread tongue. Sianon's creamy liquid was running down the Chamberlain's naked forearms. Her sex overhung the edge of the table; the gold balls drew her labia down. Each time she moved her legs she could feel a deep pulling. Each time her sex contracted, the gold balls tapped together. The dark-haired lady noticed her. She came closer.

'Suck,' she said. Sianon took her middle finger that had poked down the penis; it had the taste of salted ham but was more pungently aromatic. The lady kept her middle finger in Sianon's mouth but put her other hand between Sianon's legs, playing with the weights, tugging her clamped labia, toying with her aroused knob. The Chamberlain had moved behind Sianon. He took hold of her breasts again. His milk-wet arms were under her armpits. She could feel the wetness against her skin. Then the spanking of the Minatyr began. Sianon watched it from the corner of her eye. The lady's finger coated with his penile juices lay against her tongue. The moist weights were being rubbed against her clitoris to excite her during the spanking.

It was an anal spanking with a tawse. The split flap of leather could cope more easily with unevenness or swelling. The anus of a Minatyr was of normal size prior to spanking. But it swelled as might any man's, subjected to such rigours. The spanking greatly strengthened the erection. All the while the naked girl below him was trying to masturbate his penis. Her arm was twisted round it like a snake. Her tongue was licking the place where the loop of the necklace emerged from the glans. Then it slipped through the loop and tugged.

After every second smack, the tongue tugged: a pearl popped out from the mouth of the penis. She gripped the glans, though her hand could scarcely fit around it. Her thumb pressed underneath it; the pearl was visible as a bump inside. She masturbated it with the pad of her thumb. He groaned and a little fluid issued. Her tongue released the loop and licked the issue greedily. Then the smacks began again. After every second one, a pearl slipped from inside him, past her thumb. The necklace must have extended all the way down his penis, which was beginning to convulse. The lady stopped spanking and began to insert the tawse into his anus just as the girl drew out the last three pearls. Her thumb pressed tightly up against the duct below the glans. The semen spurted over her head. She squeezed the duct tightly. The lady pushed the tawse in then drew it quickly out and smacked again. Another constricted squirt came. There were droplets in the girl's hair. A thick diagonal streak of white lay across her tethered wrist. She held the penis till the pressure dropped and a heavy dribble of semen flowed on to her breast.

'They come several times,' said the dark-haired lady in a silken voice. 'The second one is generally the fullest.' She took the dilator from the Chamberlain. 'With the anus stretched, it can be spectacular.' Leaving Sianon in the Chamberlain's arms, she joined the other lady and started to coat the end of the dilator with the spillage of semen. The other lady, having tasted the emission, began coating her entire hand with it. The giant erection was back and the girl was kissing it; then she masturbated it with her middle finger poked all the way inside. He started moving against her. He seemed excited by the sight of the dilator. But the dark-haired lady brought it back to Sianon. 'Lie down,' the lady said. 'Quickly ...' Then to the Chamberlain she said: 'One cannot resist. Now – would you look at it, just waiting. I see now why you brought this instrument.'

'Then permit me to hold her.'

She lay half on her side. The cold metal touched her anus, which wanted to contract. But the semen had made it slippery. 'Oooh!' she gasped. The lady pressed. The Chamberlain drew one of Sianon's buttocks up. The nozzle of the dilator went inside her. It slipped slowly, coldly deeper, expressing its coating of semen, sucking her breath away; it felt as though its progress would not stop. She wanted to resist. 'Lie back ... She is too tense. Turn her so she can see the others. And put a tie between her ankles.' They stopped to do this while the dilator was only half introduced.

The other lady stood behind the kneeling creature, whose erect penis had been drawn back between his legs so it was pointing down. The girl, now freed, was milking it with both hands. The lady's hand that had been lubricated with semen had formed a fist. At the very time it pushed against him, the Chamberlain started smacking Sianon's buttocks, slapping them with his bare hands as her lady applied renewed pressure to the dilator. Her anus opened wider. She watched the fist slipping ever deeper into the groaning creature, watched the girl tonguing spittle all around the head of his penis, watched his balls retracting tightly. The fist went almost to the elbow. And between Sianon's legs, the lady began to stimulate her sex, which was soft and partly open. She began to strum her clitoris with the backs of her nails until Sianon wanted to sit up but could not, on account of the instrument. And when the lady forced her knees more open, they would only go so far because her ankles were now fastened by a leather rope. Then the lady began to turn the dilator – applying little turns, small stretchings, interspersed with the Chamberlain's smackings of her buttock-cheeks.

The other lady started to rock her fist back and forth inside the Minatyr and flex the muscle of her buried forearm. And then the creature came – in such a flood, and the fist kept rocking, the forearm flexing, and the girl's upraised hungry lips could not cope. Her chin and breasts were white; the goo was squeezing through her fingers and enveloping them. Sianon's lady grasped the projecting knob of Sianon's clitoris in her fingertips. The Chamberlain gave the dilator another turn. Sianon's toes curled up. The lady put her fingers inside Sianon's sex and sucked her breast. The milk came and Sianon's head bowed down and kissed the lady's cheek. The lady just kept sucking the milk from her breast and holding her knob in the tips of four fingers. Sianon's knees were open as far as they would go. It was like a climax, not a full one but it continued long. The Chamberlain held the rope between her ankles and held the tight dilator, now tugging it gently. Her milk kept squirting into the lady's mouth. From the other breast it welled under the lady's cheek. Sianon's lips kept reaching for the lady's earlobe. And in her belly was this overwhelming sexual feeling. The Chamberlain opened her toes, individually, rubbed between them, sucked them, tugged her dilator. She moaned in pleasure; her milk kept coming. The lady's hair was shiny wet. She could feel the lady's fingers inside her, pressing through her against the dilator, and she could feel the shudders coming through the lady's tongue and lips.

Afterwards, they turned Sianon over and loosened the dilator. 'Just look at it,' the lady whispered longingly, caressing the hot aroused folds. 'You must surely keep it thus? You must – for the banquet. She will be there?'

'If my lord decrees it.'

'He shall – if our best endeavours count for ought.' Suddenly she stared into the doorway. Janna stood there with the girl in suede. The girl was breathless; she was staring anxiously at Sianon. Janna called the Chamberlain over. When he returned to Sianon, his expression was grim. He bundled her up. 'My lady Marquise – please excuse us.'

When they reached a quiet part of the tunnel he whispered: 'Josef is in grave danger. Shh!! We must act quickly. It has only come to light through Leah: she did not see the import of where he was being taken.'

12

Kelthlings

Before Josef was an open door which seemed to beckon. Without thinking he stepped through. He was in a garden. It looked almost like the garden of Ladyseer but there were differences: the plantings appeared less contrived and more luxuriant, and the air was warmer and more humid than expected, engendering a feeling of enclosure, as though everything were inside a vast glasshouse. But he could see no frame or panes, only the blue of the sky. And though it was early afternoon the lighting was peculiar and golden; all the flower colours seemed intensified and surreal. Even the grass felt warm against his bare feet. But there were no insects. And when he turned round the door had disappeared.

His mind jarred. He closed his eyes and tried to think: had he taken any steps after passing through the door? Was it hidden in the foliage? He opened his eyes: the nearest bushes were too far. There was no door. In desperation he even began testing the air with his fingers. The disorientation he was experiencing was far more distressing than any anxiety he might have felt at simply being lost. He panicked – he did not run, but still, his heart was palpitating. He was not thinking straight and it was panic. He must have covered several-hundred yards at a rapid walk, circling – he hoped – the area. There was no door, nor artefact of any kind, and soon he was back at his starting point. So this was not a dream: for the scene had retained its integrity, nothing had shifted. And there was no feeling that his consciousness was elsewhere. It must therefore be that somehow, the way that he had arrived here could not provide an exit. But there had to be one somewhere.

The ground sloped away from him; he reached a clearing. A warm breeze was blowing upslope. He decided to walk towards its source, hoping it might yield an exit. For many minutes he continued, through several open thickets between the clearings, all the while telling himself that, however beautiful and fragrant his surroundings, as long as the way out remained undiscovered they were nevertheless, a prison.

Then he felt very thirsty. No sooner had the thought crystallised than he heard the sound of running water. Ahead and to the right was a sunlit dell. There he found a stream fed by a spring of sweet refreshing aerated water. Sitting on a smooth rock in the warmth of the sun, he drank copiously. Gradually the refreshment calmed him. The still warmth of the dell in sunshine left him almost pleasantly lethargic. Stretching back he closed his eyes for a few seconds and inhaled the powerful fragrance like the frangipani and oleander he had known in the hothouse as a child. He could hear birdsong in the distance, but a more intricately melodious birdsong than any he had encountered. And for the first time he felt almost at ease with being naked.

Suddenly his eyes snapped open. There were sounds much closer by: someone was running through the bushes. He sat up quickly, automatically covering himself. The sounds came nearer. By the time he knew he had to hide it was too late.

Crashing down above the opposite bank came a young man as naked as himself. The newcomer was totally unsurprised at meeting him.

'Have you seen them?' the young man cried agitatedly, scanning the woodland and the valley, mopping his brow. He was wild-eyed, urgent, but pale and so thin as to be on the verge of emaciation. Yet he was very visibly well endowed and his penis bore a thick vein which testified to intense and vigorous usage. Seeing the bubbling water, he scrambled down and began drinking thirstily before repeating his question.

Josef shook his head: 'Seen whom? What is this place?'

'Then you've only just arrived?'

Josef nodded.

The other stared at him then gave a low whistle. 'Then welcome to heaven. My name is Brandreth.'

'Josef.' They shook hands. 'Why are we –'

'Shh!' Brandreth cocked his head. 'Listen – can you hear?'

Josef frowned. There was only the birdsong from the valley. It chimed again.

'Kelthlings. Come on . . .' And the young man hurried off down the valley and was soon out of sight. Josef followed cagily at a discreet distance, sweeping a wide arc. Soon he could hear the rush of a small waterfall. Then the distinctive birdsong came again, growing louder. Crouching, he picked his way through the dense aromatic foliage above the stream. Then he saw them.

It was like a magical painting. Again he wondered if he could be dreaming. They were strange, beautiful and fragile – sylph-like creatures – pure-white of skin, with hair in golden wavy cloaks down to their hips, breasts small and full, nipples perched like bright-red cherries. And through their pouted lips these softly musical chortles emerged like birdsong. One creature sat on the bank; two stood in the stream, their naked bellies bulging, water bubbling through their open thighs, drawing the tips of their golden cloaks downstream like trains behind them.

There was a noise beside Josef. It was the young man Brandreth, now peering with avid eyes through the leafage. 'If we can only find their nest now, while they are occupied, we can cuckold them. If they return and find us they will not think it strange.'

None of this made any sense to Josef. But he could not take his eyes from the beautiful creatures. 'And then?' he whispered.

'They crave it – this,' Brandreth pointed to his thick-veined penis. 'Once you have been with them, no human girl can ever match them.'

'No human?' said Josef. The strange pleasure of the Succubus haunted his mind.

A few minutes later, the two men were standing at the foot of the largest of three ancient spreading oaks. Its lower branches were draped with tangled chains of ivy which provided easy footholds.

'Can't you smell it?' whispered Brandreth, throwing back his head.

'Oleander,' Josef answered. 'But there are no bushes of it here.'

'Exactly. Wait here.' Josef watched his accomplice's naked thin form disappear rapidly into the canopy. When nothing more happened, Josef stepped back and began circling the tree. Its girth was enormous; the trunk was cracked and gnarled. As he continued to move round it, he glimpsed amongst the foliage of the highest branches, close to the trunk, a large pale coloured structure, like a cankerous growth or a giant beehive. When he stepped further back it was hidden in the canopy of green. Taking hold of a thick mat of ivy against the trunk, he tried to pull himself up to gain a clearer view. The ivy broke away revealing a hollow like a doorway into the trunk.

Once inside he was standing in a lofty chamber and staring up an irregular chimney lit by shafts of light from on high. A flimsy spiral narrow ropewalk of vines ascended the inner circumference. As he began cautiously to climb, it sagged and groaned under his weight.

Several times he bumped his head on protruding knots of ivy wood and clumps of aerial root. At intervals there were narrow landings leading out on to the major branches. There was no sign of Brandreth. Josef kept climbing. At the top he emerged but not into daylight.

The space in which he stood was cocoon-like, with no clear division between floor and walls, which tapered upwards to an opalescent silken uneven dome glowing with a creamy light. Curvilinear undulations radiated across the floor; he realised they were the buried branches over which the cocoon had been woven. The interior was wholly covered in a substance resembling fine fleece; the surface on which he stood was soft, as if underlain by layer upon layer of it; it shimmered like spun silk. But this place was nonetheless a home and not a nest: the walls were garlanded with flowers; there were fragrant pomanders made of woven reeds and there were other artefacts, even some brightly coloured scarves and blankets. In a hollow he found a cache of gold and silver chains, bright beads and jewels, men's rings but also veined stream-pebbles and worn fragments of coloured glass. In another place he found a small store of food – nuts and fresh fruit and bunches of leaves, but also pots of honey and silver flasks of cordial. There was a multiplicity of silk ropes of various gauges. But there was no true furniture, only fleece-covered cushions and raised shaped places with hollows for the limbs. It was a sea of fragrant softness with waves and troughs.

The structure, although built around the trunk of the tree, was irregularly shaped; it was also very extensive, with tunnels leading off at waist height in several places, following the branches then expanding upwards into miniature versions of the main cocoon. These he assumed to be the bedchambers. Cast about were objects of cork and rope silk and smooth wood but also gold. And there were flasks and clysters, instruments which seemed unnaturally out of place here.

205

He heard a rustling sound behind him.

'Where were you? They're coming back,' Brandreth whispered hoarsely. 'Lie down!'

'Where?'

'Anywhere. Just keep quiet. Don't do anything until they accept you. Have you anything you can offer as a gift? Never mind. Keep quiet.' Brandreth sat perfectly still against the curve of the wall.

Josef lay on his side and watched the entrance. There was no sound. Then suddenly they were in the cocoon – Kelthlings, two of them, pale and nubile, cherry-nippled, doe-eyed, staring inquisitively at him. Never had he seen creatures so perfectly formed. They were naked but for thin silvery-grey silken panties. Their reaction had been of surprise but not fear. They began to speak to each other in their musical tones, discussing the two intruders. Then Josef realised what their pointing and giggling meant: they were choosing. At that thought a soft sinking feeling moved inside him.

The Kelthlings appeared to be twins, not quite identical, but equally perfect, each one a distillation of fragility and primal beauty. Yet they were distant, other-worldly, as if they had been cast from a human mould but were not of human substance, not of human soul. Their eyes spoke this. But the mould was delightful. They were exquisite soft blonde doll-like creatures, open-lipped, small-breasted, yet full-nippled; and he could see the shape of each naked sex through the clinging thin silver-grey panties. They communicated in this strange beguiling musical speech he could not understand. But they had no problem in communicating their desires to the two men whom they would take as lovers.

Brandreth held his hand out to the one who had shown an interest in him. In it was a gift of a pebble bisected by a shiny vein. She took it with obvious delight and studied it. Then she showed it to her friend, who admired it then stared expectantly at Josef. He had nothing to give and she was looking at him with such trustful anticipation. His eyes sank away, downcast. And suddenly this beautiful perfect creature was upon him, whispering musical words of selfless comfort, staring into his eyes and leaning over him to take the first kiss, a kiss so perfectly soft and beautiful that he could not have contained his arousal even should he have wished to.

She wanted to play. She pointed to Josef's naked penis and said something, tilting her head to one side. She had asked him a question. Mystified, he shook his head. Brandreth could not help. He was sitting with the other Kelthling, who appeared more shy. The first one took Josef by the hand and led him to one of the larger side chambers. Again she pointed to his penis then she swept her arm across the surface of the fleece and nodded eagerly. Josef moved closer. Nestled in the fleece were various toys. They seemed so out of place here. She indicated one of several dildos, so realistic that it might have been cast from a penis. It had balls that moved independently. It had a hole down the tube and a piercing point in the same place as Josef's. And inserted through it was a ring. This was what she had wanted to show him. His being pierced had aroused her fascination. She kept touching the piercing and the ring through the dildo and crooning to herself. Then she touched Josef's chest; her fingers were soft, her skin oily smooth. Scattered across the silken fleece he saw other toys, straps and braided silk ropes, gold balls, clamps and small chains. A little further away he glimpsed clysters and broad glass flasks of cream – instruments of the Abbey. He stared down: the fleece was marked. He touched it. Amongst its soft curls were others that were firm and shiny, glued by the juices that these sweet beautiful creatures, in their love play, had exuded.

The girl closed her soft lips about his nipple and

sucked it. Her fingertips kneaded his breast just as if it might give milk. His erection came on hard. Brandreth with his girl now joined them in the chamber.

Josef's girl proudly displayed the dildo, rubbing and squeezing it where the ring was pushed through near the tip. It seemed uncannily like his own piercing. The balls rested on her naked thigh. When she sat back he could see her sex lips pouting through the tight silk of her panties.

She pointed at the other girl and said something in that sweet shrill voice. It sounded like 'Lhirrahje'.

'Lhirrahje,' Josef repeated: it must have been her name. Brandreth had her on his knee.

'Herazhaan,' the first girl pointed solemnly at herself.

Josef opened his mouth to tell his name. Herazhaan cut in quickly: 'Zhozef.'

Dumbstruck he turned to Brandreth but Brandreth was too immersed in the delights of Lhirrahje. Her panties were down; she was on his lap trembling – everywhere that Brandreth was touching – jellied breasts, smooth soft thighs, slim bare sex, small dimpled pot belly.

Herazhaan was at first concerned by what Brandreth was doing to her friend. But very quickly she became interested and was soon wanting to help him. For Lhirrahje, despite her shyness, was experiencing pleasure at his hands: her legs stayed freely open. She looked so sweetly alluring in that pose. Watching the two Kelthlings – their innocent expressions, their unleashed lubricity as the games progressed – swept Josef's inhibitions aside.

Lhirrahje's silk panties were round one quivering ankle. Herazhaan, sitting very erect and still, watched absorbedly with the dildo still in her fingers. Every so often she glanced excitedly at Josef. Each glance of those wide doe eyes made him want to melt inside. Her hair hung like a curtain not quite touching her back.

Like her friend she was long limbed, very slim – with prominent shoulderblades, small immature-looking cuspate breasts, plump red areolae, a deeply recessed spine, and tight buttocks balanced on the upturned soles of her delicate feet. Her fingertips moved continuously, nervously playing with the dildo above her small pot belly. Even as she crouched there he would have loved to draw her panties down and slide his fingers down from back and front – just one finger from each side to tease apart the creases.

His erection had firmed to constancy. He did not move to hide it. She gazed at it. Then Brandreth called her over. She seemed to know to kiss him – her reassurance to him, but with no concept of any jealousy Josef might feel. Her full lips lingered on Brandreth's. She touched his long stiff penis, pressed her small fingertips knowledgeably against the thick vein as if testing its pulse. Then again she glanced happily at Josef. Her wide eyes flashed at him, transmitting the pleasure she was experiencing at this touching of the living penis. Her friend Lhirrahje murmured. Brandreth was completing the detachment of her panties. Against the emaciation of his body his engorged cock looked very thick. He put her ankle down in such a way that her legs stayed open. For this last part of the operation, she had been turned face down on his lap, covering his large erection, which pressed against her belly.

Josef moved across. His penis too felt large between his legs. It swung, brushing against the cool fleece as he squatted. Herazhaan had expected him to come to her. Now her head turned slightly to one side as if questioning him. Then she glanced down at her friend lying prone across Brandreth. Josef could see the girl's bottom properly. Brandreth was lifting her to make his cock more comfortable against her. When he put her down, her legs were more open.

There is something very deeply arousing about

perfection in a female anus: its beauty is intrinsic, its skin is velvet to the fingers, its embraces are illicit, sensual, wanton, profane. It is not simply the vision of its distension as the prober goes inside it. It is more the witnessing of the responses in the victim to the pleasures that distension brings. And Lhirrahje's pleasure-seeking anus was responding. Her friend was doing her by hand – two upturned fingers rimming, reaming deeper. Josef felt the sexual pulsebeat in his erection.

Brandreth made a swishing motion with his fingers. 'Smack,' he ordered. 'I want to smack her in here.' Herazhaan seemed to understand. She slid her fingers out then scampered away across the silken fleece. Lhirrahje understood too. She became restless. Her legs which had been so open to the fingering now began to close from sexual fear. Recollections of the discipline of the Abbey came to Josef. It was always so before a spanking, however much a human girl might want it and even if she subsequently came to climax while the spanking ran its course. As it was with the novices, so it seemed to be with Lhirrahje. Everything about her behaviour was entirely human.

Brandreth turned her head so she was lying on her cheek and looking at Josef. When a girl is made to look upon her watcher, her pleasure runs deeper. He drew aside her long wavy tresses of golden hair and rested his open hand against her neck. With this gesture he was holding her anxiety in check and her body in place for the spanking. This pose looked so erotic. Her buttocks made a smooth white whaleback breaking through the waves of golden hair. Then he split this smooth whaleback gently open, making it clear to her what she would get and exactly where she would get it. He gently prised the deeper cheeks apart. Josef's erection began to throb and pulse again when he saw her lovely rosebud. Soon this tight young rosebud would be made to swell.

Herazhaan had returned with a crop made entirely of

silk. It appeared specifically designed for anal whipping – the stem being wound stiff and very flexible, and carrying a thick shiny knot of silk loosely fastened to the end. She handed it to Brandreth then took on the responsibility of keeping Lhirrahje's rosebud intimately exposed.

The whippings by this knot of silk quickly brought on a kind of erection specific to that place. She squirmed; he whipped it; after every few strokes, he gently teased the swelling rosebud with the rounded tip of the stock as if using a finger or the apex of a penis. And all that sweet while, cheek to the silk, Lhirrahje kept her eyes open, looking at Josef, and her lips were parted, and Brandreth's free hand lay gently but firmly at her neck, keeping her down. But her open bottom was rising gradually into the air – reaching for the very smacks – and her legs were getting wider and wider open to allow the snapping knot of silk to focus ever more precisely to the sexual mouth of the spreading rosebud in the crack. But oh, it must have hurt so sensitive a place, more used to being licked or tickled or gently stretched by a well-oiled clyster.

Her friend now sat back on her heels, her fingers again playing with the dildo agitatedly, her breathing in concert with Lhirrahje's, each breath locked up inside her beautiful breast then expelled by the next snap of the silk.

Brandreth then displayed his handiwork: there was a raised hot ring where once there had been a cool inviting crater. Brandreth pushed the silk knot inside it. Lhirrahje squirmed. The crop hung between her legs. Herazhaan shivered. It was like the shiver that comes when a girl is trying to conceal or delay a climax. Josef reached across, taking hold of Herazhaan's foot. 'Come here,' he whispered. The ankle in his hand seemed so cool and frail. He wanted to kiss it and kiss her there between the legs where she had shivered, and let his tongue slip

211

down to linger in the tight place where her friend, gently trembling, was very slowly yielding up the knotted silk to Brandreth's tugging fingers.

Herazhaan made directly for Josef's erect penis, placing her cheek against his belly. She stared up at the clear fluid welling down his shaft. Soon it would come thicker. She nuzzled closer. Her fingertips made contact with the sticky fluid. They stroked it back up the underside of his penis and touched the piercing. The flow lazily increased. But inside he was aching. She put her fingers to her lips, painting them with his fluid. Then she ran her tongue-tip round her lips and put her fingers back to where the fluid issued from the mouth of his penis. This time she sucked the issue coating her fingers. She closed her other hand round his hot shaft. The flow strengthened. She kept gathering it on the tips of her fingers and transferring to her mouth as if she were collecting honey from a leaking comb. Then, turning on her back, she stared up at him so innocently. Her arm was back, her hand still gripping his penis, her armpit nakedly smooth. But her little finger was through the ring of the dildo. She tugged it, milked the tip. She put her head back. Her lovely face was pillowed in the fullness of her wavy golden hair. She shaped her lips to an inviting 'o'.

'You want me to suckle you?' said Josef. Her lips widened. 'You want me to feed you?' Her tongue made a sucking movement against her upper lip. She still had hold of his penis. A drop of his fluid was sliding down her little finger. She raised the dildo to her lips and took the ring between her teeth and tugged until the ball of the torc pulled through the piercing. Then she drew herself upright and sat back on her heels, the gold ring glinting between her teeth, her belly pushed out, the lips of her sex pouting suggestively through her panties.

She murmured when he pulled the waistband open, took the ring and dropped it down the front of her panties. As he eased her back, her thighs stayed open so the shape of the ring was very visible through the tautness of her panties. Her flesh inside was nude. Josef had seen it when first he drew the panties open, nude perfect pubic lips sitting pressed against the silken gusset.

Progressing only through the gentle pressure of the tips of Josef's fingers, the protruding ring moved ever down under the taut silk skin. It now balanced on the ridge of stimulated flesh. Josef gently rubbed it, squeezed it against her, turned it, worked her slippy flesh around it, pressed it gently in. Herazhaan gasped. It disappeared inside her. He kept his hand there, squeezing her sex gently through the silk.

Lhirrahje was being turned face up. Brandreth's cock bounced up from under her then brushed between her legs. But it was not destined to be used: he had not finished with the crop. He asked Josef to help. And he showed him a little clitoral shield that he had found and now intended to use. 'I want to whip her sex – just inside it, on the lips,' Brandreth explained, then, 'Oh, my – she understands. Look at her.' Josef left Herazhaan spread and sitting on her heels and he moved closer to Lhirrahje.

All her tremblings had returned. 'Down here, my dove, is where I shall whip you,' whispered Brandreth. He took her by her ankles and pushed her knees back. Her sex opened. 'Never whip too hard, Josef, not in here. If you whip too hard, they go too tight. But when you get it right – oh, God – and go inside them then, hard after the whipping ... So hot, they are, so puffy ...' And now he touched her anus, already so visibly subjected to the rigours of the knotted crop. 'Feel it. There, you see?' Her hot bulging crater tightened round the tips of Josef's gently stroking fingers.

Behind Josef, Herazhaan's breath snagged; she was jealously aroused. But Josef persisted, examining her friend's anus intimately and not attempting to hide the ferocity of his erection. Brandreth continued: 'Lift her up. We must put this on you, darling, so you do not come from the kiss of the crop.' Its cord, interthreaded with gold, encircled her waist and dropped down between her legs. It carried a tiny silk cup to shield just the clitoris. Below it, at the end of the cord, hung a polished gilt stopper. She shivered sexually when Brandreth fitted the cup. He tightened it by twisting the cord around the stopper which he then inserted into her sex. The fat, near-buried stopper pushed her labia partly open. He clamped dangly gold weights to them to keep them so. The gold strings radiated like tiny sunbeams out across her belly. Her sex was out-turned, openhearted, moist, soft pink. 'Angel wings . . .' Brandreth whispered, detaching the silk knot from the end of the crop, leaving it bare-stemmed. 'Fine kisses are what they need.' He whipped them – quickly, with her knees tucked up beside her breasts – small breasts whose jellied areolae bulged and shook. Then he opened her bottom with the stock of the crop. 'Let the stings bite awhile,' he whispered, one hand stroking her brow, the other drawing the weights radially out again across her belly, stretching her naked angel wings, now adorned with fine raised intersecting lines.

Josef returned to Herazhaan, who was still kneeling. He slid behind her. His penis was against the hollow of her back. He put both hands down the front of her panties and toyed there while she shuddered. His fingers teased her labia open. His fingernails gently scratched the moist inner surface. He felt the knob of the thick torc that was still inside her. He pressed it. She moaned. Her head fell back against his shoulder. Her little jellied breasts stood out as she watched the stock being withdrawn from her friend. Josef felt that Herazhaan would climax in his fingers if she saw another whipping.

'Come on, now, drink from me.' Sitting, he drew her

down and made of his thigh a pillow for her cheek. She kept one knee bent, still inviting him to touch her while he suckled her with his cock. His arousal, with his hand down her panties, holding those nude wet lips, made his fluid run heavily. She was milking him with her mouth. And he could suckle a girl continuously now because of what the Succubus had done to him: the flow never really stemmed while he remained erect. Moist greedy murmurs issued from her lips. She became demanding of him when she heard the crop, and she slid her fingers up inside him to stimulate the gland.

The crop began snapping down inside Lhirrahje's pubic lips. Herazhaan suddenly moaned, stopped sucking and her belly turned rigid. Her fingers slid limply out of Josef.

He gently eased her up, with his fingers still inside her. She sat against him, her knees up, splayed: she was near to climax. He slid his free hand underneath, drew her panties down and nipped her anus as his other fingers searched about inside her for the ring. He kept pausing to suck those small bright-red fat-nippled teats. The ring had worked in deeply. Eventually he drew it out. Her anus tightened. He nipped a little whorl of skin and gently pulled it. The perfect symmetry of her anus was now blemished by this small skin flap. Then he sent her for the dildo. As she began to crawl away, he stopped her, pressing his hand into the small of her back until her breasts were in the silky fleece. He wanted to look at her again, her panties round her knees, her naked bulging sex slung under her little anus with its small temporary skin protrusion, so sexually teased out of her, and now in need of wetting. He did this with his penis, which was still leaking seminal fluid. The mouth of her bottom turned slippery. Its little bulb of skin slid back inside. The cap of Josef's penis followed. He drew apart the cheeks. She moaned. Her bottom opened properly. Her back hollowed deeply. The cap disappeared inside.

The mouth of her anus clutched it lovingly. As Josef stroked the edges of Herazhaan's labia with the tips of his fingers, her hips rose sensually up and down, her bottom sucked the end of his penis as neatly as had her mouth.

He drew out. She collapsed sideways, reaching for him open-mouthed, panting gently, her lips now secure round the fluid-soaked head of his penis. The little bulb-crowned mounds of her breasts poked out to each side. 'Oh – you little beauty,' Josef murmured. Her open sex was lifted like an animal in heat as she sucked the scent of her anus from the end of his penis. 'Oh, you sweet little fucker,' Josef groaned in pleasure.

'Tl-*fugher!*' she blurted round the mouthful of his flesh.

Brandreth was beside him. He had left Lhirrahje spread-legged and swollen. He was fastening a thick cord around his waist. A second cord went through it, then round the base of his penis, above his scrotum, then up between his buttocks. He drew it tight. His cock immediately expanded larger than ever and the balls were drawn back, making the shaft longer. 'Let me,' he said. Josef baulked, but Herazhaan, knowing, wanting, stretched out on her back, her mouth yawning open. 'Look – she wants to swallow it whole.'

'Oh, God,' Josef murmured as he watched it sliding, inch by thick-veined inch, down her willing throat. Her legs writhed gently with the pleasure of swallowing. She was like a snake gorging on its prey. Brandreth crouched to get the angle, pivoted to get the depth of thrust.

Josef spread her lovely sex and held it open. She moaned with sexual pleasure at the stretching. And her lips were still seeking, her head pushing up between Brandreth's legs. It seemed she wanted every inch of shaft. She tried to get her fingers inside his anus. Josef shuddered to see her; he felt her sex tighten, wanting to close; then he saw her throat rippling, contracting like a soft squeezing sheath round the glans of the pumping penis.

Brandreth drew out stiff and dripping. The Kelthling licked the last thick drops, then groaned. Her head twisted to one side: Josef still held her sex lips open. Her clitoris was in hard erection, her labia very soft and yielding to the touch. He resolved to keep her that way.

He made her fit the heavy gold ring on to his own penis. Then he lifted her on to it, open-sexed, legs astride. It went all the way up inside her. He felt it press against her womb. And she was gasping, holding herself open, wanting to get it deeper yet. She moaned, rubbing the torc against her. Her bare wet open sex lips suckered to his pubes. Her knob was standing out from its swollen thin-skinned hood. Josef took a silk cord to it. The cord quickly turned wet and slippy as he rubbed it back and forth. She pressed her little breasts against him, kissed him, sucked his tongue. He kept the taut cord moving, masturbating her gently with it. She started gasping, chirping words he did not understand. Suddenly she sat bolt upright against him, very still and put her head back, groaning. Her labia stood open, her knob bright-red. He made to rub the cord against it, but she stayed his hand, then leant against him and clasped her hands around her buttocks. 'Udtha-cock. Fugh-it.' And she pressed her breasts tightly to Josef's chest, pressed her lips against his neck, because it would hurt, it must surely be too full a penetration. There seemed so little space from front to back to take even one fully extended penis. Her anus was already compressed and pushed up by the thickness of Josef's shaft, which was by the second gaining girth.

He felt the other penis push, the anus stretch and tighten. Then the push came again. She gasped sweet sexual tongue-filled shudders into Josef's mouth. He felt the other penis sliding up against him – tight, so tight

217

and small, her anus felt. He tried again to get the cord across her knob. He pulled it down; she bucked; he pulled it up; her knees jerked outwards. She started riding, writhing on the two shafts. Brandreth drew her back, squeezed her little breasts to bursting, kissed her. The Kelthling tongued his open mouth. Between her legs, her sex was bulging out. She put her hand down, pressing as if to stop Josef's ringed penis bursting out. Josef tried to close her labia. He rolled the wet cord into a ball and rubbed it against her. She arched away from him and came. And because the two knobs were enveloped in the compass of her sucking muscle, with the ring trapped between them, stimulating each bunch of nerves, the semen flooded. It just kept coming. Her muscle just kept sucking.

After this they watched her do her friend with the squirting dildo. She pushed it up her bottom. The girl was on her back. The oil-filled balls were between her legs on the fleece. Herazhaan teased her knob and when the pleasure was about to come, she stamped on the balls of the dildo. The squirting of the oil up inside Lhirrahje brought on the climax. Because her knob was no longer being touched, the climax was prolonged, driven only by the squirtings up inside her.

Herazhaan was kneeling over her friend. Josef made her stand, then spread her slim legs and bend from the waist. As he fingered her and opened her, the fluid stored hot inside her sex and bottom started escaping down her thighs. Lhirrahje drank of it greedily. It seemed to fuel their desire; Herazhaan was thirsty again.

Josef languorously watched the two of them making love to Brandreth to the point of his exhaustion; still they wanted to continue. It was as if the later issues of fluid were more intoxicating to these creatures. Lhirrahje was sitting astride his face and letting him suck her clitoris which now stood out like a nipple. It seemed to be secreting some form of liquid. Brandreth was becoming wild eyed, groaning with pleasure. Herazhaan was sucking his penis so strongly that the thick vein stood out purple. He passed out but she kept sucking; he climaxed while asleep, the fluid overflowing her lips. And once Brandreth was left drained and comatose they turned to Josef.

The balance was changing; these beautiful creatures were now stirred by desire. They came to Josef. Herazhaan crouched over his face and Lhirrahje removed his penile ring and sucked him. His glans slipped beneath her tongue, which seemed to mould around it, holding it, milking it, inducing a peculiar pleasure at the mouth of the penis as if something fine and narrow were being pushed very slowly down it. He imagined the fine beak of a humming bird drinking, or the proboscis of a butterfly, delicate and long – that was the feeling. The pleasure was unique. He gasped; it felt as if it were extending down the full length inside his erect penis, licking keenly, searching out the entrance to the inner gland. If the inside of the penis could taste then the taste that she was somehow putting there was as tantalisingly sweet as aniseed. And at the other end, the secretion Herazhaan was delivering from her clitoris into his mouth was like sweet almond oil, softly dripping. All the time it was coming he could feel the other one's proboscis slipping down him and now sucking inside. He tried to resist the urge to climax; the pleasure was exquisite; it made him shiver; his shivering stimulated the steady flow. Lhirrahje put her fingers into him and massaged the gland. The dull ache came: it felt as if the proboscis was going down the very tubes into his balls. His climax came and he passed out into a delicious sleep.

He awoke with the feeling that he was about to climax. They were using a clyster on him. Herazhaan, open-mouthed, was awaiting his ejaculate. She held his penis clasped tightly at the base. When the plunger of the clyster pushed the contents up inside him, Josef spouted. And Herazhaan drank his liquor as if he were a fountain. Again she fed him almond oil from her clitoris. Again they used the clyster. Again he passed out with the intensity of the sexual feeling. Each time he slept he awoke more tired.

When he awoke again it felt as if a thick silk tube was emergent from his penis. It filled the girth and felt attached. The slightest movement brought peculiar pleasure. He could not see what had been done because one of the Kelthlings was crouched astride his belly and was gently slapping his balls to stimulate the flow of fluid. He could feel one of them taking suck from the tube. He felt as if he was in sexual bondage deep inside. She sucked deeply and the feeling was of belly-piercing pleasure.

He had not the strength to move. But still they somehow kept inducing pleasure. Eventually he did not know whether he was was asleep or awake. Darkness followed daylight repeatedly. It was like a slow delicious creeping fever which never would abate. He saw his home, he saw Sianon – he reached for her then he passed out yet again.

13

Malory

Lady Belangaria stared sullenly down through the roof
of the glass enclosure. The beautiful creatures frightened
off must surely return to their charge who was lain upon
the great fleece-clad bed. Into what new visions would
they then inveigle him? She had no way of knowing for
the Kelthling mindspell touched only men. The time for
their mating had almost passed yet they seemed to want
only to drink his living semen. Would they render him
a wraith like all the others, and after all the portents had
been so good? So near to success; could it be too late?
She would persist. She must. She rounded on the perpe-
trators.

'Who sent you?' she demanded, lashing the crop on
the marble top.

'No one,' Danime muttered with head bowed.

'Was it Janna?'

Danime vehemently shook her head.

'Her poisoned claws are in this somewhere.'

'My lady,' said the Chamberlain, 'they had no busi-
ness to be in there, but –'

'If my Seerguard had not intercepted them, who
knows what damage they would have done? You have
no idea what is at stake here.'

'Then nor have they. Yes – they must be punished for
the misdemeanour – a grave misdemeanour. Danime is
the more culpable. I could arrange –'

'Arrange nothing! Chamberlain – you arrange too much.'

He spoke through gritted teeth: 'My lord expects at the banquet the presence of the one in milk. There are our visitors to be considered.'

'Keep your counsel. I want them taught a lesson.'

'As I suggested –'

'Shut up! And you! Mistress Free-woman –' she grasped Danime's hand and wrenched the symbolic ring from her finger – 'your freedom is hereby truncated. And before you go to the Milanderan banquet as a slave for common usage I shall have you dealt with in a way you shan't forget.'

All the bravery was long gone from Danime's eyes. Her lips were sealed tight. She was trembling all over as the guards carried her away.

In the subterranean suite of the Milanderan tower they shaved Danime from toe to head – in every nook and cranny, over every inch of skin. They took all body hair, even the finest and palest. 'Don't leave a single filament,' said Lady Belangaria. And they took her luscious eyebrows. When Sianon was brought in Danime was shrouded in lather. It was her second shaving. Only her sex lay exposed: it had been re-shaved first, that she might be masturbated throughout the remainder of the shaving. They used varnished sticks with elongate bulbous projections which, re-oiled and slipped into her sex or anus, would be gently twirled while the razors swept up swaths of lather to re-expose newly sensitised skin.

Fingers sometimes delved directly inside her small bare sex. Little cusps of lather clung to her erect nipples. An attendant clasped them in his fingers and shaved the undersides of her breasts. Another reshaved her head. Repeatedly they returned to the sexual places: the insides of her thighs, the skin around the gold love-ring, her aroused labia, her breasts, her buttocks, her lower back and the deep smooth sensitive channel to her anus. Every surface nerve and some just within the sexual infolds had been teased by this stroking or twirling. She did not seem to be fully aware that anyone was watching. She looked drugged. She kept murmuring; her mouth kept opening and reaching as if to make lip to skin contact with her tormentors.

Lady Belangaria whipped Danime front and back, her breasts and open sex then her anus. Then she departed, leaving her for the comfort of the men.

Amongst the onlookers was a visiting master whom the Chamberlain had escorted here. The Chamberlain appeared to hold him in esteem but addressed him only as 'Malory' or 'Deputy'. He was young and not ornately robed like the native lords – he wore a light open jerkin, soft boots and belted trousers. And he bore this affinity with Danime: his head was completely shaved. But he still wore eyebrows. The shaving ennobled his countenance and made him appear older than his years.

He had watched with apparent absorption every stage of Danime's shaving, discussing its progress with the Chamberlain. But then the Chamberlain had pressed a small package into his hand. Malory had examined it then stared across at Sianon before putting the package into his breast pocket. Shortly afterwards she was called over.

Behind her, Danime was moaning and the master's attention was constantly being diverted in that direction until the Chamberlain made his apologies and withdrew.

'Would you like to take her place?' The master looked directly into Sianon's face. She shook her head, aghast. Her lips were stuck together. She could not swallow. 'In any case your hair is too beautiful ever to be taken away.' When she looked up again, his gaze had moved away. 'And I confess to having requested that you not be whipped. I saw you at the muster. Each time I return here I find something to capture my interest.' He turned

Sianon round. Danime was being oiled. Her legs were trembling. 'Your Chamberlain asked me to give you these.' He took the package from his pocket; it was a box. Inside were two large pendant earrings. 'She made them for you.' Sianon, open-mouthed, reached to touch them: the pendants were exquisitely decorated large pearl droplets clasped in silver filigree. She had never seen anything so beautiful. She gazed in admiration at Danime. 'They are for your nipples. It would please me if you were to wear them when I escort you to the banquet.'

He turned to one of the attendants. 'Call for my valet. We go to the long gallery. Then we shall need a quiet place where she can be taken to be pierced.'

The heavy door boomed shut. The long room evoked in Sianon memories of the Abbey – in the still, cool, dusty air, the filtered daylight, the dark reflections from polished wood. With a high window at each end, it must have spanned the diameter of the tower. One wall was completely clothed in broad panelled mirrors. Down the centre was a punishment bar at belly height. This was why he had not wanted her whipped: he wanted to do her himself. Every nerve upon her skin waited. The master entrusted the nipple-rings to his valet. Then he disrobed. She could see his tall athletic physique in the mirror. There was no hair on his chest, none on his back or belly or legs. Apart from his eyebrows, his skin was totally naked. His countenance in profile was noble. She wondered whether he had an entourage of slaves to do his shaving and to attend to his sexual needs. She pictured girls of clean beauty like Danime. But he had not seemed to express more that a casual interest in Danime.

The master slipped into a short red silk dressing robe. His valet knelt before him to fit a thin blue silk yoke about his genitals. The red robe when fastened did not fully conceal him. Malory glanced across at her through the mirror. She glanced modestly away. But she had seen his sex, which was attractive and quite naked.

He took her to the middle of the room, where the mirror facing her stretched symmetrically away on each side. Before her was the horizontal bar. The valet placed on the floor below it two shallow wooden blocks. 'Stand on the blocks,' Malory whispered. He must have done this thing often. Her nipples came erect. The valet handed him a leather.

He spanked her to the point of tears. In this long, quiet room she sobbed. Her thighs pressed against the bar. In the mirror she could see him. She could see her legs, wide open, her feet balanced unsteadily on the blocks. For the duration of her spanking she was not permitted either to close her legs or to hold on to the bar. The lashes drove her buttocks forwards and her sex pressed out above the bar; he could see it through the mirror. Then suddenly the lashing stopped. The only sound was Sianon's laboured breathing, the only movement her fingers by her sides, clutching at air to try to dispel the burning shivers across the skin of her buttocks. The air being sucked into her lungs was cold; across her buttocks it felt like the searing draught from a furnace.

Malory walked to the end of the bar. His sex was fuller yet not erect. He poured water tinkling from a jug into a bowl. Then he dropped a cloth into the bowl. He brought the bowl back and placed it on the floor between her legs. She could see him lift the dripping cloth by its corners. He placed it, saturated and freezing cold, flat against her lower back.

'Ughhh!!!' Her back hollowed deeply; his nostrils flared; her sex pushed out above the bar for him to see. Her nipples tightened painfully. The freezing runnels ran down her buttocks, down her legs, making wet twisting tendrils round her thighs. Then he stood to the side, raised the broad leather strap and spanked her bottom until her gyrations dislodged the cloth stuck against her and it dropped into the bowl to be recharged with freezing water. He replaced it freezing against her back and spanked her again. He never said anything to her, never gave her any directive, never even touched her sex or breasts. But he spanked until her tears were continuously brimming – until they had reached the point where tears fed tears and she could not stop.

When that point was reached he asked the valet: 'Did you find a bed?'

'Close by, there is only a humble one – a cell, almost.'

'Close by is what is needed.'

He lifted her in his arms as tenderly as a lover and carried her to her cell. That first time, her arms and hands were afraid to make the contact with her master; they rested across her breasts and belly. Yet she felt a curious security in his arms.

Her bed had a grey woollen blanket stretched tightly over the mattress. There was no pillow. He laid her on her side. She was still sobbing. He sat near the foot of the bed, just watching her. Then without warning his fingers closed about her foot so reverently and lightly that she could feel explicitly the contact of each single one. Butterfly wings of anticipation trembled inside her. He moved up the bed. 'Hold out your wrists,' he softly instructed. He tied them together with a velvet strap. Then he sat beside her on the bed, stroking her hair until her exhaustion swallowed her up.

She must have slept for two or three hours. She woke with her wrists still tied together. He was still sitting on the bed, caressing her hair. She stared up at him. His head, naked of hair, was smooth as a statue's. This nakedness made his ears stand out; it gave him strength of countenance. Unaware she was awake he was gazing straight out above her as his hand massaged her neck. They were point and counterpoint, his profile so inscrutable, unflinching, and his touch pure tenderness. His hands were large but did not abuse their strength; his arms were bare to the elbows; his eyes were dark, deep but kindly; he might have been handsome but the shavenness made him other-worldly. She found herself wondering what sort of lord he was in his own land. And now he was looking at her, unsurprised at her being awake. His fingertips smoothed her temples, brushing the hair gently upwards and away until all she could hear was the soft bristling rush. The feeling in her belly was of warmth; the sleep had relaxed her. Her buttocks were still tender. 'I must spank again,' he whispered.

His words were like a cold hand grasping her belly and squeezing. Her eyes said: 'No.' Her lips opened; no sound issued. He bent close to her face, examining it with glittering eyes; she thought he would kiss her; his mouth trembled open; he was drinking her breath. No contact occurred other than his hand making love to her hair and neck, and his eyes caressing her, and his lungs drawing her expelled breath.

He took her hands in his. 'Shall I untie your wrists?' She shook her head. 'Do you want it here, on the bed?' She nodded. 'Then it shall be our tryst.' Gently he turned her on to her belly; gently he lowered her breasts; gently he drew her fastened wrists over the edge of the bed. He used a cane on her buttocks, not gently, thrashing the sobs out of her from a place so deep inside her heart that she felt she was drowning. Her sex thrust down upon the coarse grey blanket as if the downsweeps of the cane were the plunges of sexual love. Her tears overflowed on to the blanket. He stopped after six lashes but again her tears would not. He sat on the side of the bed. Her body was rising, trembling and falling, her breathing hoarse, her lips dry, her face wet, her earlobes burning. Then she felt his sweet double-palmed, ten-fingertipped caresses sweeping pleasure repeatedly and gently from her shoulders to the tip of her spine.

He untied her wrists. She reached for him. 'No,' he told her. 'Use your hands for your pillow.' He laid her cheek against them. She was facing the wall. He ran his fingers gently up the back of her neck and under her hair. She drew her legs slightly open, wanting to encourage him; her sex was throbbing to be touched. She felt his hands enclosing her ribcage then, thumbs first, thumb-tips in the groove of her backbone, sliding down. When they reached the small of her back, her buttocks arched and opened. Still he did not touch her there. He moved down to the foot of the bed and slowly massaged the balls of her feet. She could not keep her eyelids open; the bed quaked and Sianon slumped again into velvet sleep.

When her eyelids flickered open she was on her back. The valet was in the room. She tried to sit up. 'No,' Malory murmured, settling beside her, restraining her shoulders. 'No. Stay still. You have been good thus far.' Her agitated gaze refocused on the valet, small and dapper, staring at her with eager eyes. She wanted to close her legs. But any such reaction had been pre-empted: there were velvet straps round each of her ankles securing them to the corners of the bed. And the valet at the foot of the bed was ogling her sex and breasts. But everything there and inside her body she had been saving for her master. She turned her face to him. 'No,' he said. 'He will not whip you – that is my job. Look at me.' He drew her hair away from her face and caressed her. 'I want to wet the leather,' he said. She shivered. She could hear the water swishing in the bowl. 'I shall smack the insides of your thighs.'

They wanted to close but could not. Malory leant across her belly to do it. Amid the smacks and Sianon's moans, she heard the valet's excited breathing. Malory whispered, 'Beautiful ...' And for the first time, he kissed her open shivering lips. All the while, he was caring for her, attentive in this curious way. He smacked until the tears came again. As her tears came fuller, so his kisses came ever gentler. 'I have to wet the leather again,' he said. First he drew her body gently down the bed, opening her knees for what she knew was coming. The insides of her thighs were on fire. He began again. He stood between her legs. Fine droplets of smacked water rained down on her sex and belly. Malory set the leather aside. The valet knelt between her thighs. 'Let him drink,' Malory whispered. 'He has waited upon you so patiently.'

'Oh, please,' she whispered. She did not want this person to do this intimacy to her when the feelings were so charged, so close. 'Please – have pity.' Compared to this the whipping was a mercy, anything but this – to be made to spill this way without recourse to her master.

Malory inserted a pillow under the middle of her back. It raised her aroused belly; it made her breasts slide outwards as if she were an offering and her bed an altar.

She saw the glint in the valet's eyes. She twisted her head away. 'No ...' she pleaded. Then his warm wet lips enveloped her sex. 'Ohhh!' They suckered to her like a limpet, drawing the ache of reluctant pleasure downwards, ever downwards, from her taut belly arched over the pillow.

Malory turned her face towards his; she did not want to look at him when she was feeling this awful pleasure of the fat warm lips around her labia, clutching her so intimately and the amateurish tongue rasping her clitoris ever closer to the nightmare of a sexual release. 'Ohh ...' she gasped. But Malory held her face and kissed her. He must have felt the tense interruption of her breathing. He slipped his tongue into her open

mouth. Her teeth closed round it then released it. 'Ohh!'
Her belly jumped, just once.

'A little one,' Malory whispered, stroking her neck. It
was a little one that made her want much more. 'Steady
– stealth, sir steward. Will you look upon those thighs.'
They were seething, writhing slowly as the valet un-
suckered himself, smacked his lips with gusto and
climbed off the bed.

Malory began to wipe her sex with a soft kerchief. He
used little flat strokes that moved her vulva gently
upwards, simulating the pressure moves of love. This
gentle sexual pressure so close upon the sucking caused
a feeling like a full lump of pleasure melting in Sianon's
womb, filling her sex with liquid sweetness. Lumps of
pleasure were growing in her breasts, pushing out behind her nipples. Her thighs were burning hot; the
creases of her legs were cool; her sex was blissfully
warm. The stretched kerchief was being moulded to its
shape. 'I can see your knob through the cloth,' he
whispered.

'Ooooh . . .' Suddenly it had almost come. Her eyes
were closed. Her fingers were round her master's wrist,
the first intimacy which she had initiated, staying his
hand, staying the moist cloth's sensual movements that
were sure to bring on her climax.

Malory lifted back the cloth from Sianon's naked
trembling sex and spread it on her belly, then bent
forwards, kissing the strap marks on her skin, placing
butterfly wings of icy pleasure there. His naked head
touched her near the top of her thigh, causing a feeling
so sexual that she was frightened that its bald rotundity
would press between her legs and precipitate her climax
with the valet still watching. She was balanced so close
to the brink. It was a feeling both dreadful and sweet.
And now the lumps of pleasure in her breasts were
beginning their melting. There was nothing she could do
to contain it. She lay back slowly, stretching her elbows

away to relieve the pressure. But what was happening to her breasts was plain for them to see.

She watched Malory's eyes, child-like, delighted. Her breasts were overflowing. Oily droplets oozed from her nipples, turned watery and ran. She could feel their progress down her skin. She saw his cock, bone-hard, projecting from under his short gown. She wanted to suck it near the root, to remove the yoke and suck underneath it, drawing sustenance from the salty flesh.

His thumb nudged gently under her enlarged clitoris, nudged and rolled until he found the slow deep rhythm and it was as if the pressure under her clitoris was somehow squeezing drop by luscious drop the milk of love from Sianon's nipples. The droplets now gathered, fattening, dangling, opalescent, creamy, running down beneath her breasts and soaking into the bed.

'Ohhh . . .' The first strong contraction came between her legs; the pleasure was too keen. His thumb released her very gently.

The areolae had fatted up, the nipples had lengthened, stiffened. Nipple by nipple his fingers sought these twin erections, milking them; she could feel her breasts turning wetter. A dull tendril of arousal linked her nipples and her belly. Every pull upon her erect wet nipple felt like a suck upon her womb. 'Bring her nipple-rods and pearl drops,' said Malory.

He sat behind her on the bed. She was sitting up. He was supporting her. Her breasts were in a silver tray which reflected their undersides in all their glory. The valet was drawing her nipples gently forwards, stretching them to make a necked teat. He kept drying them but her flow of milk would not abate. It lay in little droplets and pools on the silver. Malory's fingers lay between her open legs. Her sex was open, its lips soft as moist paper, her clitoris throbbingly erect. Every time the valet drew her nipple, Malory's fingertips closed around her knob and held it.

Her head lolled back against his shoulder. Her mouth fell open. She started to gasp in the throes of climax. Malory's fingertips started to slap her wet clitoris, delivering little slaps from underneath then downwards from above. She felt something freezing cold around her nipple. She heard a click. The searing pain of puncture melded with her exquisite climax. She was still coming when the freezing searing happened a second time and both nipples, now impaled on fine gold rods, were spurting milk like ejaculate through the valet's fingers.

Then Malory lay behind her, drawing her knee up between her pierced leaking breasts, caressing with his fingertips the soft lips of her sex and holding her with her knob protruding and his yoked balls and naked penis hot against the groove of her spine.

14

Above the Banquet

When it was time to take Sianon down, the valet
brushed her hair. Malory studied her nude profile: the
underbellies of her breasts were beautifully full; the
nipples poked like blind worms speared on their gold
studs. From behind he cupped the underbellies in his
palms and teased the gold studs with his fingers. Sianon
murmured; the blind pink worms came fully erect.

'Tender?' he whispered.

Sianon nodded.

'Good.' He fitted the large pearl droplets to her studs.
'Beautiful . . . and readily detached when your breasts
are bared for whipping.'

The valet said: 'One should take care with the studs.
They ought not to be removed till the piercing is quite
bedded.'

'Oh – but is she not beautiful?' Malory drew her arms
up behind her head. He opened her legs. 'Look!'

'Indeed sir.'

Her sex was still aroused. Every movement of her
thighs, every brush of naked fingers on her belly, induced pleasure there. Her master too was in erection.
Through all her punishment, all her pleasurings on the
bed, he had remained unsatiated. She had felt his penis
leak against her back but never spill. His thwarted
satisfaction acted as a bond between them, making all
that was befalling her pleasurable to bear.

'Bring me the cane,' he asked the valet.

Afterwards he lifted her chin. 'Oh,' he murmured. 'Look.' Fat white droplets swelled on her nipples then slid down the pearls. He tapped them with his finger and smeared the milk around her teats. Then he cupped her warm breasts in his hands. 'What escort could any man crave which might be sweeter?'

He carried her in this naked whipped state downstairs through the tower, past rooms where she could hear sighs and sounds of preparation. Through open doors she glimpsed scenes – erect penises, nude girls standing on tables, fingers reaching up their legs, girls sitting shaved and knickerless on polished floors.

At the next flight of stairs he put her down, staring at her parted lips. 'I cannot go another step.' He took her by the shoulders and lowered her kneeling to the floor. He drew aside his robe, showing his erection, which was large indeed. His balls and penis were shaved completely naked. The silk yoke clasped them. With trembling fingers Sianon pushed his knees open. She coaxed his foot on to the step behind. His sex projected out above her. She turned her head to one side, reached up, pouting wide and sucked the flesh behind his balls. His erection stiffened bone hard. She sucked and sucked this underneath place. His penis gulped and wavered in the air. She wanted him to come like that, to feel his sticky juice running thickly down the side of her neck.

'Oh God.' He wrenched away from her. Then he fell to his knees caressing her face, bestowing gentle sighing kisses upon her warm full open lips. Her fingers crept tentatively behind his shaved smooth neck, teasing the bare base of his skull.

When he carried her again she could feel that his erection had not gone away. They reached a place where the door of a long raised gallery had been thrown open. At its far end was the hubbub of a gathering.

Guests converging from three directions funnelled

down the marble staircase into the entrance hall. There were lords and ladies, envoys, advocates, soldiers, merchants and slaves – many slaves, brought by the lords and ladies. But there were also slaves-in-waiting and slaves displayed as sexual ornaments against the walls. In this public hall was a modicum of restraint. Sianon remained at Malory's side. She saw Janna and the Magus; they moved separately through the crowd. She saw several of her friends at a distance; she saw Leah with a lady. She thought again of Josef. Her eyes darted round the room looking for him, wanting to see him safe yet not wanting him to be there. The more she thought of him the worse she felt. Waves of conflicting emotions suddenly threatened to overwhelm her.

'What is it?' Malory asked. He held her chin. She shook her head, her lips trembling. She could never tell him. She could not even admit it to herself. A bleak despair was welling inside her. Oh for the sweet deliverance of the lash.

'Malory – tut-tut . . . Harsh man,' said a silken voice. 'Harsher than the creatures of the pit, what has he done to you?' The bright eyes of the bejewelled Marquise were staring down at Sianon. 'Here – drink this. Let her drink it.' She forced her glass into Sianon's shaking hands. Sianon swallowed the warming liquid. She tried to wipe her eyes. Her lips were swollen. Her nose felt blocked.

'The Marquise is kind,' Malory said quietly. He was staring perplexedly at Sianon.

'Malory, show a little tenderness for once, show the girl you care.'

'Oh but I do, my lady,' he murmured. A strange light was in his eyes. He picked Sianon up and carried her, sweeping a swath through the surprised assembly. When he found a quiet corner he sat her down on a solitary couch. 'Now – what is it? Tell me.'

'It is a friend. I am afraid for him. His name is Josef.'

'Oh yes. Your Chamberlain told me something of his situation.'

'Perhaps you can help him?' she whispered.

He shook his head.

Her tears were coming again. 'You are lord.'

'I have no jurisdiction in this land.'

'Nor compassion for a slave like me?' Her outburst spoke volumes. She tried to turn away.

He picked her up again and held her. 'Sianon, Sianon.' He had spoken her name and she had not thought he knew it nor even cared. The tears rolled down her cheeks; her burning lips caressed his naked neck; she had never felt like this since Josef. Her thighs tried to close around his erect penis. He lifted her bodily and laid her face down across him. His hand slid under her belly. His middle finger slipped up to his gold ring inside her. Then he spanked her with his bare hand, spanked her bottom while her sex squeezed round his finger and her knob pressed hard against the shiny ring. When her climax came she felt as if pure sexual honey was welling in her throat to drown her.

'So – you have made amends,' came the silken voice. 'It gladdens the heart.' The Marquise had materialised at the end of the couch beside Malory. Her hand was poised as if to caress his naked head. 'We have a coterie of friends upstairs – away from the masses. Your Consul is there somewhere. Our Empress is expected. There are many who would wish to see you – and your new-found friend.' He did not answer. She bent to his ear to whisper: 'You cannot deny me this.' After checking there were no prying eyes in the vicinity, she leant over and kissed him. He offered no refusal. The scent of powder and warm jasmine billowed from her breast.

After that Malory no longer carried Sianon. She was made to walk. The Marquise remained by his side. The three of them ascended the staircase above the general banqueting area into an altogether more exclusive

236

world. At the entrance Malory paused. 'And your husband?'

'He will hardly make a scene.' Again she kissed him. Staring pointedly at Sianon and making no more pretence of modesty she clasped him expertly to erection. As she led him by his penis she whispered to Sianon: 'This one is mine. But despair not, my beauty – tonight shall see you importuned by paramours aplenty.'

The suite was an open network of beautiful pastel rooms of varied shape, height and lighting. It was not easy to tell whether any one of them was drawing room, dining room, bedroom, closet or gallery. In each was a handful of masters, ladies and slaves.

The Marquise drew Malory into a large room where a triad of kneeling girl-slaves had been slotted by their manacled hands and feet to short pillars through separate marble tables spaced around the centre of the room. Other girls lay on chaises and low tables. Some of the girls were vessels of food and drink. Two male slaves kept in permanent erection were standing by. The Marquise went to examine them.

Of the girls on the pillars there was a black-haired one to whom Malory seemed especially drawn. He led Sianon closer. The girl's skin was very white but her hair was very black and between her legs where she had been freshly shaved the density of hair roots had left a bluish shadow as if the area around her sex had been colourwashed in dilute indigo. But the inner lips were pale pink, soft and wavy as a consequence of prolonged masturbation. The hood was swollen and its skin very thinned above her strongly erect clitoris.

One of the younger masters placed between her knees on the table a curious device, a small blunt short rod of gold, little thicker than a quill attached to which were leather strands. He swept his hand gently up under her nipples and almost at the same time smacked them with a strip of leather. He smacked just the underparts of the

237

nipples. Then he drew back her hood and fitted a little weighted clamp directly to her clitoris. The clamp shook when he smacked her nipples again. Then he opened her sex very gently and stroked the tiny pee-hole with his thumb, making the weight on her clitoris loll from side to side. He picked up the curious instrument. Her head sank back on to the cap of the pillar and she started murmuring. 'One must be careful with the insertion; one would not wish to trigger her pleasure too soon.'

He turned to Malory. 'One can use the lips – her lovely mouth, for a slower build up to pleasure. Her mouth is quite responsive to the penis. But hold the weight up, would you?' As he began inserting the gold quill, so she began moaning.

'Shhh ...' he murmured, his eyes brimming with perverse delight. 'Bring a slave – her mouth needs comfort.' And the Marquise too was drawn to this spectacle as the male slave crouched above the girl on the table; with her own hands the Marquise directed the penis through the waiting lips. The girl's hips began to move. Between her thighs the strands of fine leather wafted like feathery grassheads in the breeze.

Malory drew Sianon away. The Marquise followed. Close by was a beautiful creature being covered in warmed honey. Her lord was pouring it down her front while her lady was masturbating her. The lady's fingertips were inside her and her cupped palm was slowly filling with honey.

Sitting at a carved wooden writing table in a secluded corner was a master of mature years, angular of frame. Kneeling on his table was a nude young girl whom he addressed as Tillen. He was holding her open, toying inside her. Her breasts were well-formed, her nipples well-erect. Her wrists were together behind her back. A painted drinking glass stood between her legs. The master was sitting on an upholstered stool bearing handles. His robe lay loosely open. His body was thin. White silky hairs adorned his chest. He noticed Sianon.

'My dear,' he asked the Marquise, 'what treasure have you brought me?'

'That, you must ask the Deputy Consul.'

Malory muttered: 'My lord the Marquis should feel free.'

'Then bring her closer.' The Marquis swung round. His robe fell open. His penis, though fringed with sparse near-colourless silky hairs, was that of a much younger man. He immediately wanted to touch Sianon's breasts. Malory made his excuses and wandered away. The Marquise stayed with her husband.

He detached the nipple-pearls very gently and placed them in safety on the table. He then examined the position of the tiny rods pushed through her nipples. 'Good,' he murmured. 'Deep in behind. One can get a good deep draw by pulling.' He took them in his fingers to show the Marquise. He made Sianon gasp. 'Does your beau not know how to do it?' It felt as if he were pulling the very milk glands. He spread his legs and pointed to his penis. 'Does he not give you this? Ah – no, I suspect not, for my lady has first call upon his while mine is doomed to perpetual youth in kissing lovely lips like these –' he touched Sianon's mouth – 'and feeding little love-birds with its juices.' He turned to Tillen and touched her sex. 'And look at this sweet mouth. I keep you ever open, don't I? Ever luscious? Was anything on this sweet earth more beautifully designed? Perfect symmetry, perfect softness, sweet aroma, delectable taste.' He hooked two fingers and drew them gently upwards under her erect clitoris. The tiny pee-hole broadened, so sexually; a little crystal-clear fluid spurted into the coloured glass. He dipped his fingers in and smoothed the fluid round his pink glans. 'Come closer,' he said to Sianon. 'Here – below the table. Yes. Kneel under the edge. Take her wrists my dear. Fasten them up here.' There were wooden rings under the table edge.

'My dearest,' said his wife, 'take it gently now. Your condition?'

'If I should die in the throes with such as these then my life was quite fulfilled. And if I do not have these lovely mouths right now then surely I will wither.'

The Marquise assisted her lord. Tillen lay back. His spindly legs slipped under the table and over Sianon's shoulders. His pink penis was hot. The wetness had dried but Sianon could smell it all over the penis and balls and in the creases of his legs, as if the girl had spilled while he was inside her. The scent aroused her; so did such thoughts; she had never done that with a man. She spread her lips willingly round his girl-scented penis. A funny pleasure came in her throat, because of that scent and its smoky taste, and because of the hot hairless fullness of the shaft, and because she could hear Tillen moaning as the master, hunching forwards, sucked inside her open sex, tried to suck the fluid out of her as if it were the water of life.

'My lord – lift up,' said the Marquise. 'You must go deeper if you are to please.'

He balanced, wavering on his frail arms on the handles of the stool. The Marquise put her fingers under, clutched his balls and drew them back. His shaft lengthened to a slim pink rigid snake. The extra few inches slipped down Sianon's throat. And she so wanted to be touched between the legs but there was no one to touch her. Her own wrists were fastened up. Her knees were splayed. Her erect knob pushed in vain to try to kiss the polished floor. All she had was this deep oral contact with her lord's penis which, as the Marquise teased his anus, threw long jets of aromatic pleasure deep into her throat while pushing, ever pushing that she might not lose a drop.

The Marquis was lifted off her by male slaves then left to recuperate on a couch. Tillen lay sprawled on the table, the painted glass vessel tipped on its side, its elixir spilt. The Lady Marquise's fingertips dipped thoughtfully into the pool.

Malory had returned. He had watched it all. He unfastened Sianon's tethers and hauled her up. 'My lord may find her lips a trifle tainted,' the Marquise whispered spitefully. He ignored her and swept up the pearl droplets from the table. Then he carried Sianon to one of the chaises and made her sit. He stared round the room. The girl covered in honey was now on her back. Her master was filling her sex with warm honey from a clyster. Her fingers were holding herself closed, that the honey might not leak. When the master saw Malory watching he said: 'It thins even more inside her, through body warmth. When it exudes it has the consistency of nectar but bears a stronger taste.'

Impulsively Malory went to the black-haired girl and lifted her off her pillar. He collected up a bunch of fat blue grapes coated in a matt bloom. Then he laid the beautiful girl down with her head on Sianon's lap. The girl's sex still had the leather strands projecting from the gold tag inserted into her pee-hole. He dangled the bunch of grapes and told Sianon: 'Feed her.' Sianon stared at him. She stared at the beautiful girl. Sweet enticing memories came to her, of the sexual things she had been made to do to other initiates in the Abbey.

Hesitantly she detached one of the grapes. Trembling, she squeezed the juice into the girl's open mouth. Breathless, she watched it dripping. She saw her master coming erect. She fed the girl with dripped juice. Then she kissed her. The leather strands, moving, drew attention to her sex. Sianon's fingers stroked the strands, then the blue-shadowed skin, then the warm weighted clitoral erection. She slipped a grape into her own mouth and bowed down. The girl moaned when it touched her erection. Sianon's tongue slid it down past the tethers to the sexual entrance which was tight. Sianon pushed. The fat grape popped in. For the next

241

three insertions of spittle-covered grapes she used her mouth. For the next few she used the head of her master's penis. All the time she was inserting the grapes she was masturbating the girl, who was wanting to spread her legs as the feeling of fullness deepened. But she could only spread so far because of the manacles round her ankles. Eventually Sianon could see and feel the swelling. She enclosed the protuberant sex in her hand. She gazed at Malory and played with the girl until he could bear it no more.

He thrust deep inside her hot sex as Sianon licked the sweet sticky purple juice his penis was expressing from inside. The girl started coming, triggering the master. Too late he pulled out, squirting white fluid laced with purple juice between her labia and over the leather strands. Sianon licked it, drank the mixture, sweet, salt and pungent. She held it in her mouth that the Marquis's spillage might be expunged and her lips, tongue and throat might be imbued afresh with her master's yield. From the corner of her eye she saw the Lady Marquise, narrow-eyed, hovering in the background. But Sianon's lips clung tightly round her master's penis. The Marquise approached, changing tack now, stroking Sianon's hair. 'She has a good mouth, that much I warrant.' The fingers began to roam, under Sianon's chin, over the girl's wet tethers then under Malory's penis, which re-stiffened though he pulled away from the touch. The Marquise forced a smile. 'Use it on her if you must. It shall come back to me.'

Sianon could feel his unspoken anger as he lifted her up and carried her. They passed into a hexagonal room, in character somewhere between a master bedroom and a large parlour. Around the periphery were steps up to low landings which led into several other rooms arranged radially. There were beds and couches, cushions, chairs, and tables well-laden with refreshments. Naked lovers were ensconced in deep armchairs. Astride the arm of a chair was Toinile – red-haired, freckled, naked, the same frightened Toinile whom Sianon had watched being painted at the muster. A lady was making her drink from a glass while spreading her sex about the arm of the chair. Across the room a mature man, evidently some important dignitary, was standing clasping a heavy goblet of wine. There were two priest-like figures in the room, one standing near one of the doorways, the other behind a table upon which a nude male slave was sitting uneasily. The dignitary's gaze left the young man and moved inquiringly to Sianon. Voices – both male and female – could be heard from at least two of the adjoining rooms.

One of the priests addressed the dignitary: 'Consul – perhaps you would care to see the others? Please bring your wine.' As they were passing Sianon the Consul halted. His bulbous eyes fixed on her. 'Malory – you seem in a great hurry. Is this the one the Chamberlain spoke of?'

'This is Sianon.'

'Then your arrival is timely. Don't leave before we make her acquaintance.' And the bulbous gaze followed them across the room.

Malory carried Sianon down several flights of steps and into a large blue-tiled room, a place of preparation. Nearby was a roaring fire. But a cold draught issued from the far end. 'There is an ice-house under here,' said Malory. Sianon did not know what he meant. 'A place where ice can be kept all year – for eating and for play. This one is like a cavern. It has pools and frozen waterfalls. One may experience pleasures that cannot come about in any other way.' He kissed her warm lips. 'Don't look so apprehensive. Trust me.'

Emerging from the stairwell was a man swathed in furs and carrying a naked girl. Sianon could see powdery ice in her hair; her skin was bluish-white, her shivering lips and nipples purple. The man laid his

243

charge on a table by the fire. He began rubbing her arms and legs. Malory went to speak to him but Sianon could see her master was in fact absorbed by the appearance of the girl. She saw Malory's hands roving over her shivering body. When he came back his hands were cold. 'Stand by the fire,' he said, 'while I get my furs.'

The girl lay across the table. Her master had requested a cistern of warm fluid. The stewards placed it on a stand on the table. Flexible pipes were coupled to it; they connected via the girl to a drain in the floor. Other girls were being brought in and made ready. One was with her mistress. Malory had now returned. He warmed the inner surface of the furs at the fire and said: 'It is better to witness first, before you undergo it.' But Sianon had undergone it. And she had watched it being done to other girls: in the Abbey such irrigation was performed for sexual pleasure.

The girl's master showed Sianon the rigid sleeve which was carefully and gently inserted to keep the muscle constantly open for the pipes and instruments of investigation to be clamped within. 'There is then no question of denial; friction at entry is reduced; she is kept stretched throughout; at every stage her degree of fullness is controlled by these taps and levers.'

Sianon watched. The girl did not want to lie down for it. So he lifted her down and she leant facing the table. When the sleeve was fully home he played with her sex. She started to tremble. 'Lie forward.' He put her cheek against her arm on the table. He put her other thumb into her mouth. Her lips sealed round it for comfort. He stroked her neck; he tickled her back. 'Open the valve, steward! Shhh – do her gently.' The pipe rippled. Subdued murmurs issued past her thumb. Her legs jerked open. Her bottom lifted. Her sex was visible from behind. Her belly bulged down. Its smooth skin touched the cold surface of the table. Her master slipped his fingers underneath her, feeling her belly then masturbating her moistly and gently, then feeling her belly again. 'Stop the inflow.' And for a few seconds he rubbed her lower back, rubbing with broad fingertips down into the hollow, always downwards, always gently. Then he played with her sex again until her lips sucked hungrily about her thumb and her clitoris looked distended. 'Let the fluid out,' he instructed the steward. She shuddered. He slapped her bare bottom vigorously with the cupped palm of his hand.

Sianon looked around at the other girls and the various means and positions of masturbation. One was on her back on a table, her knees bent outwards, the soles of her feet held pressed together by her mistress's clasping hand. The pipe rippled. Her belly bulged – an involuntary reaction to the inflow.

The senior irrigator turned to Sianon. It was her turn. The first girl was being refilled. The second was being turned over on the table. Sianon chose to take it freely standing. But she asked that Malory stay close by her. She wanted to touch his penis while she was being filled. She spread her legs for the sleeve to be fitted. 'Hold me, my lord, I beg you,' Sianon whispered. He held her sex in his fingers, stroking her erection. She slipped her hand beneath his balls. And she could feel his firmness even there. The first rush of fluid warmed inside her. He supported her breasts on his arm. She was near the fire, which warmed the front of her body, bathed her breasts in its radiant glow. The fluid kept coming, filling her, stretching her. 'Keep your legs spread,' said the irrigator. Malory's hand moved back and forth between her sex and swollen nipples, just toying, gently pulling, half milking her. Though she was gasping now, still her distraught fingertips tried to stimulate his penis and balls. Then suddenly she was being emptied. 'Stand up – straight. Good. A little fuller this time.'

'Ohhh!' It felt as if she would burst. Malory put his fingers up inside her sex, pressing gently but deep. He made her retain the fluid for longer. When she was drained she felt hot inside, hot, open and empty. They filled her for purposes of masturbation twice more. Each filling was more prolonged; each time during filling she clasped her master's aroused penis. 'It is as if the filling feeds your breasts,' he said admiringly. He was touching her nipples and underneath her arms. Then he slipped his fingers up her sex again while she was being emptied for the final time. And suddenly she wanted so much to be held by him; she reached for him and before she could close her lips round his earlobe, a little climax came. She was holding his penis in one hand, squeezing, stroking her thumb about the tip and it was turning oily: he was secreting through watching her arousal. Sianon sucked his earlobe; she reached down underneath his naked balls and felt his erection stiffen bone hard against her arm.

Nearby the girl's sex was being penetrated by her master's penis while she was being filled. The filling had both warmed and excited her. He was lifting her from the floor, holding her safely while the tubing rippled.

'So warm,' Malory murmured, continuing to touch Sianon as he donned his furs. 'Let me carry you to down the ice-house.'

She had never witnessed such a scene. She had never been so naked in such cold. It was a glittering cavern deep below ground, lit by myriads of candles. Ice dust glinted on the rough-hewn ceiling. Frozen pools spread across the floor. Wisps of white breath issued from the tight-lipped ladies; clouds of frozen steam billowed from the naked bodies of the young men. Erections burgeoned. Stubby icicles glistened in fervid, gloved stabbing fingers. Glasses of crushed ice clinked as the semen copiously spilled.

Malory stood Sianon on a fur-covered pedestal then fastened her wrists to a ring in the ceiling. He spread her legs. 'Keep still,' he said. She could not. An icy draught was sweeping round her like a stream. He tied her hair up round her head, baring her neck. She started shivering uncontrollably. Standing before her he took hold of her sex and gently prised it open with his thumbs. He kept rubbing it open and it went colder and colder, and drier as its moisture evaporated. Then it stayed open. The skin of her breasts was painfully tight; the gold studs through her nipples felt like icicles. He stood to the side and watched her.

There were ladies clutching balls in fistfuls of crushed ice. There were icicles with deep circular grooves melted into their basal rims by strong contractions of the sphincter. There were labia being bathed in ice water.

Malory warmed his hands inside his furs against his chest. Then he took Sianon's paper-flat dry cold labia in his fingers, as many fingers as could make simultaneous contact with her, drawing the cold from them. 'As smooth and velvety as frosted peach,' he murmured, 'as supple as cats' ears.' Then he sucked her freezing nipples and groaned in appreciative pleasure. She experienced a dull sweet numbness near the base of her spine which craved a hand to be pressed there gently.

When she opened her eyes the Lady Marquise, swathed in furs, was watching. 'Malory – you must not keep her here too long lest the benefit to pleasure be lost in the chill. See . . .' She was carrying a trug. She drew back the cloth to reveal a serried array of icicles. 'I am dispatched to pick them. Come back with me. We are now rid of my lord for the night. Bring your little toy. She will not be disappointed. We have dildos warmed by the fire.'

'Is it not fitting that we share a bedroom?' The pupils of the Marquise's eyes expanded to dark treacherous pools for Malory as he watched the pleasuring. 'I drew the inspiration from the practices of our Empress.' Danime

247

was spread open on the bed. Her wrists were sleeved within warm human manacles. Two naked male slaves lay on the pillows, their feet tied back behind their heads. Each sex was shaved; each erection stood fiercely; crop marks crisscrossed the smooth skin under their balls; Danime's fists were deep inside the creases of their buttocks. Leah was licking her. Each time Danime moved her arms, the manacles of flesh visibly tightened.

But Sianon was caught in the midst of the Marquise's game with Malory. 'If I take your little friend away – for just a minute,' she teased him, 'shall you then survive?'

It was a calculated ploy to separate them but, distracted by Danime and Leah, Malory did not refuse. The Marquise led Sianon across the room. She raised a finger: an attendant appeared with a tall glass for her on a silver platter. The Marquise sipped the drink, stared aloofly at Sianon then turned to the slave tethered to the upright frame. His body formed a standing cross above her head and facing away. 'The male form is quite exquisite. Malory is a supreme example. My one regret is that he will not let me punish him. If I cannot punish beauty I am quite forlorn. I sense this may be true of you.'

The Marquise smiled complicitously. She fitted a little leather collar to the slave's balls. The leash hung down. She told Sianon: 'Hold it while I spank his arsehole.'

The same strongly sexual feeling came to Sianon as she had experienced seeing the male slaves being punished by Janna. She could feel the smacks vibrating through the taut leash; she could hear his moans. 'Here, you take the strap to it.' Sianon gritted her teeth and lashed.

'Oh, beautiful,' said the Marquise, loosely sliding her tubed palm up and down the rigid penis. 'I see you as a rider in a chariot, lashing the whip-tip deep inside the cracks, hauling back the balls.' Sianon lashed again and again. Then suddenly she knew to stop. She held the choker firm and steady until his urge to climax had receded. The Marquise held his cheeks wide and licked deep into the crease. And the Marquise too knew exactly when to stop licking.

'Give him something very watery to drink,' she told the attendant. 'With the bladder full, it takes just the edge of keenness off the pleasure. We can masturbate him for that much longer. With a man I like to go for one really good one.' She looked sidelong at Malory, who was leaning against the bedside table and was quite visibly erect. But swelling inside Sianon was this feeling of empowerment. She started to imagine sexual things she might do to Malory.

The fullness in the slave's bladder was making his erection extra hard. 'Let us leave him awhile. There are those next door we must attend.' Smiling at Malory, the Marquise led Sianon into the next room.

A young man lay half shaven on a narrow table. In the middle of the room a waist-high marble pedestal bore an erect broad phallus, so polished by intimate usage that the whiteness of the stone was smoothed to glassy grey. A nude slave was being gently lifted on to it. The Consul supervised. The Marquise hurried to support the slave's heavy scrotum in her fingers. His sex reached ceilingward, driven by the broad stretching pleasure of the phallus; his toes reached vainly for the floor. Then the Marquise and the attendants stood back and left him balanced intimately on the hard shiny phallus. His balls retreated to a tight fat pouch – the sign that the deep stretching if left unchecked would bring his climax.

They eased him off and made him walk stiffly erect around the room. Then they made him stand against the wall and the Consul whipped his buttocks.

Malory was now in the room and staring at Sianon. She looked away, neither at the male slave nor at the

Marquise, who pointedly took Sianon gently by the wrist and edged her forwards. She held her – again gently – by the shoulders. The slave was being lifted back on to the phallus. His balls were drawn up; his weight descended. His trembling rigid penis looked so swollen.

The Consul drew the gasping slave's leg open, wanting to examine him. He pressed his thumb into the soft skin of the crease of the thigh. And the Marquise pressed her thumbs softly into the sides of Sianon's breasts, about two inches from the gold studs. A little milk exuded from her. The Marquise sighed in pleasure. The Consul now forced the slave's other leg wide open, pushing it up so far that his body lifted slightly from the phallus. The throbbing penis and naked scrotum were exposed on all sides. The Marquise's hand slipped between Sianon's legs, rubbing the creases of her thighs. 'Open like he has.' Sianon bowed her legs; her inner lips were fattening; the Marquise pressed her fingertips in at the sides. The Consul was stroking the selfsame place on the slave, stretched far more open than Sianon. And he was starting to come, impaled on the phallus. Immediately the Consul stopped stroking and the climax was prolonged. 'Quickly – let her kiss,' urged the Consul. Taking hold of the slave's feet, they pushed them high, exposing the bulging penis.

Sianon, reaching, pressed her soft open lips against the side of the shaved scrotum swollen so hard by pleasure. 'See – she understands his needs,' said the Consul. Her lips clung to the side of the round smooth naked skin; her breathing changed; she closed her eyes. A funny feeling came deep inside her at the moment she felt his contractions coming: she could feel them through her lips. Then his semen sprayed and sprinkled in silvery droplets in her hair.

The Marquise gazed at her as she crouched below the spending male, whose sex was still quivering, with the

Consul massaging the hard round place now impregnated with a purple suck-mark and slippy with her spittle. Little bubbles of the thicker yield of semen sloughed lazily down the penile shaft. The Consul caught them on his fingertips and tasted. 'Precious liquid, yield of love.' Then he stared at Sianon. 'Pearl drops for her lovely hair.' And the Marquise smoothed her thumb tenderly across Sianon's eyebrow. The semen was still running down the shaft.

The Marquise turned her attention to the nude male on the narrow table. She took on the responsibility of completing his shaving. The Consul, now on the far side of this table, stared at the young man, admiring his body, then he looked at Sianon. His lips mouthed silently the words: 'Come over here.' Sianon moved on tiptoes round the table. 'Let me look at you – your Chamberlain spoke of you – so full, so beautiful.' His fingers lifted her breasts very gently, stroking to the sides and up under her arms. He knew how to coax them. She could see her reflection in the mirror on the wall. She saw how full her breasts were becoming. They looked as if she were pregnant. Then she looked at the nude young man.

The Marquise was bending over him, with fingers stretched, drawing the hot skin taut, carefully and minutely shaving under his scrotum. His sex was soft but thick, as if a long-standing erection had just abated. And beside him was a string of gold balls on a chain: someone must have been using these anally to excite him. But there was no sign of his fluid having been expelled. Around each of his ankles was a loose leather strap. The table was covered in stretched suede. It was heavily scuffed and discoloured; the edges were smoothed by long usage for such examinations. If a girl were to have been bent across it, her toes would scarcely have reached the floor; her aroused sex would have protruded below its surface, invitingly to the fingers. At

251

intervals along the edge were centres of discoloration. On the rounded corners were smoother darker patches where the love-slaves must have been made to sit for their masters.

The Marquise was drying the young man. 'Will you look at him – a pure submissive.' A sweet surge of excitement came inside Sianon. 'Shall I use the gold balls?' the Marquise asked. 'Shall you hold his penis steady?' She was talking to the Consul but staring at Malory. The Consul handed her a heavy tongue-shaped leather strap. 'Do the spanking.' –

The young man's ankle straps were fastened wide apart to the ceiling. His heavy balls and sex lolled down towards his belly, leaving bare and convex the area beneath them. The Marquise began by wetting only the anus with her spittle; she kept reapplying it with her fingers until the spittle would not absorb and the skin stayed wet. Then she wetted the flat round end of the strap. Then she started spanking – but only the place she had wetted. When the smacks made it dry she rewetted it.

'The skin goes hot,' the Consul said, 'the body's defence. The wetting slows the swelling so one can take things that much further. Wait . . .' He licked his fingers. Then he too gently rubbed the anus, wetting and rewetting it. The rubbing action made the swollen penis roll and shake. Then he slid his middle finger in and rubbed from side to side. The young man began moaning. His erection boned. The Marquise smiled. The Consul took out his finger and sucked it. Then the Marquise wetted the anus once again before the spanking recommenced. 'He's a good one,' declared the Marquise. 'For me he lasts a good long time. And he is copious.'

'Turn round,' the Consul told Sianon. She faced the mirror for him. Her thighs moved open, her toes turned in. His hand pressed gently into the small of her back, urging her almost to lose her balance. Her buttocks thrust back, spread open. 'Oh my . . .' he murmured. Her head sank back. With half-closed eyes she saw her body in the mirror, her brown impaled nipples ripe for sucking. She could feel his middle finger entering her bottom. He lifted her on his hand and she could see her naked sex, wanting to be kissed and stroked, and she could see the second joint of his finger disappearing up her bottom, pouting to receive it. She could hear the smacks and the young man moaning. The Marquise was asking again about the gold balls. Clearly she wanted to use them on him. Sianon's bottom wanted to tighten round the wet pushing finger.

The Consul, his finger up inside her, her legs tucked up, carried her to the young man and lowered her on to his face. His anguished lips closed round her sex for succour. Then the sexual smacking of his anus recommenced with Sianon's sex inside his mouth. She felt the hot moist tip of his penis touch her backbone. The continuous spanking was stimulating him to leak. He became agitated, very agitated, groaning. Her sex was in his mouth but his lips lay passively open and his tongue would no longer suck inside her. She tried to reach behind to clasp the shaft of his penis and bestow relief. 'No, no . . .' The Consul lifted her away. 'See – how near he is. We must make him save it.'

Sianon was sitting on the Consul's hand, sitting with his middle finger inside, and helplessly watching the young man fighting against the need to deliver. The taste of her sex would be on his lips. The Marquise had cast the strap aside and held the gold balls in readiness, rolling them in her fingers, keen to slip them up inside, unable to do so safely in his present pulsing state. 'Too zealous a spanking, I fear . . .' the Consul said to her.

'My lord, I can never resist. And now my fingers itch to get these up inside him.'

'Any insertion now might bring him on. We must allow time.'

In all of this, no direct stimulation of any kind had been given to his penis. But it was curving like a bone inserted inside him. Every few seconds it gulped. With each gulp the Consul pressed the finger he had inside Sianon back towards her spine. 'Anal spanking is a keen mistress.' He lowered Sianon to her feet. The Marquise was filling a clyster. Shivers came between Sianon's legs. Her nipples tightened against their studs. The Consul put his arm around her from behind, gathering her breasts. He put his lips to her ear. 'See – his sex is softening. A little more time then you shall make it hard again with the delvings of the clyster.'

With Malory still watching from a distance, the Consul sat Sianon on the edge of the couch and masturbated her until her jaw fell slack and she was panting. Then the Marquise placed the heavy clyster in her hands.

Her thighs were trembling. She stood at the end of the narrow table. The Consul stood at the head. The slave was looking at her pleadingly from between his spread legs. His penis lolled, even began to retreat. His naked balls looked heavy yet vulnerable. The whole area was shaved pink and smooth. The shaved anus protruded as a cratered rim. 'Go on,' urged the Marquise. She took hold of Sianon's limp arms, directing the spout of the clyster. But it was Sianon herself who pushed it in. And she felt an acute surge of pleasure as it slipped inside his anus and his erection started, sluggishly though her victim was already groaning. Then she depressed the plunger and his penis stood right up. His head arched back. 'My Lady Marquise, I fear it is I who cannot resist,' begged the Consul. And his own stiffly aroused penis slid down the victim's throat. Sianon was trembling, pushing the plunger ever deeper. The slave's penis kept inflating. The Marquise played with Sianon's sex from behind until she could not stand up straight. She hunched. The Marquise's finger found the erect wet tip of Sianon's clitoris and masturbated it. 'Keep filling him, he needs it all – and more.' With every drop of her sapping strength, and through all the young man's stifled moans of pleasure, Sianon depressed the plunger to the hilt. And with the Marquise still playing with her, she collapsed, her breasts against the smooth suede of the table. 'Now suck his balls, just his balls, take them both into your mouth.'

The tortured penis rocked from side to side under Sianon's deep sucking of the scrotum. Then it started spouting. The Marquise quickly nipped the mouth of it shut and the semen squirted copiously through her fingers. Her clenched fist could not contain it. Each deep suck that Sianon took upon the scrotum drove another squirt. It was running down the Marquise's wrist. The Consul was climaxing in the young man's mouth, and driving hard and deep, urgently replacing the semen being lost through emission to the Marquise's gripping fist.

'Malory,' said the Marquise, 'had you ever thought to find in a girl such sweet lechery?'

In answer Malory swept Sianon up in his arms and carried her to the vacant phallus. He kept his arm around her shoulder and his arm under her knees and gently lowered her. 'Your bottom, not your sex. Let it find it. Take just the glans inside.' She moaned when the polished stone opened her. 'Beautiful,' he murmured, his tongue delving inside her open lips. Her knees were tucked up, her sex was exposed. She wanted someone to kiss it. Cuddling her, he rotated her gently back and forth. Then he carried her back to the bedroom. The Marquise and the Consul followed but went to the tethered male. The Marquise ran her hand up the back of his leg. The leather cord hung from his balls. She put a golden egg on a chain inside him. 'Now his penis cannot go down.' It curved up as if attached to the ceiling by a string. The two of them walked round him, discussing him and touching him. Then the Marquise showed the Consul Danime in her human manacles. Leah had been moved down on to the floor. The Consul examined intimately Danime's manacles, nipped each firm erection near the base, taking hold of the undertube and squeezing, making the slaves moan, then gripping Danime's forearms, moving them gently to make the penises rock.

'Do you not find her total nudity exceptionally beautiful?' asked the Marquise. And the Consul felt for Danime's beauty, felt her gold ring between her legs, felt for beauty deep inside her bald sex. The Marquise kissed her shiny head, her tongue lingering on the naked eyebrows. With eyes half-closed the Marquise gazed at Malory. Danime looked drowsy; the Consul thumbed her clitoris, tried to press it back inside her. The Marquise's tongue was near to Danime's mouth. Danime turned her head and kissed it and trembled on the verge of climax.

On the bedside tables were the recharged jugs of aromatic cordials whose scent would soon be fortified, whose temperature would be at body heat, whose taste would be imbued with salt-bitterness as they issued from the various founts of sexual love. This watery form of love could not be hurried. After a whipping the male erection lingered long. The Marquise now proved this. As Leah next continued to re-administer the cordial to the two male slaves, Danime sucked Leah's chained pouting sexual lips; she sucked her swollen little anus. The cordial was frequently spilled. Leah's responsiveness was a cause of enquiry by the Consul. Because the male erections softened only slowly there was time for Leah to be explored and enjoyed. The Consul took upon himself the honour.

Malory was on the couch with Sianon. Her head was on his lap. She could feel his penis swelling against the back of her neck. She twisted round and pressed her lips against it near the base. It felt so hot, this skin. Every male in the room was erect. Malory kept touching her anus where the cap of the marble phallus had been inside it. He kept touching it and watching Leah.

The Consul had lifted her off Danime and had taken her to a sturdy pedestal table just wide enough for her sex to ride. He hitched her up until her sex spread open on its polished surface and her toes were off the floor. The pressure made her anus close and pout. His penis could not easily gain entry, so he licked her, left her wet and tried again. He had to stand on tiptoes and direct his penis downwards to open out this upturned well of love. Then as her anus, still compressed under her weight, tried to accommodate the extra girth of the glans of so desirous a penis, the vision of her body squirming on the pedestal caused Malory's erection to become even fatter against Sianon's lips, and caused his fingers to want more deeply to explore her anus.

'I want to soften it and stretch it,' Malory whispered. A little shiver came in Sianon's breasts. He moved her up so they were now against his penis. He drew upon her nipples by pulling their studs. Her nipples made fat buds which pressed into his balls and under his penis. Between the pulling of her nipples, he rubbed his shaft against them then squeezed them between thumb and finger like maple buds that would burst and weep.

The Marquise was with the tethered slave. She was under his legs, filling a leather drawstring pouch with crushed ice. This she fitted round his dangling balls and drew the string tight. His anus immediately tightened and his cock began to pulse as if it would spout. Gently she pulled the gold chain attached to the egg inside him, and the pulsing began again. But only a very little juice overflowed. Gradually the Marquise coaxed the anus sufficiently wide for the egg to be yielded. She buried it in the bucket of crushed ice. Then she warmed her hands by the fire, rubbing them sensually and staring at

Leah. She went back to the male slave, detached the pouch of ice and dropped it to the floor, then clutched his balls in both hands, pressing both thumbs in a rubbing motion up towards his anus. 'Give him some more to drink,' she instructed the attendant.

The Consul, seeking deeper anal penetration, had lifted Leah from the pedestal. Her sex was open to limits of its chain. The Marquise donned her gloves. In one hand she held a warmed dildo, in the other an icicle. She stood between Leah's lifted legs. The icicle slipped gently under the chain, between the lips, tip to clitoris. Leah gasped. Her little nipples stood out hard. The icicle slid out, the warm dildo slid between the lips. The nipples came harder. The icicle was simultaneously pressed to the tip of the clitoris and Leah climaxed. The Consul groaned and drew out of her. His shaft slid back up between her legs, ejaculating a few little drops of semen on her belly before he managed to stay his climax. The Marquise sucked them off her. Then she went to Danime, who took the proffered tongue between her lips. Her forearms writhed. The two erections trembled. The Marquise whipped beneath them with the crop. She called for more cordial to be administered by Leah. Then she returned to the standing tethered male. She grasped his penis round the base, pressing the point of her thumb into the undertube. He started to groan. She was masturbating him in slow strong movements of her wrist. The thumb was pressing into him and his balls were lifting. He was panting. Her hand stopped and just squeezed his penis tightly with her wrist quite still. His panting continued. She drew the freezing gold egg from its ice bucket and pushed it up between the spread cheeks, up into the reluctant hot anus. When the cold egg touched his gland inside, he began spurting. Her thumb pressing into his shaft could not stay the flow. So powerful were the jets that they detached completely from the penis and struck the wall.

258

Eventually, despite the kissings and lickings, the erections on the bed partially subsided. Then the warm weakly scented crystal jets, guided by Leah's clutching hands, arched up, cascading over Danime's breasts, naked underarms and head. The Marquise held Danime's mouth open so the warm jets fell inside.

The Marquise lovingly kissed Danime's open mouth. Then she brought an empty, glass-stemmed clyster. It had an elongate slim glass teat. Danime shivered. The Marquise held the empty clyster in the air and depressed the plunger fully home. Then she laid it between Danime's legs, its teat nestled against the spread lips of her sex. Danime lay splayed on the bed, her two fists captive. The Marquise then retightened the human clasps by whipping the slaves just below the balls. When she was satisfied that Danime's wrists could not be extracted, she knelt between her thighs and got to work with the clyster. She oiled the teat and pushed it up the tiny pee-hole. Danime's belly bucked. The Consul held her thighs down. He began masturbating Danime very slowly until Danime started to writhe and plead. The tugging of her wrists served only to urge the erections. Leah twisted round and her lips reached between the Consul's legs to take his penis. The Marquise pushed the clyster firmly up against Danime and drew the plunger. Danime moaned as the tube began to swell with her nearly colourless pee. The area around Danime's clitoris stood out in erection. The plunger of the clyster continued its slow drawing.

The clyster was full. The Marquise clasped the barrel. 'So warm,' she murmured. She left it in place and sucked Danime. She leant over to drip spittle on to the two erect penises then slapped them wet. Then she took hold of the clyster and pressed the plunger slowly and relentlessly back in. Danime started to gasp. The Marquise kept pressing. Danime tried to sit up. 'She needs an icicle – quickly!' As her gold ring was drawn up and the freezing pleasure nosed into her tight bottom mouth, Danime's fists, clenching, pulling, precipitated the two climaxes. White columns of semen shot into the air, collapsing on the balls and Danime's forearms. Leah licked the balls, the Marquise scooped semen in her fingers and smothered it over Danime's pulsing clitoris and sealed the naked creases of her sex.

Sianon's breasts were starting to leak against Malory's penis. He turned her nipples up so he could look at their leaking. Her milk was watery, spreading out over the fine hairs coating her breast-skin. It soaked her gold studs. He made her kneel across him on all fours so her breasts hung down. The pressure made the milk form fat swelling droplets which dripped upon his erect penis. 'Ooh ... So hot.' He threw his head back. Glistening runnels clothed his shaft. Hot droplets splashed directly on his naked balls. He put her facing away from him on her side. She held her breath and lifted her leg. Her breasts were still leaking. He felt for her anus. It opened. His milk-oiled shaft slid deep inside it. His balls pressed up against her. He smacked her clitoris. She moaned. His shaft slid out but slipped back deep inside her sex and kissed the mouth of her womb. She gasped in pleasure. He rode her sex and anus with these deep alternate strokes. Her breasts kept slipping through his fingers. Her clitoris stood hard. He began again to smack it. Her shaking breasts squirted milk all over his arms, all over the couch. And suddenly he moaned, trembling, then he froze. Sianon glimpsed the Marquise's resentful gaze; it spurred her on. Reaching down, she sank her teeth into his forearm. He shuddered, drew out. She twisted round. His semen was already coming. It squirted up her clitoris, across her breasts, vying with her sprays of milk, before her lips caught his rampant bouncing penis and sealed round the glans, sucking it so strongly that the fluid squirted between her tongue and teeth and burned the back of her throat. She sucked the juice right out of him. The sweat was dripping from his skin and he did not stop moaning. His penis kept pumping to her sucks even after it was empty.

Then she rubbed her breasts across his lips, dripping her milk into his mouth. She put her fingers up inside him to make him more erect: she wanted it inside her again. He murmured: 'I have never met a slave who so cut me to the quick. I love you, Sianon. While I am with you, you shall never come to harm.'

She kissed his nipple contentedly and lay against his breast. When she looked up, the Marquise was staring down at her. 'Savour him while you can. Did he not tell you that he leaves at dawn?'

15

Requital

Josef opened his eyes. The light was softened by a fine misty gauze across the broad window. He lay on his side. He heard a murmur behind him. He jerked round. Staring at him was a pair of dark secure eyes.

'Minette . . .' he managed. She was sitting on the bed.

'My lord?' Her nostrils flared. She sighed deeply, slowly shaking her head.

By degrees he became aware of his surroundings – the panoply of elegant furnishings, the rich draperies, the scent of flowers. This was the Empress's bed. Swiftly but silently the great door opened.

'Lie still. The Kelthlings have sorely weakened you,' said Minette.

A steward had entered the room.

'He will need sustenance,' said Minette.

The steward bowed. 'Your Highness . . .' And he departed.

Josef frowned. 'Are you . . . Are you then kin to the Empress?' he whispered in bewildered awe.

'I am Empress,' said Minette.

His mouth fell open. She raised her head – just a little – and stared at him with those secure eyes. 'I am young. I know I have much to learn. My powers are yet restricted. But I am Empress.'

'But the one who – What of her?'

'My mistress? We play games. You surely have them

262

where you come from? It is simply that I love her very deeply and with her I sublimate my soul. But Lady Belangaria is wont to take her games too far.'

The door reopened. A beautiful girl entered. She had no hair nor eyebrows. She stayed near the door.

'Come and see him now, Danime,' said Minette. She turned to him. 'It has been many days. She almost relinquished hope of seeing you conscious. Yet we have Danime to thank for your being here at all.'

Minette then explained about the abortive rescue bid which had alerted her to his plight. Josef listened, and looked at this brave girl to whom he owed so much.

'Thank you,' he said to her. 'You put yourself in danger yet you did not even know me.'

Her gaze was fiercely independent but shy of praise. 'I did it because of Brown-hair.'

'You said that she was with you.'

Danime stared accusingly at Minette. There was a long silence. 'I have to tell you . . .' Minette hesitated. 'Sianon is gone from Tormunil.'

The devastation swept over him like a pall.

'I could not have prevented it even had I known. That would be seen as officious interference. She is not a free-woman like Danime. We live by trade and she was bartered.'

Josef could scarcely recognise in the Empress any of the shy Minette he had first glimpsed in the gardens. But she still bore her integrity and goodness. He murmured: 'I am not a free-man yet you stepped in to save me from my lady's clutches.'

'Josef – you are a free-man: fate decrees it.' She took something from the bedside table. 'Lady Belangaria is gravely misguided. Yet she is right on one count.' Minette held up a ring. At first he did not recognise it, until he touched the cold black metal.

'The Talisur,' he whispered.

'It was sent back here in advance of your arrival. I

instructed that it be kept safely and that she should not be told.' Gently she slipped it on his finger. 'It was wrested from you by trickery. Now fate must take its course: you have your freedom. I bestow it. The Talisur empowers it.'

A wave of coldness flowed over him; a feeling of agitation moved inside him; he felt the awesome power of the ring.

'Do not seek to run before you walk; the mind must first become attuned.'

'You mean I can go after her?'

'Sup first. But yes – and there is one who would go with you.'

He looked at Danime. She smiled, shaking her head. 'One day perhaps I may seek her out. On that day – beware.'

The steward returned with soup and soft bread. Josef was ravenous. He cleaned the bowl. When he looked up, Leah was standing in the doorway.

At dusk Leah looked up at her master sitting gazing at the road ahead. She snuggled up to him. 'Does the Talisur make my lord forget the night we spent together?'

He shook his head. 'How could it?'

'Does it take away the ache of wanting that the lady made inside him?'

'It makes it worse.'

She shivered as she kissed the Talisur ring.

'Then feed me,' Leah whispered. And her soft lips closed again about his throbbing penis. Down and down they sank, swallowing it completely. She would not release it. She clutched his aching love-heart in her fingers. He could not remain passive through the long ejaculation and the sensuous sucking feeding.

Malory stared out over the dry plain below. The last rays of sunset clipped the far dusty hills beyond which his destination lay. There was no sound. He watched the quiet hand of night descend upon the land. But he was thinking of the strange beautiful creature who had evoked in him such powerful feelings. Life and love were liquid droplets melting in the drift of time. Yet he was jealous of the Consul and jealous of his own men. He could not share her in the way that was ordained for her. And of all the other slaves in the contingent he could not bring himself to touch a single one.

He turned and walked back to the hostelry. The last of his men were leaving the stables. He waited until all were gone. Then he went inside. Only one lamp burned at the back. She was in a stall. They had suspended her by her wrists and drawn her legs out horizontally in the position of a chair. Her ankles were fastened to two posts. Her eyes were closed as if she were asleep. He moved closer. Her breasts looked as if she were heavily pregnant. He had taken her nipple-studs out but nobody had whipped her breasts. They looked as if they were bursting with retained milk. Her hair hung down over one shoulder. Her sex was open. He could see the nodule of her clitoris standing proud. Her belly glistened with spilt semen. It was on her breasts and thighs. It would be running down the groove of her spine.

She opened her lovely brown eyes. And all he wanted was to kiss her beautiful precious face. Fervently her lips took his. They burned against his. Tightly he held her in his arms. Tenderly he wiped the emissions away. When he began to untie her she cried: 'No! Just hold me. Hold my breasts.' He slipped his arms round from behind. Gently his fingers squeezed. 'Oooooo ...' He pressed his open lips against the pulsebeat in her neck. The milk began oozing sexually from her nipples. Pure-white and thick it traversed the rich-brown areolae in two broadening curtains running down, converging below her navel.

He went round to her front and gently spread her sex

265

lips wider. The rich milk ran inside to coat the glans of his erect penis reaching up to drink. As he unfastened her arms, her sex slid down to sleeve his penis. He reached back, tugging free in turn the tethers from her ankles. Then he carried her on his penis out into the arms of night.

When he reached his room she was clinging round his neck asleep. He sank back into the armchair. He did not relinquish her. He could not. His penis stayed erect inside her. She did not wake. One nipple stuck to his bare chest, the other had burrowed into the infold of his armpit. He could feel her clitoris pressing against his pubes and her sweet warm sex, exuding her precious lubricant, squeezing his shaft, milking it at intervals while she was asleep.